IT WAS OVER A DECADE ago that Robyn Mundy first went to Antarctica, and she has managed to return there every year since, working as an assistant expedition leader for a Sydney-based eco-tour company. In the summer of 2003–04, she spent a season living and working at Davis Station, Antarctica, as a field assistant. In 2008 she over-wintered at Mawson Station, Antarctica, where she worked on an emperor penguin project. Robyn has a Masters Degree in Creative Writing from the University of New Mexico, USA. She wrote *The Nature of Ice* as part of a PhD in Writing at Edith Cowan University in Western Australia.

THE NATURE OF ICE

ROBYN MUNDY

ALLEN&UNWIN

First published in 2009

Australian Government

This project has been assisted by the Commonwealth
Government through the Australia Council,
its arts funding and advisory board.

Allen & Unwin
83 Alexander Street
Crows Nest NSW 2065
Australia
Phone: (61 2) 8425 0100
Fax: (61 2) 9906 2218
Email: info@allenandunwin.com
Web: www.allenandunwin.com

Cataloguing-in-Publication details are available
from the National Library of Australia
www.librariesaustralia.nla.gov.au

978 1 74175 576 3

Set in 12.5/16.25 pt Garamond Premier Pro by Bookhouse, Sydney
Printed and bound in Australia by Griffin Press

10 9 8 7 6 5 4 3 2 1

To Nancy Robinson Flannery, with love and admiration

AUTHOR'S NOTE

MISSPELLINGS AND ORIGINAL PUNCTUATION IN the archival material have been retained.

After Antarctica, nothing is the same . . .

—Thomas Keneally, 2003

Tasmanian Club, Hobart
2 December 1911

THE SCENT OF BLOSSOM CAUGHT the night breeze and drifted into his room. He stood naked in the darkness. Beyond the open window a bow of streetlights; far away, a mopoke owl. On this, his final night in the known world, he tried to imprint on his memory each sound, each smell, the lightness of summer, the touch of air against his skin. He imagined Paquita's tortoiseshell clip falling to the floor. He had never seen her dark hair loose.

THE ANTARCTIC EXPEDITION

The *Aurora* sailed from Hobart for Antarctica via Macquarie Island on Saturday afternoon, having on board Dr Mawson and nearly half the members of the Australasian Antarctic Expedition, the scientific instruments, and wireless telegraphy equipment, a large quantity of stores of all kinds, provisions, clothing, sledges, 266 tons of coal, etc. She is to proceed direct to Macquarie Island, where the party which is to remain on the island will be landed . . .

Hearty cheers were given by those on shore as the vessel drew away, and these were answered by the occupants of the *Aurora*, while there was much waving of hats and handkerchiefs. Cameras were busy in all directions, and the cinematographs were not idle, so that the memory of the departure of the first Australasian Antarctic Expedition from Hobart should not be lost as long as pictorial records can preserve it. Occupying a prominent position on the *Aurora*'s rigging was a signboard with a finger pointing ahead, supplied by the Tasmanian Tourist Association, bearing the words "To the Antarctic and Success".

TO THE ANTARCTIC
AND SUCCESS

AURORA AUSTRALIS YAWS IN THE roll of the storm, four days out from Hobart and hurtling southward beyond the edge of the known world. Freya's world, that is. During the night the cabin has turned into a dance floor for Blundstone boots, a fluffy seal, an empty water bottle missing its cap. As if in an act of surrender, a drawer flings open and jettisons a roll of large format film. Freya Jorgensen watches from the top bunk as it tumbles over carpet to join the motley collection.

From along the hallway, sounds of retching spill from a cabin. A tingle rises through Freya's jaw and spreads across her lips as she teeters on the edge of nausea. If she could only open the porthole, stand before the moonlit night and draw in great gasps of cold ocean air. Her stomach rises and falls like an untethered buoy, its rhythmic wave keeping time with the curtains that fringe each bunk and glide freely on their tracks. She wedges her body diagonally and determines again to concentrate on breathing, dismiss each new thought that entices distraction. She weighs up the energy required to maintain purchase on her bunk with that of abandoning sleep and escaping the cabin altogether. Her travel clock reads 2:20 a.m., forty minutes since the last time she looked. She gives sleep one more chance, though she knows a lost cause when she sees it.

FREYA REELS ALONG THE SHIP'S corridor, out through the heavy double doors and onto the covered stern deck where she pulls on gloves and zips a padded jacket over her pyjamas. She leans against the railing above the trawl deck and looks out at the rolling mountain of ocean lit by the floodlights of the ship. With the wind screaming and steel groaning, the ship ought to tear in two, continually pummelled and pulled by the yank of the storm. Yet she feels secure aboard this ice-strengthened vessel, her feelings a contrast to the mix of dread and excitement she remembers as a child—seesawing across oceans and hemispheres to a strange southern land.

Flood lamps bathe the protected surrounds with an amber glow that drains the hurry from the ship's lurid orange paint. Freya relishes the mood of this working deck where few stay longer than to smoke a cigarette. In the roughest seas she can stand at eye level with the ocean and watch wind peel back the caps. In daylight hours she photographs albatross and petrels wheeling across the wake, their wing tips skimming the waves with a precision that astounds her. How easy it would be to mistime the peak of the swell, to fly too low, to flounder. And yet the sea birds toy with the ocean, spiralling upward, weaving in great playful arcs, circling the ship time and again.

Aurora Australis slides into a trough and shudders to a standstill. A wave of vibration stutters down its spine, reverberating through her hands and feet. Before the ship has time to regain momentum, a new crest of water gallops forward, lifting the hull on its shoulders.

Freya moves to the first run of steps leading down to the trawl deck, but even from here she sees how easily she could lose her footing in a roll. She grips the handrail and leans out into the night.

It takes time for her eyes to grow accustomed to the dark, to realise that what she took for cloud-covered moonlight is something else again. The movement is subtle at first, little more than a mystical shroud tinted with the softest hush of green. The wisp of colour begins to swell, its edges inhaling and exhaling like a creature stirring into life. She has an image, fleeting, of lying beneath such a sky roiling with emerald and gold. But Freya is not inclined to rely on childhood memories; her first eight years are filtered through the countless recollections of her mother who, after three decades in Western Australia, still yearns for the seeming perfection of their Norwegian homeland. Is she so very different from Mama, always wanting more?

'Willing us to get there faster?'

The man pauses at the top railing before walking down the steps. Adam Singer is one of the carpenters heading to Davis

Station. A few of the younger girls have been talking about him and Freya understands why: drop-dead gorgeous is right.

'Didn't mean to startle you.'

His gaze disarms her, and though it seems foolish—a married woman of thirty-six—she suddenly feels unsure of herself. 'Do you think that's an aurora out there?'

Adam leans into her side and nods. 'First time south?'

'Is it that obvious?' She smiles. 'I still can't believe I'm on my way to Antarctica. That it's not a dream.'

'A year-long dream. If Davis is like Macquarie Island we'll have plenty of good auroras through winter.'

'I'll have to find a way to come back. I'm only down for summer.'

'That's a shame.'

The ship heaves and jolts. Freya grabs for the handrail but misses. She feels herself teeter backward, stopped by Adam who snags her waist. A rush of ocean cascades over the stern and jams open the trawl gates with a deafening ring. Beneath the gridded steps they stand upon, water floods the deck. Adam does not loosen his hold and she in turn lingers, registering, in this surreal light, the invitation proffered. As intimately as a lover, he combs back threads of her white-blonde hair blown across her face while she stands mesmerised, leaning towards his touch. With an air of fascination Adam traces his finger around the birthmark that spreads across her cheek like a stain. Perhaps his blatant trespass onto tainted skin, perhaps her own returning sanity, makes her break away, her discomposure heightened by the hardness in his eyes.

He holds up his hands in a gesture of retreat. 'Only wanting to help. Nothing more.'

Freya turns her blemished cheek away, confused, stammering thanks and apology in a single sentence. She stands rigid until Adam has gone. She looks back to her shining sky but not a wisp remains, nothing but stars strewn across the night, wind scouring the waves.

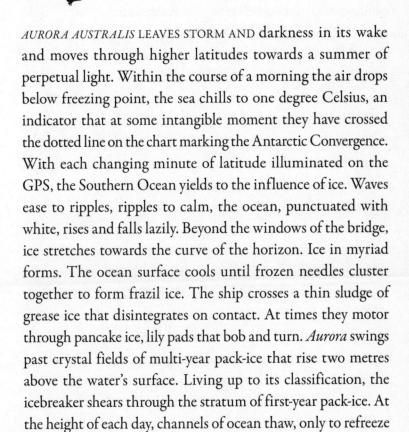

AURORA AUSTRALIS LEAVES STORM AND darkness in its wake and moves through higher latitudes towards a summer of perpetual light. Within the course of a morning the air drops below freezing point, the sea chills to one degree Celsius, an indicator that at some intangible moment they have crossed the dotted line on the chart marking the Antarctic Convergence. With each changing minute of latitude illuminated on the GPS, the Southern Ocean yields to the influence of ice. Waves ease to ripples, ripples to calm, the ocean, punctuated with white, rises and falls lazily. Beyond the windows of the bridge, ice stretches towards the curve of the horizon. Ice in myriad forms. The ocean surface cools until frozen needles cluster together to form frazil ice. The ship crosses a thin sludge of grease ice that disintegrates on contact. At times they motor through pancake ice, lily pads that bob and turn. *Aurora* swings past crystal fields of multi-year pack-ice that rise two metres above the water's surface. Living up to its classification, the icebreaker shears through the stratum of first-year pack-ice. At the height of each day, channels of ocean thaw, only to refreeze into fragile sheets that raft one upon the other—panes of glass the vessel snaps in two. On the radar, a tabular berg edging the sky measures fifty kilometres in length; Freya mistook the berg for a long, low cloud.

Aurora's captain, no older than she, has a pageboy haircut that moves in one slick motion with each turn of his head. He reminds her of photos of her husband Marcus as a boy. The captain veers the ship towards a stretch of 'water sky', an ominously dark band that on any Australian horizon would signal rain. Here, the sky is a chameleon, stained dark by an underbelly of ice-free ocean. 'Look at the difference there.' The captain points to where the sky brightens to a luminous glow. This he calls 'ice blink', an upward reflection from pack-ice and bergs. 'That's where we don't want to end up, stuck in heavy ice and chewing through fuel. Ice blink and water sky were all they had to go on in the early polar days,' the captain says, flicking his hair as he leans down to scan the radar. 'You've got to hand it to 'em, finding their way south through this.'

Aurora eases past bergs whose skirts of icicles thaw in the late afternoon light. Freya sets up her camera on the flying bridge, wishing they could turn off the engines and listen to the streams of water, could simply drift awhile with no direction in mind.

Ice crunches beneath the hull. Squadrons of cape petrels keep pace with the ship, the small birds with their black-and-white chequered wings forming a graphic blur against the electric orange hull and crystalline ocean.

Behind the viewfinder her focus is rarely deflected. She has tempered the promise of the perfect photo into disciplined restraint, resisting the wonder of the moment to weigh shape against tone and texture, to balance shadow and light. Marcus calls her driven, seldom as praise. Freya is reminded of the difference between herself and her husband when she sees him in their overgrown garden where he will sit and read for hours, seemingly oblivious to a litter of leaves, the influx of snails and weeds. Occasionally she still arms herself with clippers and a faded memory of a garden once so lush with colour and native birds, she never questioned the time she used to put into it. She has let her photography become so consuming, she wonders has she lost the ability to be part of a world beyond the boundaries of a 4 x 5 inch transparency? *Not part of the programme*, she averts the subject to stem her mother's not-so-gentle reminders of *time marching on, and women who want it all then leave it too late*. This, she persuades herself, is all she wants. Thoughts of home and things she'll never have eased by the unutterable beauty of ice. Freya draws back from her camera to absorb the vision that spills beyond the frame. She turns slowly on the deck as she feels against her pocket for sunglasses. She had anticipated the glisten of white, the glare of ice painful to the unprotected eye. Her collection of oversized books picked up from discount bins had long since imprinted her mind's eye with the blue of bergs. Never had she expected this opalescence of light and colour. How can any camera capture such an impossible expanse?

She was first drawn to Antarctica through the images of Frank Hurley, photographer on Douglas Mawson's 1911–14 Australasian Antarctic Expedition. *An Antarctic heaven*, he named the pack-ice. Freya was still a photography student when she gazed in wonder at Hurley's black and white photographs, fell through them as if to touch the ice. She wonders now how Frank Hurley reconciled himself to the knowledge that every nuance of colour displayed before him would be reduced to tones of grey.

Freya catches sight of a familiar face at the far railing. She knows Travis from her pre-departure training in Tasmania where he helped untangle her prusik loops and distinguish alpine butterflies. She makes her way towards him but is intercepted.

'Freya? I'm Kittie. Davis Station weather forecaster. *Fine*-weather forecaster, I'm known as.' Kittie holds out her camera. 'I was hoping you could give me a rundown on my new toy.'

'Happy to.' Freya takes the camera.

'They say when all else fails consult the manual. All else has failed, including the manual, which I managed to leave on the kitchen counter at home.'

'Mind if I listen in?' calls Travis, holding up his point-and-shoot.

The three sit down on the flying deck in a circle. Freya could be running one of her university extension weekend courses, giving Travis tips on how to override the automatic settings in tricky lighting scenarios, working through the different modes and menus on Kittie's high-end SLR.

She glances up to see Adam Singer propped against the railing. He nods in her direction but declines her gestured invitation to join them.

'You'd be all digital?' Kittie asks.

'For small format work. And stuff I play around with in Photoshop. I still use film for images I want to enlarge into murals.'

'Film?' Travis banters. 'We're talking acetate, chemicals, darkrooms? I wouldn't have pegged you for a luddite, Freya.'

Freya shrugs. 'Part of me still likes the idea of creating an original transparency. Something you can hold in your hand.'

'Digital artist meets traditional craftswoman.'

Travis is a volunteer field assistant who will be stationed out at the Amery Ice Shelf. He looks scarcely old enough to have finished a science degree, let alone be sporting a wedding ring. Like Freya, it's his first time south. 'Fine-weather' Kittie, a title that seems to extend to a sunny and boisterous disposition, has summered and wintered twice before.

'Any tips for the uninitiated?' Travis asks her.

Kittie snorts. 'Out at the Amery Ice Shelf all summer? An hour's flight away from the politics of the station? My advice, you lucky bastard, is to pinch yourself now and again.' She raises her camera in a toast: 'To Antarctica.'

'To the Antarctic and success,' Freya seconds.

Travis checks his watch. 'And to one more sumptuous five-thirty evening meal, never mind the nursing home hours. See you down there.' He springs to his feet and bounds away.

Kittie points at Freya's camera. 'What exactly is your project?'

'My husband and I are putting together a travelling exhibition of Antarctic images, my photos alongside Frank Hurley's first photos. A sort of Antarctica-then-and-now.'

'Whoo-hoo!' Kittie gives her a mock punch. 'A breath of fresh air among the science and trades projects.'

Freya is tempted to explain more but thinks better of it. *Not everyone shares your passion for Hurley's art*, Marcus would caution.

In her first, unsuccessful application to the Arts Council she had worded her proposal *Themes from Hurley's photos linking to my own.* When the Council recommended further development, Marcus had comforted her: *It's certainly not a failure. What you have is the kernel of a very good idea.*

'Is he a photographer?'

'Frank Hurley?'

'Your husband, you schmuck!'

Freya laughs. 'Marcus is an academic. Communications. Though in some ways he knows more about photography than I do: he taught visual theory in the early days.'

'Dr Marcus didn't try to stow away as your field assistant?'

'He has teaching commitments,' she offers, 'and he's busy with some research.' Freya hesitates. 'To be honest,' she confides, 'my husband tends to be a bit of a homebody.'

'Ah.' Kittie gives her a knowing nod. 'My partner's a *would-be* homebody. Has visions of being a stay-at-home parent with a brood of kids.'

Encumbrances, Marcus had dismissed children the one time she broached the topic. 'You have children, Kittie?'

'Not yet. Diana and I are hoping to adopt.' Kittie registers Freya's blink of surprise. 'Believe it or not,' she says, 'I do tend to be closeted when I'm at the station. Doesn't pay to stir up the homophobes.' She taps a finger in the direction of Adam Singer at the opposite railing. 'Case in point,' she whispers.

'How do you mean?' Freya leans closer, curious in spite of herself.

'I get the weirdest vibe from that dude. I'm here to tell you, I can pick out the egomaniacs and misogynists from a hundred paces.'

Adam? She can't be serious. Freya is unsure whether to laugh. 'That's a bit harsh. You make the place sound like a hornets' nest.'

'Nah, there's always one or two that come crawling out of the woodwork. The difference from home is there's no ready means of escape. As for the rest of us, it's a mandatory requirement to be off-centre. You would have had the unspeakable joy of the psych assessment?'

'Oh, yes.' Freya shudders, remembering the written test, the hour-long interview, the evaluation. *You appear to be fiercely independent and professionally self-assured, yet the written tests indicate a tendency to be submissive—at times you operate out of a sense of duty.*

'It went on forever,' she recalls. 'How would I integrate into a tight-knit community after working so long on my own? Did I have my husband's full support?' Who wouldn't feel on edge with some of the intimations?—*an underlying vulnerability, a lack of self-esteem*—the psychologist's focus all the while

15

honed in on her birthmark. He had quizzed her at length over Marcus, interjecting: *But outside of the house, what do you do together—for fun?* Freya had found herself back-pedalling, defending her husband and her marriage. 'I half-expected to be told I wasn't suitable.'

'At mine,' Kittie says, 'the security guy escorted me up in the lift. When the interview was over I said to the psych, *Shall I let myself out?* She gives me this go-crawl-back-under-your-rock look and says, *Unless you'd rather jump out the window.*' Kittie twirls her fingers. 'And a good day to you too, Dr Happy!'

Freya drums her fists on the deck with a peal of laughter. She opens her eyes to catch Adam's smile.

'So there you have it,' Kittie says. 'We're both certifiably insane enough to go to Antarctica.'

FREYA ARRIVES AT THE DINNER table in time to hear Charlie, the Davis Station radio officer, expound on the pros and cons of modern-day communications compared to earlier technology. 'Telegraphy, it was back then at the Melbourne GPO. Twenty years before I started coming south.' His weathered face bears a kind smile.

'Phone calls, emails, faxes—and now bloody sat phones and SMSs,' Charlie emphasises each word, 'the ruin of many a relationship, in my opinion. These days you get wives and partners calling up all hours of the day and night, checking up. Coming to Antarctica won't solve any problems you've left at home.'

'A somewhat cynical view, Charlie,' says the woman at the end of the table whose name eludes Freya.

Charlie shrugs. 'Three decades south. Three marriage bust-ups.'

'Why do you keep coming down?'

'The buggers won't let me retire! Each time I tell the Division this is my last year—*yes, yes,* they say, then call me up four weeks before the start of a new season, knickers in a knot because someone's pulled out. Gave the winters away a few years back,' he says. 'A lowly summerer nowadays.'

Freya laughs. 'Plenty of us would kill to have your kind of summer every year.'

'What about the female perspective?' Travis says. 'You're married, Freya. Your other half mind you running away to Antarctica?'

'Hardly running away,' she tries not to sound defensive. 'I've been freelancing for ten years. Marcus is used to me going away for work. Though, admittedly, not for five months straight.'

'You're on a humanities grant?' says the woman, a PI as she introduced herself yesterday—Principal Investigator—distracting Freya from remembering her name with yet another Antarctic acronym.

'A Commonwealth arts grant. I'm working on a photographic collection for an exhibition.'

'Courtesy of the Australian taxpayer.' The woman sniffs. 'What a lark.'

Charlie winks at Freya sympathetically. 'As I understand it, that privilege extends to us all, sciences and trades.' He leans conspiratorially towards Travis. 'They've got a cubby hole set up for Freya above the helipad at Davis Station.'

'Is that so?' Travis grins agreeably, though, like Freya, he seems mildly perplexed.

Freya addresses herself to everyone at the table, ignoring whatever bait is being dangled. 'They've lined-up a studio that an artist-in-residence used a few years back. The station leader says it has views across Prydz Bay. Is he right, Charlie?'

'Million-dollar views.' Charlie nods, gathering the plates. 'A million decibels of racket thrown in at no additional charge.'

FOR EIGHTEEN BONE-SHAKING HOURS *AURORA Australis* bashes through ice that seals Prydz Bay, her progress best measured in hours per kilometre. Forward the ship rumbles, struggling to gain momentum, engines screaming with an insatiable thirst for fuel. *Aurora* charges at the fast ice like an orca seizing prey from the shore.

In her cabin, Freya scrolls through the bank of Frank Hurley photos she keeps on her laptop, opening a folder of images of the original *Aurora*'s journey. *Steam Yacht* Aurora *breaking through pack-ice on her voyage south.*

She wonders at her desire to peer in through the sphere of Hurley's lens, to focus on the man looking out. She can easily picture the larrikin Hurley defying danger and cold as he precariously balanced on the slippery bowsprit with his big box camera to photograph the ship, those watching from the bridge shaking their heads at his showman antics.

What a lark. *What a lark.*

Frank Hurley wrote that every photograph, like an auto-graph, bears the stamp of the photographer's personality. Freya flags this image for her exhibition; it is as striking a reflection of a tour-de-force photographer as of a voyage of discovery. As she considers the photos she took today—technically sound but not one of them involving risk—she suddenly questions if she can meet the challenge Frank Hurley has set her.

Through the porthole, Freya spies two crosses marking an outlying island—a grim welcome to Davis Station. She hears a commotion in the hallway and follows others up the stairwell onto the deck. Beyond the island, the ice of the Antarctic plateau shimmers like a mirage. On the ship's bow, a group dressed in yellow freezer suits link arms and sway back and forth. And there, directly ahead, nestled among rock, sits a cluster of green, blue, red and yellow buildings, a bright and shining station at the edge of the world. Why the anticipation of arrival should flood her with apprehension she doesn't fully understand. She feels eight years old again, shuffling on a crowded deck towards a gangway and clasping her father's lifeline of a hand, overwhelmed by baking heat and the salty air of Fremantle port, by booming voices and indecipherable words. Now, just as she did then, she wishes she could turn back time and sail on, remain in no-man's land for just a while longer. Her trepidation strikes her as absurd, yet she can't shake off the foreboding: before her is a threshold beyond which there can be no return.

Steam Yacht Aurora
*breaking through pack-ice on
her voyage south*

The seventh continent
19 *January* 1912

DOUGLAS MAWSON GLANCED THROUGH *AURORA*'S porthole
at a foreshore strewn with provisions, a line of tents, timber
stacked beside the foundations of the hut already referred
to as winter quarters. Beyond their base, the great domed
icecap could be mistaken for a blanket of cloud pressing
down upon the horizon, so mighty was it in breadth
and depth.

From his cabin he could hear Frank Hurley crowing
about photographs of *Aurora* he'd printed to send home to
the newspapers, *The old girl ploughing through a glorious
band of pack-ice.* Inglorious ice, Captain Davis would argue.
Douglas dared not think how close Antarctica's gauntlet of
ice had come to undoing the expedition. Days wasted
circling the pack, a sickening volume of coal consumed in
searching for an open lead. And then the bittersweet sight
of a stretch of ice so vast they had at first mistaken it for the
continent. The quickening of the pulse, the realisation that

within a gunshot was the greatest glacier tongue known to
man, their eyes the first to witness it. Less magical was the
ensuing backtracking, hours spent on *Aurora*'s open bridge
or frigid in the crow's nest, scouring the coastline for a tract
of ice-free land on which to establish this base. He'd had no
option but to amalgamate the smallest subsidiary party into
his own, reducing them to two continental bases instead of
the planned three.

Some from the Geographical Society had scoffed at the
magnitude of his plans—he, a twenty-nine-year-old
Australian geologist mounting an expedition with science its
sole objective. During 1911 he had given his fundraising
presentation *ad nauseam* throughout Britain and Australia:
*Bound up with the general mystery of the seventh continent
are volumes of facts of vital importance to science and economic
problems. The object of the expedition is to investigate the
Antarctic Continent to the southward of Australia. Our
intention is to land several self-contained wintering parties at
widely separated points, each to make continuous scientific
records at the base station, and to investigate the surrounding
region by sledge journeys.*

He should thank Providence that they were here at all,
the relay party successfully landed at Macquarie Island
on the way down, the newly erected wireless mast now
crowning the island's North Head. *Wireless telegraphy
will be used for the first time in polar exploration, our
Macquarie Island station transmitting Antarctic news
to Hobart.*

Douglas wound the sheet out of the typewriter and read over his instructions to Captain Davis: *Motor at least five hundred miles west, there to establish Frank Wild's continental base.* He could hear Davis above decks, bellowing orders to heave up the anchor and make ready to depart. *Westward ho, lads!* Douglas scrabbled for a new sheet of paper and took up his pen.

Adelie Land

19 January 1912

My Paquita,

Just a hurried line to say goodbye for a year—we are just about to go ashore at winter quarters, having landed all the needful.

What has happened in the last fortnight you will hear from the press. Suffice it to say that everything has gone off well enough though we had hoped to find a more rocky coastline.

You will not get this letter until the end of April or May and by then we expect to have the wireless in operation so you may hear earlier.

We have made a successful landing and I don't anticipate anything in the nature of disaster. Your wandering Dougelly will return with the Olive Branch to his haven of rest in a little over a year's time. Of course that is if he is still wanted—from what you have said anyway, he is coming back to enquire. You will be quite a woman of the world then—perhaps quite too fine for me? Eh. Well don't let that be, for in this stern country

of biting facts ones love gets frozen in deeper and there is plenty
of time here to think over all the happiness that may be ours.
The very fact of your loving me seems all that I want, and
I could live always in that beatitude.

Know O'Darling that in this frozen South I can always
wring happiness from my heart by thinking of your splendid self.

There is an ocean of love between us dear.

Your loving Douglas

IT WAS AS THOUGH HE had folded and sealed all his personal
emotions inside the letter to Paquita, tenderness put away in
readiness for the task ahead. Indeed, the parting at Commonwealth Bay may have seemed a matter-of-fact one to those
watching from the ship. Hurried handshakes on the poop
deck, a round of cheers from the ship's crew, their smaller
boat pushing off from large. As his eighteen men pulled away,
each on an oar picking up the rhythm of the stroke, he heard
Aurora's boatswain mutter, *Poor beggars*. Captain Davis's
remark skimmed across the mirror-calm water for all to hear,
She's a godforsaken country to spend a year in.

Douglas watched the arc *Aurora* made as she slid her
nose around a half-moon, his men gauging the broadening
distance between whaleboat and ship with a growing sense
of realisation. In the time it took to angle their course
towards shore, a wave of melancholy subdued the men of
main base left on their own at Commonwealth Bay. The
whaleboat rocked in *Aurora*'s wake.

DAVIS
STATION

AURORA AUSTRALIS GIVES THREE DEAFENING blasts as she swings away, nudging back along the channel of broken sea ice and out between the islands of Prydz Bay. Davis summerers congregate along a snow-encrusted road that winds from the station down to the sea ice. Freya stands at the foreshore adjusting her tripod. She focuses on a line of bodies crowning the hill, each with a maritime flare held high, a line of statues posed in farewell. Shouts and laughter are punctuated by a report of cracks and whizzes as their makeshift fireworks cascade in a blaze of orange smoke. Freya leans into her camera, her motor drive burring, trying to summon, through the pall, a feeling for this place—and a sense of her own place within it. In the space of a week, people around her have eased into a pattern, returning tradies reminiscing with old workmates, a comradely chatter among those Freya has worked alongside during resupply— dozens forming a human chain to transport provisions from shipping containers, sort old food stocks from new.

The ship slides from view and the crowd of well-wishers slowly disbands, lured indoors by the promise of warmth. Freya folds her tripod and turns to see Adam Singer waiting for her.

'At last she's gone,' he says of the ship. 'Our summer can finally begin.' Adam walks beside her up the road; ten o'clock at night and the station gleams, buildings edged in sunlight.

'How are you settling in?' he asks.

'This reminds me of my first week of school in Australia. Everything new and different and my head still spinning.'

'Found your way around the buildings yet?'

'Mostly. I now know where to muster if the fire alarm goes off, and not to mix burnable rubbish with non-burnable.'

'You're doing better than some. I'm impressed. What would your hero make of the place, a century on?'

'Hero?'

'The famous Hurley. He's your inspiration, I hear.'

'I imagine Frank Hurley would be right at home in the twenty-first century. He'd own the latest digital camera and image software, and would be out there scaling one of those icebergs to get the most dramatic viewpoint.'

'He's the one who stood on railway tracks snapping photos of oncoming trains.'

'That's Hurley,' Freya says, surprised at Adam's knowledge. 'Master of photography and daring pursuits.'

'Can we expect the same of you?'

Freya blinks. 'I'm not much of a daredevil. I've also been told there'll be no exploring off station until I'm field trained. First time and all.'

Adam scoffs. 'Anyone's guess how long that will take with the boffins all raring to start their science projects. You'll be way down the list.' He slows and turns towards the sea ice. 'Down here, Freya, there are times when what they don't know won't hurt them. Make the most of every moment. Summer comes and goes in a heartbeat.' He strides away to the living quarters and calls back to her, 'If you and your camera want some company, I'd love the chance to help.'

'I'd like that too,' she says, flattered by his attention, a bounce in her step as she climbs the hill toward her studio.

EVENING SUNLIGHT CATCHES THE CORNER of the window above her desk. Freya's upstairs studio perches on the brow of the hill, flanked by helicopter landing pads. She scrolls through the backlog of daily emails from her husband, registering his impatience at having to wait days for a reply. 'Dear Marcus,' she writes.

>> I'm sorry! The ship left tonight and this is the first chance I've had to write. The week has been a blur with vehicles trundling back and forth across the sea ice, helicopters slinging in loads from the ship. Everyone on station worked around the clock while an astronomical amount of fuel was pumped from ship to shore.

A crate with my gear and belongings finally turned up today and I've begun setting up my studio—make that my sea container, 1990s-vintage, heated, with a freezer door, windows and—joy of joys!—internet connection. It's wee, and a little bit decrepit in a way that reminds me of the first studio I had in Melbourne, but warm and cosy with bench space and beautiful natural lighting. I love it! I share my little parcel of real estate with the helicopter crew downstairs and with Romeo and Juliet—yes, those are the call signs of our two noisy helicopters. Hopefully things will quieten down now the ship has left.

There are eighty people here for summer and we've already been assigned our weekly duties. Think of me tomorrow sweeping and mopping cold porches! The LQ (Living Quarters) is the main building where we squeeze into the dining room, with some overflow to the lounge and bar. The 'deluxe' bedrooms upstairs have been assigned to those who will stay on for winter, while we summerers are scattered far and wide. Tonight I was relocated from a bunk room to my own tiny room in the temporary accommodation module.

I see you've spent every night this week reading diaries from Mawson's expedition! I've been flagging some Hurley photos for the exhibition and can't wait to hear which excerpts you think will work with them.

The sun is still up, but my weary head is telling me it's late. Time for a shower and sleep. More soon.

Sending warm thoughts across the frozen ocean.

Love, Freya x

Before shutting down her laptop, Freya clicks through Hurley's images from January 1912 of winter quarters under construction, the small wooden hut prefabricated in Australia and brought down in numbered pieces. Eighteen men, pioneers, starting from scratch.

The earthy hues and muted tones of timber, canvas tents—even straw from packing boxes—belong to a photographic world of black and white. Alongside them, her first digitals of Davis Station scream with colour and glare, angles and moulding, the shine of triple glass. She thinks of Adam's question. What *would* Hurley make of it all? Could any one of Mawson's men have looked at winter quarters and imagined an Antarctic future with these elaborate trappings?

Freya leaves her studio and grips the blizzard line to negotiate a slick of ice leading to her accommodation module. She tiptoes inside and gingerly closes the door whose printed notice, *Please Close The Door Quietly*, has been annotated by some sleep-deprived occupant: *That means YOU, dickhead!*

Hot water tumbles over her bare shoulders, steam fills the tiny shower cubicle. Freya stands naked in a sea of warmth, combing her fingers through her hair as water rains around her, her body aglow with the simple, sensual pleasure of moisture on skin.

She reflects on Adam and his apparent interest in her, on the seductive power of his charisma—perhaps the lure is in being made to *feel* attractive. Freya catches her reflection in the mirror. Its film of vapour fails to soften the burgundy smear stamped upon her throat and cheek, a mark of birth that still, after so many years and assaults on her senses, has the power to make her wince. *Who else would want you?* Marcus had once said in the height of an argument. Freya reaches for the switch and snuffs out the light.

Winter quarters under construction

Winter quarters
26 January 1912

THE OVERWHELMING IMPRESSION WAS THE voluminous body of light. Douglas stood beneath the hut's apex, with diaphanous streamers pushing down through the skylights and flooding his clothing and hands, oiling boards of Oregon and Baltic pine. Every part of the room was plated in light.

Eighteen bodies crowded into winter quarters, men snuffling and snoring in reindeer fur bags, mattresses slung across the floor between stacks of pre-cut timber ready for assembly into bunks.

At midnight, the room was still bright enough to read by. Though he was not a church-going man, the comparison Douglas drew was to stand inside a stone chapel, motes caught in the light of a leaded window, air chill and undisturbed while beyond the walls the world might rage with wind as it did tonight. The reverence he felt was not a measure of the existence of God but a belief that this simple structure, built with willing hands in the place he had named Commonwealth Bay, would withstand all manner of tempest and storm. In Antarctica, it was nature that ruled.

HE LAY ON HIS CABIN floor looking up through the skylight at a world turned white, mesmerised by horizontal showers of snow that scoured and pitted the new panes of glass. Inside, the hut felt snug.

Already his men acknowledged the benefits of an Australian homestead design with its large interior room shielded from the elements by a perimeter of enclosed verandahs. He'd opted for two exceptions to the open plan: Frank Hurley's closet-sized darkroom in the corner behind the cooking range, and his own eight-by-eight-foot cabin. A decent break in the wind and they would have the surplus hut from the abandoned base tacked to the front wall as a workshop and laboratory.

Men were staking claims for a bunk site by decorating each six-foot stretch of wall. Johnny Hunter, the biologist, had hung a framed photograph of his sweetheart Nell, seated in the front row of Sydney University's women's hockey team. Xavier Mertz—the Swiss dog handler and ski expert they called X—frequently went into raptures about the hockey girls, in particular a Miss Meares in the front row whom he intended to woo and marry the moment they returned to Australia. X had on display postcards of the Swiss Alps and a series of miniature Swiss flags alongside a portrait of his mother. He'd begun a trend by nailing to his section of the wall a canvas holder for his tobacco and pipes.

The second dogman, Ninnis—nicknamed Cherub on account of his propensity to blush—had unpacked a carnation given him in London by Anna Pavlova which he'd framed, and a signed portrait of 'Anna on her tippy toes' in a performance of *Swan Lake*. Ninnis must have looked even taller and ganglier next to the petite Pavlova, in whose honour he'd named the prettiest dog.

Douglas propped a pillow behind his back and the journal on his knees. He felt too weary to pencil an excess of words.

General turn-in in Hut. Wind outside, roof on just in time.

He turned to the art print tacked to his own wall. The naked nymph sat in a meadow threading yellow daisy buds; reclining on a branch above, a faun serenaded her with panpipes. Douglas suspected that Paquita knew nothing of desire beyond a lover's kiss: a caress left her teary and bewildered. He found her innocence both charming and unsettling. She had lived her twenty years coddled by family, more cloistered, surely, than most Australian-born girls. Could he expect such a woman, beyond her sense of duty, to understand the drive of men or fathom *him*, whose public persona he could educe as easily as the opening of a blind? Love and science, domesticity and exploration: separate carriages on a single train. He had teetered along such a track, away to London at the start of last year to launch the expedition just weeks after announcing their engagement. The final months in Australia had passed as a blur, every bone-wearying source of funding exhausted. He had plunged his own savings into the expedition, sold off his shares, spent beyond his means on Paquita's diamond ring. Still, Douglas Mawson's girl belonged to a family unaccustomed to thrift.

Stoicism had become a necessity, had guided him through otherwise heartrending decisions leading up to the expedition: he felt no regret in dissuading Paquita from attending the official departure in Adelaide, or from coming to Hobart to farewell the ship as she'd so much wanted to do. His fiancée was a darling, a sweet and loving angel, but he had sacrificed everything to reach this point and he would not risk a public outburst of emotion, tearful embraces before the keen eyes of the press. She was a good girl, a dutiful girl; of course she bowed to his ruling. *And don't waste your time writing letters*, he'd instructed. *I won't get them until the ship returns in a year and I'll have no time for reading then.*

Yet here in the privacy of his cabin, he felt as brazen as a voyeur, free to touch the print on the wall, to trace the long raven hair of the painted maiden; he saw where sunlight caught her skin. He fancied, in her likeness to Paquita, the promise of the future, the allure of the explorer's return.

STEEL
CROSSES

EACH AUTUMN THE OCEAN SURROUNDING Antarctica begins to freeze. By winter the sea ice will have grown to a metre and a half thick, sturdy enough to carry the weight of Davis Station's heaviest plant vehicle. But Chad McGonigal has been south enough times to know that by early November, the sea ice has begun to melt from the underside up. At some indeterminate time it will take on the structure of honeycomb, turning rotten, its bearing capacity halved, strength and structure reduced to a veneer.

Squalls whistle by. Chad pushes on the auger and winds the hand drill, the steel bit slowly grinding down through the sea ice while Indie stands back, hands on hips. A chute of sea water burbles up through the hole, freezing as it washes over the ice. Indie thinks him a lost cause for insisting on testing the thickness of the sea ice firsthand. For not trusting a mate's word.

Indie drops the weighted tape measure into the hole. 'I told you, you fuckwit.' He brandishes the measure. 'One point six metres. I've been driving the Hägglund across it all frigging week.'

Chad refrains from telling him about the Hagg that broke through the sea ice at Mawson Station. Never mind its state-of-the-art Swedish design, Mercedes-powered turbo diesel engines, automatic bilge pumps: try as she might, the old girl did precious little amphibious travel that day. For those in the cab it was a scrambled exit through the roof hatches, the Hägglund hanging on for five desperate hours before giving up and gurgling out of sight.

Chad clambers into the cab of the D8 bulldozer. The path left by *Aurora Australis* now runs as a frozen scar across the ice. He lowers the blade and begins the job of clearing sastrugi from the runway; the two Casa planes are due any day.

Adélie penguins march across the sea ice, their return signalling the start of the breeding season. For a time the penguins form an orderly line until, for no apparent reason, one renegade diverges and a second stops dead in its tracks, bringing a confused halt to the rest of the troops.

Spindrift flurries past the windscreen. Still visible are two steel crosses that mark the high point of Anchorage Island. The first time Chad saw them from a distance he pictured them crafted from Oregon pine, stately things, the grain scoured into ridges, the wood bleached blond with weather and age. He knew neither man—accidental deaths a decade apart. Inscriptions on brass plaques unite them in death.

His own epitaph, he thinks, might read:

CHAD McGONIGAL—DIEHARD LONER AND FEARFUL WASTER.
WOODEN-BOAT BUILDER. ANTARCTIC CHIPPIE. A LIFE GIVEN TO
BROKEN RESOLUTIONS AND SHIRKING IRKSOME CROWDS.
BAD-MOUTHED IN ABSENTIA BY HIS HAPLESS MATES.

The horizon blurs with the milky swirl of sky. He can see the bergs a kilometre away, but has trouble making out the surface a metre ahead. The lack of definition threatens to disarm his senses—he could plough through a wall of ice and still have trouble seeing it. Twice he's been called out of the carpentry shop in bad weather to operate the bulldozer; twice the new plant operator has been laid up with one thing or another. Chad fits the headphones and turns up the station music, clipping to a drone the engine noise that vibrates through bone.

Fifty metres away, Indie turns the Hägglund in an arc and trundles back towards the station where he will load drums of aviation fuel on the sledge. Indie has the new plant operator pegged as a malingerer, says it stood out like dogs' balls during their training in Hobart. Nine winters here, and Chad is still floored by those who turn out to be trouble.

As for him, he should be on his way back to Hobart, but is one of a handful from winter who have been asked to stay on and help. There are worse ways to earn a living than work a second summer at Davis Station. Even his place on the east coast of Tasmania loses some of its shine at this time of year—the onslaught of tourists and stink boats, infernal jet skis that carve up the bay from morning to night. Even on an afternoon as bleak as this he still jumps at the chance to be out on the ice.

See? Some things stay the same. The ghostly voice still haunts him.

Fingers of mist inch across the side window. Images flicker and fade like spliced frames of film played too many times. Chad can't block out these illusory hands that paw at the window struggling to escape but he takes a cloth and wipes the glass clear, turns the demister to high, attempts to stave off the wretched woman who returns to him in snippets of black and white. Still the echo lingers, her hands as familiar as his own.

Static from the VHF radio cuts the music; Chad unhooks the handpiece. 'How's tricks, Charlie boy?'

'Can't complain, Chad. Warmer in here than out there. Got a couple of things for you. Our esteemed leader asks when you'll be back on dry land. Malcolm wants a powwow with you.'

'Give me an hour, sooner if the weather claps out. He say what it's about?'

'Nope.'

It must be nearing the end of Charlie's shift. He's in no mood to chat.

'What else you got?'

'Message from Adam Singer. He and your other new chippies are hosting this week's happy hour. Five o'clock, Adam says, if you can lend a hand. A couple of them are rummaging round the dress-up room now, picking out a frock to wear.'

Chad shakes his head. 'Doesn't take long, does it? Will we see you up there?'

'After the day I've had, fella, the only happy hour I'll be having is a nap.'

Chad lines the D8 up for a second run parallel to the first. He watches the Hägglund wind up the hill towards the fuel farm. Chad's waiting to see whether *Ginger* and *Gadget*, the new Casa planes, will perform as well as the old Twin Otters.

Wind buffets the cab. Chad turns up the music. He can hazard a guess at the day's slushy from the choice of music the job privileges them to play: a member of *The Whalers* who, complete with harmonicas, Hawaiian guitars and tropical shirts, have cut their first demo tape. Wailers is right, Chad thinks, the band's signature song the product of hours of racket from the music practice shed.

The Whalers croon while Chad provides the bass. *The frozen sea. The frozen sea. When we said goodbye*—he catches a sudden movement over the top of the blade and jams on the floor brake. He yanks the steering control to avoid the figure crouching directly in his path. The right track locks and the D8 slides like a chord on *The Whalers'* guitar. Steel grousers warble over a slick of ice. The woman before him grabs at her equipment, tumbling over herself in an attempt to leap clear. *The Whalers* strums. Chad yells. The woman skates on one knee, legs tangled with those of her tripod. How the twenty-tonner doesn't collect her he'll never know, but the D8 completes one lithe and graceful loop before easing to a stop.

'Are you hurt?' he shouts, jumping down from the cab.

The woman scrambles to her feet, her clothing caked in snow. 'I'm okay. Are you alright?'

He picks up her camera from the snow. The housing of the lens comes apart in his hands. 'That ain't good.'

'An understatement,' she says wryly, though the words catch in her throat and when she collects the pieces from him Chad sees her hands are trembling.

He's about to offer to take the lens back to the station, to see what can be done, but is seized by a sudden urge to shake her. 'What the hell were you doing there? I nearly wiped you out.' When she takes a step back, he realises he's shouting.

'I'm very sorry,' she says. 'I was trying to get a close-up of the blade. I misjudged the distance,' she adds, sheepishly.

'Misjudged the distance! Do you make a practice of springing out in front of moving vehicles?'

The wind carries her answer away, leaving only the residue of an accent. The squall blows back her hair to uncover a birthmark stamped upon her cheek and throat. The other side of her face is as white as her tangle of blonde hair. He finds himself mesmerised. She retrieves her bags and shakes snow from her fallen hat.

'How long have you been out here?' he asks.

'Not long.'

'Apart from it being a no-no,' Chad speaks evenly, 'it's not a smart idea to be out on the sea ice alone, particularly in weather like this.'

She slides on her hat and rearranges her hair around her face. 'Please. You won't say anything, will you?'

He may be many things, but a dobber he's not. 'Come on,' he says. 'I'll drive you back to the station.'

They trudge across the ice, her body leaning into the squall at the same angle as his own. Chad climbs onto the track of the bulldozer and holds the door open against a gust that given half a chance would tear it from its hinges. She clambers up beside him but halts at the sight of the single-person cab.

'I get a bit claustrophobic. Do you mind if I walk?'

'I can't leave you out here on your own. Please get in, before we both freeze.' He slides her survival pack onto the floor beside the single seat. 'Sit up on the ledge and nurse your gear. There's enough room.'

Chad is grateful for the engine noise that drowns out any need for talk. What other joker hits his forties still burdened with the shyness of his teenage years? She sits at his right, squeezed between his bulk and the door, her legs straddling the steering clutch. Each time she attempts to sit upright her head grazes the roof. She hunches, one arm hugging her tripod, the other clasped around the camera bag as if it, too, were under siege. Her body doesn't stop shivering—from cold or shock or discomfort at the confinement, he can't tell. She seems clueless about what the place can dish out. He gives the woman a sideways glare, but if she registers his disdain she does a fine job of ignoring it. She scowls through the window at the pail of sky. Her birthmark radiates across her white cheek as fierce as a burn. Stay on in Antarctica to escape the summer airheads at home? Call him a luckless bastard; he never was one for timing.

'McGONIGAL. PERFECT TIMING.' THE STATION leader lowers his head to look over the rim of his glasses. 'How would you like to play tour guide over summer?'

Chad casts Malcolm Ball a look of despair. 'Passenger ships already?'

Malcolm gives a manic shake of his head. 'Not on your Nellie.' He concentrates on placing a stack of loose pages into the bite of Jaws, his beloved electric stapler. He rubs a thumb over the copper staple that transforms the corner of the page into an equilateral triangle. You could run a set of parallel rules over Malcolm's desk and find not a blade of paper out of place.

'Freya Jorgensen.'

Chad shrugs.

'Photographer. Tall girl.' Malcolm goes to pat his cheek but apparently thinks better of it and sweeps a hand through his number two crew cut. 'Mop of fair hair. Run into her?'

'Almost.'

'The thing is, Chad, she's emailed me with all the places she wants to photograph.' He fans the stapled pages. 'A list as long as your bloody arm. She'll be lucky to get out to half of them. I've already told her she can't go gallivanting off on her own. It's Freya's first time south. We'll see how she goes on field training later in the week with Simon, but I'd like a qualified trip leader, someone with your know-how, to go out with her, keep an eye on things.'

Keep her alive, he means. 'What about the work on the summer accommodation module? Isn't that why I've been asked to stay on?'

Malcolm shakes his head again. 'It won't be every day, nothing like that. She can hook up with the seal team once a week, the skua mob will let her tag along if they can ever get their act together. Just now and then, when you see your way to setting up the boys and letting things roll for a day or two. The building work takes priority. I'll tell Freya that she'll need to slot in with your schedule.' Malcolm waits for a moment. 'What's the problem, McGonigal?' He gets an edge to his voice when things don't go his way. 'Your boys are all crack tradesmen, aren't they?'

'You know they are.'

'Adam Singer would jump at the chance if I gave him the nod. He's taken quite a shine to Freya and her project.'

'I bet he has.' The Predator, is the name those Adam trained with in Hobart call him on the quiet. Bullshit artist or Casanova, in two weeks at the station Adam has already mentioned enough conquests to make Chad feel inadequate.

'Come on,' Malcolm urges, 'you and I are used to juggling balls for the Division. Any other time you'd be panting to get off the station.'

Clearly taking Chad's grunt as a yes, Malcolm runs a neat line of correction fluid over jottings in the margin of one page. Both of them know Chad has no recourse. Ultimately, the station leader calls the shots.

'Let's see. You'll be able to bike it on quads as long as the sea ice is good. Freya's project has been allocated five hours' helicopter time. That should get you out to some choice spots. You never know, you might end up large as life on some art gallery wall, immortalised in print alongside Frank Hurley's photos.' He rolls up the pages and loops an elastic band around them, once, twice, three times to be sure.

Chad can feel his hackles rise.

'I know you'll like this.' Malcolm lowers his voice as he leans across the desk. 'There's a chance I can get the two of you out on *Ginger* or *Gadget* later in the summer. Up to the plateau, Amery Ice Shelf, Beaver Lake.' He presents the scroll to Chad on a platter of upturned hands. 'No promises, mind.'

Chad can't help himself: he takes the roll and smacks the edge of the desk with the same flick he'd use to nail a fly. 'Always glad to help, Malcolm.' Dislodged by the sudden movement, loose papers billow and waft across the trim and tidy desk.

Ski training
February 1912

SKI TRAINING WAS A DISASTER waiting to happen.

'It's all well and good for you, X,' Walter Hannam, the big wireless operator, grumbled. 'We weren't all born Swiss long-jump ski champions.'

The trouble, Douglas realised, was that few Australians had encountered snow before, let alone trying to move about with eight-foot wooden planks lashed to their boots. Douglas could see the group losing heart while Xavier Mertz, the embodiment of optimism and goodwill, insisted they relocate to a higher rise where they could make use of the gradient down to the hut.

'We make our own championship!' X sang. Douglas gave a half-hearted nod of approval and away they went, the vaudeville ski patrol shuffling like penguins behind their instructor, Douglas bringing up the rear.

Snow sparkled, the ice cliffs shone, snow petrels in their dozens swept across a sky gilded with evening sun. Over at the headland, Frank Hurley stood caped beneath his black cloth, his camera's cyclopean eye framing the landscape.

Commonwealth Bay was a glorious place when the wind stopped blowing. The men had asked him about the uncanny pattern of wind—how one could stand in relative calm while thirty yards away another would be blown off his feet in a gust. At times the harbour had been struck with ferocious squalls, when, at the same time, the foreshore registered nothing more than a whisper of breeze. No one but Douglas had reason to wonder at the uniquely fickle nature of Commonwealth Bay—his men, first-timers, assumed this weather was normal for Antarctica. Ninnis joked that they needn't bother filling the gaps in the hut walls—already the verandahs were knee-deep in snowdrift; in another month, Ninnis said, the snow banked around the outside of the building would be *up to pussy's bow*.

Another sixty weddell seals had come ashore during the day to join the hundred-odd lounging on the ice. Along the foreshore, two adélie penguins shot out of the water and sped off on their bellies before striding off to feed their fledgling chicks. Penguins were leaving Commonwealth Bay and would not return until next spring. Tomorrow, if the weather held, he would have the men start stockpiling—five hundred adélie carcasses to supplement their diet, ward off scurvy through the dark months of winter.

Mertz demonstrated the stance again, crouching to a squat and shifting his body weight forward. He eased down the hill, made a clean sweep in the snow and came to a stop near the back wall of the hut. Douglas applauded with the others.

'Who'll give that a crack?' Walter Hannam said.

Mertz gave a nod of encouragement to Johnny Hunter. Though Hunter initially tucked himself down low, he shot up like a duck the moment gravity took hold. He hadn't travelled nine yards before he keeled to one side. Douglas watched two more men topple like skittles and tumble down the slope with limbs and skis akimbo. Hannam collapsed in the snow, his raucous laugh echoing across the bay and setting off the dogs. 'Championship! Championship!' Hannam roared at each man who fell.

Mertz loomed over Douglas, panting in his thick accent his latest English word, 'Golly!' He added, 'I bet our chief will make the *A-one* sportsman.'

Enough was enough. Douglas unbuckled his straps. 'I didn't bring men all this damned way to break arms and legs in the name of sport.'

A wild squeal rang out and Douglas looked up to see Walter Hannam tobogganing towards the hut, his hefty body prone along the length of a single ski. Men dived clear; Hannam shot past, hooting and shouting and slapping his thigh—his glee cut short when he registered the hut's back wall fast approaching.

Douglas closed his eyes.

'Championship! Championship!' the onlookers roared, then cackled hysterically when Hannam careened into the hut.

'Have the men pack away the gear,' Douglas barked at Mertz. 'They won't be needing skis again.'

He dumped his own skis near the hut and strode away, choosing to seek out Hurley's company by the rocks over that of a crestfallen ski instructor and a now-subdued group of men.

Beyond the hut the Greenland dogs sat stretched along the length of their chains, looking perfectly at home. Ginger lolled on the rocks licking her paws, Basilisk and Gadget sat blinking at the yolk of the sun. Douglas always marvelled at the warmth trapped inside those dense, matted coats. To be so naturally adapted. To be so well equipped. There was no clear explanation as to why so many had perished.

They had begun with forty-nine dogs. Frank Wild had taken eight for his western base but that still left half the original count dead. Mertz and Ninnis had spoken of the voyage out from London on *Aurora*, some dogs collapsing with distemper while one beast turned rabid and roamed the decks after tearing free of its chains. *It was kill or be killed*, X explained.

Between the group's setting up the radio relay station at Macquarie Island and arriving at Commonwealth Bay, ten dogs had died. Fitting and foaming at the mouth, paroxysms of shivering, some of their faces disfigured with lockjaw— illnesses the likes of which no one had seen before. Doctors McLean and Whetter's post-mortem diagnosed gastric inflammation, collapsed lungs, a gangrenous appendix. It was as if some hidden evil had poisoned their bodies from the inside out.

Hurley stood at his tripod, sunlight catching the glass of his camera. 'Hannam survive his field training?' He grinned.

'Which of us should be more grateful?' Douglas spoke without caution. 'Hannam for his surplus padding, or the rest of us for nailing extra braces to the framework of the hut?'

'Poor old fat boy.' Hurley chortled and Douglas chided himself for disregarding a rule of leadership he'd admired in Ernest Shackleton: be fair, firm and friendly, *never familiar*.

The men had all filtered indoors except for Mertz, who pushed away on skis, head down, moving out of sight beyond the rise.

'Look at her sitting there, timbers gleaming,' Hurley nodded to winter quarters, 'an outpost of the Empire amid all this untamed glory. And beyond that rise, Doc, who knows what's in store for us?'

'We, and your camera, will be the first to explore it.'

'It's the kind of adventure every fellow dreams of.' Hurley turned to him. 'From what I hear, a number of us were up against some stiff competition—older, more experienced chaps.'

'Youth and vigour, Hurley. I needed men with the recuperative powers to withstand harsh conditions and extreme discomfort.' That was another thing he'd learned on Shackleton's expedition, hauling across an endless tract of ice not just a laden sledge but also an ageing sledging companion—his old geology professor and mentor; cajoling

the Prof to keep moving, at times admonishing him as
though he was a badly behaved child, turning at the sound
of his cry to witness the horror of him scrabbling on hands
and knees while their companion kicked him like a dog.

'And here was I thinking I'd impressed you with artistic
talent.'

'Don't misunderstand me, Hurley. The need for a first-
rate photographic record is the sole reason you are here.'
Every camera enthusiast in Australia had applied for the role
of expedition photographer. Though his colleagues thought
Hurley a remarkably fine photographer, he had no cinematograph experience. 'From personal know-how, some of the
best scenes are to be got on sledging journeys. As fortune
would have it, you came equipped with the necessary build
and constitution.' Indeed, Douglas would have sacrificed
the photographic results rather than include a weak link in
the team.

He recalled the drive to raise fifty thousand pounds in
less than a year from a British public who had already given
generously to Scott's South Pole expedition. The appeal in
London's *Daily Mail* to raise enough money for a ship to get
started; months in their Lower Regent Street office first
sending out requests to manufacturers, then letters thanking
firms for tins of rabbit, plum pudding, sewing machines and
tobacco, glaxo milk powder, candles—and soap, of which
they'd received enough to lather the Southern Ocean. He
could happily go on travelling for the rest of time, but to
organise another expedition . . .

Douglas saw Mertz reappear, a compact figure weaving down the slope on skis, seeking out undulations that sent him gliding through the air. He watched as X eased to a standstill near the dogs.

'The first Swiss to ski in Antartica,' Hurley said. 'He makes it look dead easy,'

Ginger would have bowled X over had her chain been longer. She nuzzled under his arm as he untethered his skis. He scratched her back and she leaned her weight against his leg, her tongue lapping at the air.

Then the dogs pricked their ears in unison; penguins halted in their tracks. Douglas watched X smile with the sweetness of the melody rising from the hut.

Ginger laid her ears flat when X hoisted her up by her front legs and placed her paws on his chest. He stepped from side to side, one hand on his dance partner's back, the other resting on her paw. Mertz and Ginger swayed to 'The Shepherd's Cradle Song'; the lullaby playing on the gramophone spilled across the bay. On each turn Ginger hopped and shuffled; with each step she licked her master's chin.

Douglas nodded. 'The first to dance.'

Xavier Mertz at Land's End

FIELD
TRAINING

FREYA SAVOURS THE HOUR: TOO early for helicopters to begin their day. Her pack and camera case rest against her studio door, everything double-checked and ready to go. She fires off a quick email: *About to leave for field training. Hoping for fine weather and photos to match. Back Sunday.* Within a minute her laptop chimes with her husband's reply: *TAKE CARE OUT THERE!*

Long ago, when he was her tutor, Marcus introduced Freya to Hurley's pictorial world, and led her to question the truth in her own photography. *Mediation and manipulation have been part of photography from its early days.* He had held up a Hurley image before the class. *Take the process of composing, positioning the subject, cropping objects the photographer considers extraneous or an interruption. In this sense, doesn't every photo lie?*

She studies Hurley's photo now. *Xavier Mertz at Land's End.* Carefully posed near the ice cliff, the figure of Mertz offers more than scale to the icescape. An enduring Hurley theme was human fragility pitted against the might of nature. Hurley captures Mertz's awe as he gazes out across the sea ice, the low-angle light dragging his shadow back across the snow. Did Xavier Mertz have any premonition of what lay ahead?

When your own shutter blinks—Marcus's eyes had swept the tutorial room—*think about the story you're showing. Then look at what you're masking.*

A memory from earlier in the week dances before Freya's eyes. *Not a smart idea*, the man driving the bulldozer had said, unable to hide his disdain at finding her out on the ice alone. Neither smart, nor her proudest moment. Marcus, if she told him, would struggle to imagine his wife defying the rules.

In a small, primitive darkroom at Commonwealth Bay, Frank Hurley brought this image of Mertz into being, meticulously retouching the negative, using camelhair brushes and developer to tease out highlights and shadows. Hurley worked like an impressionist painter, drawing on brushstroke and colour to create light and shade, to reveal a deeper truth.

Sensate truth, Marcus termed Hurley's art, and framed Freya's face with his gaze.

At the end of her final semester at the photography college, Marcus had encouraged her to stay in Melbourne and urged her to take her portfolio to a dozen contacts on a list he'd prepared, convinced she had the talent to strike out on her own. Of course she accepted his invitation to celebrate her first paid assignment. *To new beginnings*, he had toasted.

'WE BEGAN HERE.' THE FIELD training officer traces on the map the route Freya had taken. 'And we were looking sweet all the way up here. Waypoint 228,' Simon taps the map, 'is where we started going walkabout.' The GPS, the size of a mobile phone and every bit as intrusive, is passed around the field training circle for all to acknowledge Freya's unplanned 5.2-kilometre detour. Latitude, longitude, minutes, seconds; dozens of satellites map the globe with frightening acuity, ten of their stealthy eyes fixed upon the ice edge where the training group confers.

'If you have access to a GPS,' asks Travis, beside her, 'why would you bother with a compass?'

Freya silently agrees.

'Chances are, you won't use anything but a GPS over summer. They're all well and good until your batteries run flat, or your LCD gives out with the cold.' Simon rests the map on the seat of his quad bike. He takes Freya's compass and demonstrates again how to adjust for magnetic deviation. 'Remember, folks,' he draws a pocket-sized book from his jacket and waves it like a spruiker touting programs at a fair, 'Simon says. Whatever you need to know, the information is all here in your field manuals.'

The four trainees, Freya now at the rear, follow Simon Says in a single line back through iceberg alley, weaving between the same towering bergs, meandering past the same field of waist-high snow, avoiding the same crests of ice that Freya led them safely by when outward bound. She can't help dwelling on her ineptitude. What if other people's safety depended on her navigation? *A girl in need of rescue*, Marcus began calling her years ago, on the night she took a wrong turn while showing him her city, and hurtled down an alleyway to a dead end. He was as certain of his feelings then as he was of his sense of direction. After she moved from Melbourne back to Perth he had appeared unannounced on the doorstep of her unit, the fragrance of the bedraggled posy in his hand engulfing, as was her image of him smuggling hand-picked sprigs of daphne across the continent.

No unlit street signs to blame out here: just her own shoddy compass work, though no one is insensitive enough to say so. Simon and the training group are kind, encouraging, which only adds to Freya's sting of failure. All day her focus has been pulled and pushed by all this wonder, her mind raking through ideas on how to photograph the ice—dismissing the notion of black and white amid all this colour and texture, the quality of light, the incomprehensible magnitude of the place. Did she take a compass bearing as often as she ought? Did she add or subtract for magnetic deviation? Travis joked that she'd lured them astray on purpose. Everyone agreed that the path she blazed out to the ocean added a brilliant photo opportunity to an already outstanding day of navigational training—the water sparkling, the ice edge alive with the hubbub of penguins.

Freya has her work cut out keeping pace with the bikes ahead, her oversized helmet requiring constant attention to stop it sliding forward. This irrational dislike she has for enclosure—what kind of person knowingly chooses a helmet several sizes too large? She releases her grip on the handlebar and pushes at the headgear. She has less than a second to feel her body rise as her bike becomes airborne, launched by an unseen wave of sastrugi. Time moves in frames. She feels as weightless as a bird. Freya looks out upon a surface of crystal blue shimmering in silver light. She sees a blur of peacock green and red, the clothing and bike of the rider ahead wheeling through the ice. In the time it takes a shutter to blink, Freya captures the spark of a photographic idea: a summer aurora, its celestial lights streaked vivid through the ice. Her quad lands with a jarring thud, skittles over ice and returns with a flick of its tail to the furrow of tracks. The helmet droops over her eyes again like a forelock from an unkempt mane.

BANDITS HUT STANDS THIRTY KILOMETRES north of Davis Station. Another ten k's, a mere hop and a skip, and they would be at Walkabout Rocks, the station's northern boundary.

Pockets of steam lift the lid from a pot of melted snow, mist upon the window waxes and wanes. Though Freya feels weary from a full day of training, she leaves her companions to the warmth of the field hut, its gas heater glowing, a clutter of Scrabble tiles spilled upon a board.

Outside cold bites at her skin. Shadows stretch the length of the frozen fjord. Bergs on the horizon rest in evening light. Below, five quad bikes nestle between the shadow of stone and undulations of broken ice—the tide crack, which can be seen rammed against every outcrop of land. Freya breaks off a wedge of chocolate, her last bar, having demolished the rest of her monthly supply in her first two weeks at the station. She savours the bittersweet square as it thaws and melts inside her mouth. No matter that it's Old Gold and five years out of date.

Granite dykes meander the length and width of the Vestfold Hills, corridors of shiny black that crisscross the rocks like a cobbled road. On the southern horizon luminescence glows from the river of ice they call the Sørsdal; the large glacier with its fissured tongue slicks out across the ocean to mark the station's southern boundary. Beyond the hills the icecap, always the icecap, beguiling in its blush of rose. She turns in circles, drawing in the wonder of the place, giddied with the reality of being here, immersed in its beauty and expanse. She will photograph it all, from Walkabout Rocks to the Sørsdal Glacier, the calm and wild of the place. This, she knows, reaching for her camera, is joy.

The lookout above the hut is capped with boulders as crimson as the evening light. The air surrounding her is charged with life. Angel wings blur in Freya's camera shutter: snow petrels darting and swooping, agile with every turn. The night is filled with the chatter of these birds no larger than doves, flashes of white fluttering into and out of rocky crevices.

Freya hears a bird call. She kneels upon the rock and whistles a quavered note, then hears from beneath her feet a soft trill in reply. She releases her camera from its tripod and scrambles down to where she can lie flat and squint into a rocky cleft. She can see deep inside a pair of glassy beads peering out. The snow petrel, small and white, could fit in the cup of her hands. How does a bird so seemingly fragile exist in such a hostile place? Freya watches and absorbs, struck by a sense of the familiar, and remembers, Frank Hurley's image of a snow petrel, identical to the scene before her. *To shared discoveries*; Freya whistles and the snow petrel tilts her head, she studies Freya for a time. Finally, the bird plumps her breast feathers, closes her eyes and tucks her head into a curve of downy white. She knows she is beyond reach, safe, protected by her hug of rock.

Nesting snow petrel

Composites
March 1912

THE CURIOUS NOISE PLAGUED DOUGLAS and Hurley all
afternoon. Douglas thought of surf breaking incessantly on
a distant beach; Hurley likened it to wind raking the tops of
trees. To the west, flurries of snowdrift lifted from the cape
while along the foreshore the bay remained still. Hurley
had abandoned his tripod and lay sprawled on his belly
among the rocky crevices, attempting to entice a nesting
snow petrel to pose before his lens. He might score more
than a photographic impression: the snow petrel's defence
against intruders was an oily red concoction that the dainty
little creature could summon from its belly and eject a
full six feet.

Douglas rested on his haunches, framing with his eyes a
panorama of the bay. The adélie rookery looked barely
inhabited. The occasional weddell seal that still ventured
ashore received a swift bullet to the head; scarlet snow lay in
patches along the foreshore where Ninnis and Mertz

butchered the meat while the dogs stood poised on their chains, fielding the scraps.

Ninnis and Mertz; their names rolled off the tongue as a couplet, never one without the other.

Hurley scrambled to his feet. 'Somewhere up there, Doc,' he gestured to the sky, 'it's blowing like the devil.'

Douglas gave a wry smile. 'If we could only find a way to make it stay up there.'

Throughout these last weeks the wind had blown with increased velocity, leaving only a few hours' reprieve before ratcheting up to blast the bay anew. This was their third month at winter quarters, the sum of their science work a boxful of specimens for the biological collection, and the daily meteorological and magnetic recordings. As for exploring further afield, blizzards had simply overwhelmed their attempts at preliminary sledging and trail-marking up on the plateau.

Hurley returned his camera to its tripod, entering his other world beneath the black cloth. Douglas looked forward to these hours more than he could say, assisting Frank with his eighty pounds of photographic equipment. Indoors, Hurley would act the eternal practical joker, but out here, camera in hand, he approached his art with scientific resolve. A seventy-mile-an-hour wind that blasted others indoors brought Hurley scurrying outside. He filmed men blown from the weather screen, photographed them hurricane walking, their bodies pitched semi-prone into the wind. *Photographing the blizzard*, Frank declared with utter certainty, *is our chance to show the world something it has never seen before.*

Not so long ago, Douglas had believed a photographer was worthwhile solely as a means of recouping funds after the expedition: lantern slides to accompany public lectures, photographs to illustrate a book, an adventure cinematograph to be shown in theatres to the paying public. Yet he could see, from the prints Frank created in the hut's darkroom each evening, that his images stood alone. His photographs evoked two Antarctic worlds, one of serene, dazzling beauty, the other hostile and stark; each mood enkindled the senses. In his images of man against nature, one could come to believe in the presence of God. In the darkroom Hurley turned alchemist, pushing the limits of photographic science. For artistic effect he could take a scene of the bay photographed on an overcast day and merge it with a negative of a sky torn ragged with cloud. *Composites*, he called these compilations. No one but Hurley could detect the real from the embellished and even he, over time, might fail to distinguish between the two.

Oregon timber for the wireless masts stayed stacked beside the hut where it had lain since January. Oh, for a spell of calm long enough to get them up. By now—the evenings dim before nine o'clock, the receding sun as pale as tinned butter—the relay station at Macquarie Island would be tuning in each night, listening unrewarded through an ether of static for a string of dots and dashes from a thousand miles south.

Douglas ran his thumb over a quartz seam in the gneiss painted with splashes of copper, crystals glowing emerald green—minerals created deep within the earth's crust. Phenomenal forces of pressure and heat transformed silica-rich fluids into a bejewelled seam of rock. While it was the order of science that shaped his thoughts, this astonishing beauty—the lustre of minerals, their exquisite crystal structures and kaleidoscope of colour—bewitched a deeper, intangible part of him.

The sound of moving air grew shrill. Hurley looked out from beneath his black cloth and stretched his arm to the sky as if to comb his fingers through a river of wind.

'See here.' Douglas beckoned him, taking his handker-chief and polishing a film of sea salt from the quartz. 'This glassy green could be emerald, at the very least beryl; under a microscope we'd see a pattern of hexagonal prisms.'

Hurley kneeled down for a closer look. 'Jewels for a king.'

A willy-willy rose from the incline behind the hut, the funnel of snow wheeling across the slope like a child's spinning top.

'This is green apatite.' Douglas brought their attention back to mineralogy. 'And all of this,' he pointed, 'is copper sulphide oxidised to malachite.' Douglas wanted Hurley to see the art in science as he saw the science in Hurley's photographic art. 'These minerals begin as separate elements—copper, beryllium, aluminium, phosphorous, calcium. The real magic happens when they crystallise and combine; then they transform into new minerals.'

'Composites.'

Douglas nodded. 'Nature's form of art.'

He caught the edge of a sound and turned to see a zinc sheet sweep into the air. It flew north over Boat Harbour like a great silver-backed gull then lifted higher again, the razor-sharp edge agleam as it twisted and turned, the sheet warbling a cry as it sailed overhead.

Hurricane walking

SLUSHY

BY ELEVEN AT NIGHT THE buildings of Davis Station gleam from the golden light of a sun that, now, barely sets. Even Freya's accommodation block basks in the glow, the orange prefab box elevated by the lustre. Quiet hours; a reprieve, she thinks, pausing at the landing of her studio before stepping in.

Freya has resigned herself to her bone-shaking surrounds; she dons ear phones and edges up the volume of her iPod to muffle the shriek of engines, the drum-beats of air, anything to disguise the quaking that rattles the engineer's workshop below and reverberates upstairs. The two Squirrels, at rest now until morning, are lashed to the ground, rotor blades pulled taut so they bow like whale ribs.

She feels a visceral shiver when she opens the image attached to Marcus's email: *Hurricane walking. Autumn 1912.*

>> The diaries make constant reference to the appalling weather at winter quarters. By autumn they experienced winds exceeding

120 km per hour. Mawson's journal speaks of Frank Bickerton, the plane engineer, venturing out with Hurley and both being swept down a slope. Johnny Hunter, biologist, remarks of men being unable to walk upright, of the struggle to simply get underway against the wind resistance. Might this attached photo of Hurley's illustrate those diary excerpts?

Indeed it would. She draws back from the image of the two men and pictures the photographer clinging to his heavy wooden tripod, snow filling his camera as he battles wind and frostbite.

Freya wants to honour Hurley and his work, pay tribute to a pioneer of Antarctic photography. She knows that there are those who disparage Hurley's photographic vision, who claim his portraits reduced the men to members of a species battling nature's forces, rather than the heroes the public of the day wanted to see. Freya clicks to her own portraits—her fellow trainees retrieving a quad bike from its simulated plunge through the sea ice during field training; scientists working in snowdrift at the tide gauge; Kittie changing the sunlight card, a parhelion filling the sky and tracing a circle around her. So far she has only a handful of images to place alongside Hurley's, yet she can see that the Antarctic environment itself is as vibrant now as it was then, as real and as complex as any human figure. In Hurley's *Hurricane Walking*, the identity of the two men was secondary to his desire to portray the challenge of working in such extremes. At winter quarters, the community of eighteen epitomised the hero, each man an integral part of a unified team. Descriptions from the diaries, Marcus has persuaded her, will add another layer to the photographic experience. Freya sits back further in her seat at the thought of all she owes her husband.

In preparing her second application to the Arts Council, try as she might she could not transform her creative vision onto paper, not in terms that Marcus found convincing. She agreed to his offer to collect impressions from Antarctic pioneers; he rewrote her proposal as *a narrative woven through the photographic work*. Marcus found, in the diaries of the men from Douglas Mawson's 1911–14 expedition, the link to Australia's Antarctic history—and to Hurley—he said her photographs needed.

Freya had whirled like a dervish from the letterbox to the house, delirious with joy at the Council's offer.

Come with me, she had said to Marcus (hadn't she already anticipated his answer?)

Whatever will I do in Antarctica for five months?

Come as my assistant, she'd offered lamely. *See the place. Experience it with me.*

Marcus had placed his arm around her shoulder. *I'll see ice aplenty through your and Hurley's photos. I'm happy here, Freya, working on the text.*

❧

FREYA RELISHES THESE QUIET AFTER-DINNER hours in her studio, a mug of hot chocolate warming her hands. If not for tomorrow's early start—she is rostered on as slushy in the kitchen—she would stay here half the night, would look up from her desk through the pane of crazed glass to gauge the lowest dip of light.

She pulls her studio door shut and registers a separate echo. Across the way she spies the figure of a man leaving the carpentry shop, hunched down: Chad McGonigal, head-chippie-turned-unwilling-photographic-assistant as of this morning's meeting with the station leader. *We've met*, Chad muttered without expression when Malcolm Ball introduced them. Freya studies his gait as he saunters down the roadway, jacket and overalls adding to his bulk, hands wedged in pockets, drawn in on himself as he had been throughout Malcolm's briefing.

He slows in his tracks, perhaps to take in the ice-choked bay flooded with pink. Does the wonder of the place fade in the eyes of a jaded man who's seen it countless times before? She watches him cross to the edge of the path and cartwheel through a bank of snow with a litheness that surprises her. When he stands and brushes snow from his hands, his long hair spills across his back.

Who deserves the most commiseration—a wounded Adam Singer, visibly put out at being denied the chance to help her; Chad McGonigal, landed an assignment he clearly doesn't want; or herself, the future of her project beholden to an unwilling man?

'Joy,' she bids the sky goodnight on her way down the steps.

THE MORNING WEATHER BALLOON RISES from the meteorological building, scudding across the sky faster than Freya can run. Cold air cuts her lungs and her hair is a tangled mess. She waves at Kittie and makes it to the kitchen just in time for her rostered day on.

Freya is not about to enquire of either chef why the second slushy hasn't shown up. The tension between Sandy and Tommo bulges like a pressure cooker lid about to explode. Enough to know that the tradies have downed tools for their morning break and are on their way, marching down the road. Among them are the nicotine hounds who peel away to the smoking shed for a longed-for drag, but the mass of hungry workers cascades into the dining room for ten o'clock smoko, mounding onto their plates a volume of food that leaves Freya wide-eyed.

More toast, slushy!

Freya slides the tray into a bain-marie of steaming porridge, beans, scrambled eggs, Sandy's maple syrup pancakes and his *grab-'em-while-they-last* cheese scones. No sooner has she topped up the coffee machine than there are empty jugs to refill. She scours the shelves in search of powdered milk, scans an out-of-reach ledge, afraid the chefs will snap at her if she asks, one more time, where things are kept. With a rising tide of despair she hears the clatter of pots being slung onto the bench, the sizzle of a pan plunged into water. Used baking tins hover in a teetering pile, tongs fall and clank, batter forms an ellipsis that stretches across the floor from the rim of the stove to a bowl bobbing in the sink.

Freya remembers that the music on the MP3 player is slushy's choice only when an opportunist takes advantage of her oversight and puts on Metallica. Loud.

'On ya, Freya!' Tommo, the big chef, springs into life, drumming his meat knife on the stainless steel counter.

'Turn it down, please!' Dr Ev calls from the furthest table.

'Hear, hear.' Malcolm theatrically pokes his fingers in his ears.

Chad McGonigal slouches in the corner, swirling syrup across his high-rise of pancakes.

Sandy pleads, 'Freya, I know we're one slushy down. I'm onto it, but for now, try and get those pots washed. Soon as you can.'

'I told her already,' Tommo growls, throwing his frisbee of a meat tray onto the bench. Blood splatters the wall tiles. 'She's slow.'

The two chefs are as glum as a pair of sad clowns. Sandy, the new summer chef who travelled south with Freya, looks exhausted as he pours filling into fluted shells of pastry, his forearms powdered with flour. Tommo, who wintered over, rocks to the rhythm as he trims fat from a weeping shoulder of pork. He throws the discards none too carefully into a bin.

Charlie, Freya's saviour, rounds the corner with a carton of milk powder balanced on his shoulder. 'This should hold back the herd. You mix up a fresh lot. I'll get a head start on the washing up and we'll round them off at the pass.'

'I'll do it, Charlie. You've been working since six this morning. Sit down and have your break.'

Charlie ignores her, pushing through the mess to the sink and rolling up his tartan sleeves. Two field assistants scuttle up from a table and run a stack of plates and cutlery through the glass washer, then launch into a tea-towel flicking match.

'You galahs got nothing better to do with your time?' Malcolm ushers them over to the drinks fridge. 'Merv, you unpack the juice and Wattsie, let's you and I get these boxes stacked away.'

Dr Ev pulls an overflowing laundry basket from under the bench. 'Freya, I'll run the tea-towels upstairs, get them started for you.'

Freya does battle with an overfilled garbage bag that splits as she pulls it free of the bin. She seizes the bag in her arms, her futile grip all that stops it rupturing further, while the innards of the bag leak onto her jeans and across the floor.

Chad McGonigal appears before her and shakes out a new bag, easing it over the old.

'Thanks,' she says.

'When do you want to start?' he asks by way of hello. 'Malcolm's given me the list of places you want to photograph.'

'I can be ready as soon as you say.'

Chad winds a length of colour-coded tape around the neck of the bag: green for wet burnables. 'It's not my project,' he says. 'I'm just along for the ride.'

'Look,' she says, frustrated at his surliness, 'I'm sorry if you feel put out. I didn't ask for your help. If I had my way—' Freya stops herself. 'I mean that I'm used to working on my own.'

'The way it looked from the cab of the D8, you're lucky to be working at all.'

Freya flushes at the reference and Chad looks contrite.

'Why don't I talk to Malcolm?' she says. 'See if he can find someone else? I don't want to waste your time—or my own. You have the option of coming down here whenever you choose. I only have one chance at this.'

Tommo squeals, throws down his carving knife and holds up a finger plump as a frankfurter, the tip burst and bloodied. 'Faaark!'

Sandy sighs. 'Call the Doc, someone. Anyone.' He looks out at the empty dining room. 'Never mind, I'll do it myself.'

Chad raises his hand. 'I've got it, Sandy.' He turns to Freya. 'I'll help if I'm wanted. Your call.' And off he marches towards the phone.

FREYA SPENDS HER AFTERNOON BREAK in the lounge, still draped in her apron, shoes kicked off. She pulls a book from the library shelf—*Mawson's Antarctic Diaries*—kicks off her shoes and spreads out across two easy chairs.

Marcus says she owes her presence here not just to Frank Hurley but to Douglas Mawson and John King Davis, Antarctic pioneers after whom two of Australia's continental stations were named. A portrait of a gaunt-looking Davis hangs framed in the station foyer, a young face prematurely aged by dourness. *1884–1967. Master of the* Aurora *1911–14. Second in Command of the Australasian Antarctic Expedition.*

Freya yawns as she leafs through Mawson's diary, her eyes heavy as she scans photos and hut notices: *Members of the Staff will be appointed in succession to the special posts of cook, messman and nightwatchman. Duties commence at 7 a.m. and continue until the washing and cleaning are completed in the evening—*

'Douglas Mawson.' The station leader's voice jolts her back to full consciousness. Malcolm stands in the light, casting his shadow across the open pages. 'A fellow we can all look up to. Thankfully no curried seal or penguin fricassee on our menu, but each man took his turn helping in the kitchen, just as we do today. Wouldn't we all give our eyeteeth to be on an expedition like that?'

Freya offers a feeble smile. 'I doubt he invited too many women along.'

'True,' Malcolm slides the chairs into an orderly circle, 'though Mawson was an egalitarian. No class distinctions on his expedition. They were all expected to put their shoulders to the wheel.' Malcolm scoops up the magazines scattered on the coffee table. He is, Freya decides, a touch too industrious for his own good.

'Sorted out your itinerary with Mr McGonigal?' he says.

Freya hesitates. 'Adam Singer mentioned that he'd love the chance to help. Perhaps he and I—'

'It's Singer's first time at Davis. Chad's been coming to Antarctica since the sledging days. He knows the Vestfolds like the back of his hand. He has a great deal of knowledge to impart, once you chisel your way through that outer shell.'

'He doesn't appear very keen,' Freya says in desperation.

'McGonigal? All bluff and bluster. He'd set up camp out on the ice if he had his way.'

'Really?' she says, unconvinced.

'There are some ripsnorting tales from the Heroic Era,' he says, dismissing further comment on the topic of Chad. 'Always been a big fan of Mawson and Davis, outstanding achievers the pair of them. They made a good team, at least in the early years. Not always an easy alliance—one man driven by a passion for science, the other responsible for the safety of his ship and crew.' Malcolm pauses. 'Not unlike the daily trials of a station leader.'

He returns the magazines to the cupboard and sorts them into evenly sized stacks.

'Hours of riveting reading up there.' He gestures to the bookshelves. 'If you want to get down to the nitty-gritty, you can't do better than Mawson's journal. Davis's is floating somewhere round the traps.' Malcolm sidles between the chairs and plucks a lilac-coloured volume from the bookcase, handing it to Freya as though it were a required text. 'Blockbusters, the pair of 'em.'

'Great. Thanks.'

He returns to the magazine cupboard and snaps the doors shut. 'Better than wasting your time on this mind-numbing rot.'

Everything shipshape and stowed away, Malcolm evaporates from the lounge as suddenly as he materialised. He leaves Freya feeling she should sit up straight, improve her posture, find better things to do than slouch about in socks. *Blockbusters*. She wouldn't put it past him to follow up with study questions.

FOLLOWING DINNER, A GROUP DRIFTS in from the dining room to gather around the bar. A clack of pool balls reverberates through the lounge, lights flood the dartboard, METEOROLOGY VS WHITECOATS chalked up on the blackboard. Chad McGonigal keeps to the sidelines, rinsing empty beer bottles for recycling. The help-yourself fridge is filled to the gills with homebrew—Adélie Ale, Davis Draught, Blizz Bitter and more. Bottling nights are a production assembly line rarely short of volunteers.

According to Fling, wintering sparkie and brewmaster extraordinaire, the reputation of Davis beer has gained international renown, confirmed by a tourist icebreaker that called in last summer. ''Twas only a matter of time,' he declares to those gathered at the bar. Chad listens to Fling ease from his usual Scottish brogue into his best Texan drawl, mimicking the couple that had declined tea and coffee. 'Howzabout a li'lla' that holm-broo y'awl got stashed away.' Always good for a yarn, is Fling.

'Wouldn't you know,' the brewmaster continues, reverting to his Glaswegian lilt, 'before Chad could summon up a fresh tray of glasses, we had a score of Americans, six German neurologists, and a family of Italians sporting designer jackets with sealskin trims forming a queue from the bar, out through the lounge and clogging up the entry to the cold porch.

Even the two wee bairns waited in line. Chad, is that not God's truth?'

Chad nods. Fling empties his glass. 'Poor old Chad's morning tour of the station was reduced to a smattering of teetotallers.'

'The fewer the better,' Chad says, though his words are drowned out by laughter.

Charlie makes a space for the new arrival. 'Here she is, the little battler. Survived your day as super slushy, Freya?'

'Barely. Thanks for helping out this morning.'

'Chad,' Charlie calls. 'Get the girl a drink before she drops in her tracks.'

But Freya doesn't need his help; she stands at the fridge scanning the homebrew before holding up a bottle marked Ginger Beer.

'Kicks like a mule,' Fling boasts.

The recycled bottle still wears the remnants of a Japanese beer label. Chad watches Freya carrying the bottle at arm's length in case the fermented brew, like a dodgy firework, explodes unannounced.

He studies her as she uncaps the bottle and pours herself a drink, the sight of the foaming liquid washing his thoughts back to his own homebrewing days.

He remembers the pinch of sunburned skin pink with calamine lotion on a night too hot for a ten-year-old to sleep indoors. Lying in a canvas swag his father had rigged between two trees, he could spy Orion through the mosquito mesh. If he concentrated hard he could add up each star that winked—his count roundly broken by an almighty blast from the boatshed. At the second explosion he sat up, resigned to a third. His latest batch of ginger beer had blown its caps.

He could hear the old man up on the verandah, *Thar she blows, Sal.*

Ma's belly laugh could fill all five rooms of the shack, roly-poly down the hill to the beach and still have enough in reserve to make the seagulls on the point stand to attention.

After breakfast Chad and Ma would be faced with the aftermath, their rubber thongs squelching on the sticky cement. *Don't go near the broken glass, love.* Ma would wear a stoic grimace as she gallantly carried the survivors from the shed and stacked them *out of harm's way* beneath the tank stand, arguing that as she came protected by an inbuilt layer of cushioning, she was best equipped to transport any live ammunition.

Even then, Chad understood his family summers were special, better by a mile than his schoolmates' back in town. Sacrosanct these things that are numbered, he thinks now, summers with all three of them together the *grab-'em-while-they-last* kind.

'Earth to McGonigal!' Simon stands at the whiteboard with his marker pen poised. 'You putting on a flick tonight?'

'Ask Freya. Slushy's choice.'

'*Amelie,*' Freya announces.

'New one on me,' spouts Fling, who hasn't watched a film since Chad's known him.

'Chick flick,' two of the dart players cry out in unison.

At the end of the bar, Kittie jumps up in support of Freya. '*Amelie* is a wonderful movie. European films are so much more creative and uplifting than the formulaic crap Hollywood spits out.'

'Chick flick with subtitles,' the met boys shout.

'I've seen it. It's good,' Chad offers, though no one but Freya acknowledges him with a smile.

Simon adds a line beneath the film title: *Slushy's choice. Uplifting and creative.*

'What are you trying to do?' Charlie says. 'Drive 'em away in their droves?'

Chad leaves the banter, intending to secure a good seat at the end of an aisle.

Freya trails him to the theatre door. 'I was wondering if you'd have any time this week. To come out.'

Chad shrugs. Freya Jorgensen has some ground to make up before she can start asking any favours of him.

'I was thinking we could head out to one of the islands. If that sounds alright.' She begins to squirm, starts to walk away.

It feels a niggardly kind of win. 'Sounds okay.'

A release of breath. 'First day of good weather?'

Chad gestures to Kittie. 'Have your mate put in an order.'

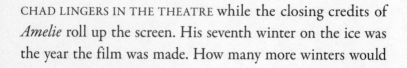

CHAD LINGERS IN THE THEATRE while the closing credits of *Amelie* roll up the screen. His seventh winter on the ice was the year the film was made. How many more winters would he put his hand up for, he who had always planned to see the world? He switches off the player and slips the DVD back onto the shelf. He runs his palm across the leather satchels that line the theatre walls. He likes the texture of the cases that house the old sixteen-millimetre movie reels; faded delivery stickers—RAILWAY EXPRESS, FILMS URGENT—speak of their commercial days. Chad savours the smell of age trapped in the leather, the sense of preservation in the straps and buckles that hold the cans in place. Film was on its way out when he began his time down here. The collection would be gone altogether, shipped back to Australia lock, stock and two smoking barrels, if not for a few sentimental stalwarts like himself who refuse to surrender to change.

This past winter, he'd screened a golden oldie twice a week. He'd fed each reel through the jaws of a fickle reconditioned beast that would, given half a chance, chew up every splice and spit out rags of film. He'd arrived at the theatre ahead of time to fill baskets with Roses chocolates and chips—it was as close as he could imagine to hosting his own party.

Chad cherishes the quality of film, the texture of the grain, the imperfections and scratches that stream down the screen and give it charm. He finds magical the razzle-dazzle, star-crossed lovers, women's satin gowns. He is drawn dizzily, hopelessly, to happy-ever-afters and uncomplicated lives.

He gathers a handful of mugs left between the chairs and makes his way from the theatre, dimming all the lights but one. A red glow spills from the glass of the projection booth. He hears the soft slurring of breath, the nasal intake of air, an ebb before each exhalation. Hair falls across her blemished cheek, her face a porcelain mask against the crimson light. Freya Jorgensen slumps in the back row, legs limp, arms folded across her chest, a rag doll out for the count.

Hell let loose
May 1912

THOSE RASCAL DOGS HAD BROKEN out of the verandah again. They emerged through the drift, slipping and slithering over polished ice, exhilarated to come across an ambulatory man dragging an extinguished lantern and groping on all fours to find his way home. Pavlova inspected Douglas's rear while Ginger and Gadget nosed the rime of ice lining his burberry helmet. In a blizzard, the forty yards from the Stevenson meteorological screen back to the hut might be a blanket of mist spread across the sea for all he could see through the drift.

The whistling of wind formed a song, a ceaseless whine that pervaded men's dreams and did its best to drown out every thought. He wore fur mittens, two pairs of woollen socks, and still his toes and fingers throbbed. Wind savaged the body, seared any flesh left uncovered. The men of winter quarters could be likened to a band of painted warriors, at one against the foe, their cheeks and brows scarred with lines of frostnip. Twice now Hurley had paid the price of operating his camera without a glove, his fingertips blackened from freezing.

Douglas patted at a shape to gain a bearing. Wind and snowdrift had scoured the boxes of food stacked along the wall of the hut, carving grooves through softer portions of the wooden casing and leaving harder fibres raised in relief. An identical process of abrasion hardened and polished the surrounding territory, channelling snow and ice into east–west ridges of sastrugi—the frozen waves a source of direction for a purblind man.

He climbed the snow bank against the western wall and eased his body down through the roof's newly installed trapdoor.

At Commonwealth Bay, abdication to the elements came in incremental acts of surrender. They had given up shovelling snowdrift from the hut's main entry; they had let that verandah go.

By 11.45 at night the wind sounded terrific. Timbers shimmied, the hut cracked as if set to explode. When Douglas emerged from his cabin, the crowd around Hyde Park Corner—the meeting place named by Ninnis—looked a solemn gathering indeed. John Close, the expedition's so-called physical fitness expert, ten years older than his application claimed and too often disposed to idleness, looked ashen-faced.

'What is it?' Douglas asked.

'This wind could sweep away the whole blooming show.' Close's voice sounded reedy and thin. 'Could lift the hut clean up and dump it in the sea.'

On a good day, Douglas found Close's timorous nature farcical—the acetylene generator for the lights would explode, they'd all perish from scurvy, if the stove ran down they would surely freeze to death in their sleeping bags. Send him out in a blizzard to collect the day's ice and you'd think he'd been banished. But tonight . . . Douglas couldn't help asking himself where they would find refuge if the hut gave way. By the volume of shrieks the gusts were nearing one hundred and fifty miles an hour. It seemed unbelievable that air could flow so swiftly.

'Not me alone what's concerned.' Close sniffed. 'You ask the boys.'

Azi Webb, the chief magnetician, unfolded some jottings from his pocket. 'Bage and I did the calculations. Eighty pound of wind to the square foot will stress the roof rafters about six thousand pounds per square inch. The full strength of the timber.'

'How does that rate in wind speed?'

'One hundred and thirty miles an hour, or thereabouts.'

'The only thing holding her in place,' Bage said, 'is the volume of snow banked around the walls.'

'Not this one.' Ninnis thumped the wall beside his bunk. He was right: the prevailing wind quickly blasted away any accumulation of snow on the hut's southern side.

'I was saying to the boys—God willing, we're all still here tomorrow—that we could build a snow bank,' the meteorologist Cecil Madigan said. 'If we stack a crescent of benzine fuel cases, say, ten yards behind the hut, the wind should dump snow between it and the back wall.'

'Put the hut in a better lee,' Douglas said. He should have thought of it himself. He left the group and pulled down the meteorological log: the day's minimum –21°F. He lingered over the monthly averages, the figures belying the wind's fury.

February	26.6 mph
March	49.0 mph
April	51.6 mph

He tried and tried again to summon memories of a world not ravaged by wind. A civilised world with freshly laundered clothes, polished fruit upon a sideboard, the softness of a woman's hand. But even his image of Paquita had dimmed, as if the features of her sweet and gentle face, the detail of her frock, were permanently veiled by snowdrift. Through these wretched months he'd written not a word to Paquita—what, of consequence, could a letter tell? That her fiancé and his men had been reduced to trogladytes, confined to a hut entombed in snow? That he, who once had hauled a sledge twelve hundred miles to the south magnetic pole—that wandering point on the earth's surface where the magnetic field rises vertically—knew naught of any landmark beyond the rise? No one outside this dismal realm could fathom conditions so brutal that the simplest task—retrieving a recording, collecting daily ice—demanded superhuman effort. The wireless masts lay fallow on the ground; the lower segments were no sooner raised than wind chafed the rope supports and he ordered them to be pulled down again. When he cast his memory back to his first Antarctic winter with Shackleton, he could recall the bitter cold, but never at Cape Royds had he known this unremitting fury. Here at Commonwealth Bay, the wind ripped and rent, bent and bullied; it had torn their whaleboat from its anchors and delivered it across the frozen harbour to kingdom come. Douglas shook his head. He would write no such letter lest the very act of doing so administered defeat.

The hut quaked. Wind shrilled. Douglas totted up wind speeds for the first half of May and estimated the average at sixty-four miles an hour.

He entered *Hell let loose* in the midnight record and placed the log back on the shelf. Winter hadn't even begun.

*Collecting ice from the
glacier at winter quarters*

A THOUSAND RIVERS

FREYA KICKS OFF HER MUDDY boots, opens her studio door, strews her gear across the floor and kneels beside the heater. It's nine at night and she's exhausted. Exhilarated. In truth, she's also relieved to have got through the afternoon without giving in. She would not have guessed, this morning, how rapidly the weather could turn, or how a minus-thirty windchill could chew through so many camera batteries. The cold had drained her own reserves.

This morning, they had driven out across the ice in perfect sunshine. There wasn't a breath of wind as she and Chad McGonigal tramped around the island in silence, he sitting down a respectable distance away each time she stopped to photograph the antics of courting penguins. She followed Chad's example and kept to herself, her novice's delight at the sight of so many penguins held in check by the muteness of her guide. They'd stopped for lunch at three o'clock, the dissonant brays and squawks from nearby penguins suddenly comical beside their own silence. She had laughed aloud, then turned to Chad: *It's a noisy business, impressing a mate*. Chad had grunted and pointed at a male suitor making an elaborate display of building a nest. The adélie waddled industriously up and down the slope, ferrying a single stone at a time. They watched him posture before his would-be mate, dip his head low in rhythmic waves and finally place each stone just so. *She looks smitten to me*, Freya had said; the female bowed her head in concert with his moves. But no. *Female adélies are a fickle lot*, Chad muttered. *She'll as easily up and march away if he doesn't get it right.*

They were climbing the hill when Freya registered a breeze and stopped to zip up her jacket. Soon she was battling to keep pace, or to even make headway in the stronger gusts, the wind savage on her face. Chad had beckoned her on—*It's worth it*—taking out his point-and-shoot. She had reached the top, breathless from the cold but transfixed by the scene laid out upon the ice. They stood side by side photographing streamers of snowdrift that could have been a thousand rivers tumbling out across the white. She couldn't help herself. *Have you ever seen anything so wild and beautiful?*

Of course he had, countless times, she reminds herself now. She had held her glove in her teeth to change batteries, then had to scrabble for a cloth to clear the eyepiece of her camera which was iced over with her breath. At home she could operate any of her cameras blindfolded; out there in the cold, wearing gloves, she struggled to locate the shutter button, fumbling with buttons and dials. But within minutes of taking off her thick gloves and switching them for liners, her hands refused to function, her fingers wooden and throbbing with cold.

Tough on hands, your line of work. You want to head back?

She had hesitated. If she couldn't handle an afternoon of poor conditions, how could she expect to carry out her project? *I just need a minute to warm up.*

They'd sheltered in the lee of boulders where she'd slid her bare hands into her armpits to gain some body warmth. As the feeling returned her fingers ached as though they had been slammed in a door.

This is about as rugged as it gets this time of year. Chad had poured hot drinks from the thermos in his pack. *It gets easier, dealing with the cold.*

Freya sipped a mug of sweet black tea, and then a second, feeling a glimmer of warmth radiate through her. *I lived in Norway until I was eight. My sister and I would walk to school during winter in temperatures colder than this; we'd play outside all the time. I don't remember feeling this cold.*

Chad had nodded. *Down here, the wind's the killer.*

Is there a trick to staying warm? She'd almost been afraid to ask.

He shrugged. *You get better at knowing what clothes work for you, at understanding your limits.* He'd offered her some chocolate and with it half a smile. *There's no formula. Somehow you figure it out for yourself.*

An unmistakable whiff of penguin now wafts about Freya's studio. She sniffs at her hands, her clothing, matted tendrils of her hair. Distracted by the acrid odour, she follows the scent across the room to her new waterproof camera pack, the base and tail straps caked in guano. Wonderful.

Freya opens her laptop and clicks on her inbox. She scrolls through an email from Marcus with the subject: *Progress on the diaries!*

>> Translated from the journal of Xavier Mertz, 18 May 1912:

At 6 pm we returned to the hut in pitch black. Such a walk has to be experienced once in a lifetime. The distance is only 300 metres, yet it took us half an hour, with great effort. The wind stole away our breath, and the severe cold bit at the uncovered part of our faces . . . First we tried our luck upright, locking arms with one another, but the wind knocked us down. For fifteen minutes we rolled about, our bodies writhing in all directions. Then the wind swept Azi away so I followed him. As we sat against a rock to catch our breath, I had to rub my hands because my fingertips were nearly frostbitten. Around the edge of my burberry cap was a bright light, 'St Elmo's fire', produced by electricity driven through snowflakes.

Battling against the wind and darkness, the distance to the hut, and our sense of time, seemed distorted. Finally, we bumped into the hut wall with our heads.

Freya should reply to Marcus, acknowledge his email, tell him the details of her day. *I want to hear about everything.* She studies Hurley's photo, *Collecting ice from the glacier*, focusing on the two figures, crawling on hands and knees through the blizzard. She feels herself transported by needles of snow, by wretched, aching cold. How did they find their way, let alone work, in such conditions? In a less alien environment the task of collecting ice might seem mundane, but at winter quarters, these two men battling nature elevates domestic duties to the realm of the extraordinary. If her own images are even half as evocative, a fraction as strong, she will rate them a success.

Wind buffets the window. Freya sits at her desk thinking through each aspect of her project: first, a series of portraits of station life, in counterpart to those Hurley took at winter quarters. Then, a collection of polaroid transfers—muted images—to echo the dreamlike colours of his Lumière autochromes. On her laptop she has blended several digital images, the beginning of a series reminiscent of those photos Hurley combined in the darkroom, composite images from multiple negatives.

Freya is still unsure how to photograph the ice. Ideas wake her in the night, parade in the shadows as if waiting for her to recognise them. Each day, vivid images glance before her eyes, tempting her to slow down time so that bikes, clothing— motion and colour—are illuminated from the ice. *A summer aurora*; she pictures it, a series of icescapes printed onto bolts of silk, dancing and billowing the length and breadth of a gallery wall. If Marcus were here she would talk it through with him—*their* project, she reminds herself. She knows she would be swayed by him—by his ability to tease out ideas, to shape and structure them with meanings she might never consider on her own. Her husband would offer his rendition as a gift, neatly packaged, near to, though not quite the delicate thing she first imagined, shades of her vision evanescing with the precision of his words.

Freya returns her focus to the screen, to Frank Hurley, withstanding such brutal conditions to garner remarkable images of time. Yet, for all the power in this image of the blizzard, already enhanced from the original, it failed to satisfy the photographer's vision. Hurley embellished each published version with increasingly voluminous swathes of snowdrift, until the two figures, and even winter quarters, were all but obliterated by blizzard. *Perhaps the cold addled his brain*, Marcus suggested the day she catalogued Hurley's images ready for her Antarctic trip, her husband suddenly out of sorts with her excitement. *What kind of photographer*, he said, *would risk their credibility with such gross manipulation, such blatant untruth?* Though Freya had remained silent, she knew instinctively, in a way she'd have floundered to articulate, that Hurley didn't falter from the truth. Only now, defrosting her fingers and toes in this wind-battered container of a studio, can she explain what she feels: Hurley's vision was not to imitate nature, but to offer an impression built layer upon layer, an accumulation of experiences that embodied the struggle with the blizzard.

A summer aurora? A fabrication, when she has access to so much that is real and tangible? She could so easily dissuade herself. *How does it link to Hurley's photos?* Marcus would quite rightly ask her. She doesn't know. At least, not yet.

Other than her digitals, she'll have no sure way of knowing, until she gets home, if a single frame is working. What kind of photographer would devote a finite supply of large format film to a whimsical idea, would risk the outcome of their project on such uncertain odds?

Freya shuts down her computer, a notch more resilient, in body and mind, than when the day began. *This kind.*

The nightwatchman's terror
July 1912

THE NIGHT SKY SWAYED WITH streamers of emerald green. At every turn daubs of light smudged the sky, the aurora masking the stars so only planets shone through.

The group huddled against the sixty-miler. Those who had raced from the hut without burberry outers now inched to the front to gain what protection could be had.

'Look!' cried Ninnis, pointing to the north where luminescence above the horizon waxed to a ruby arch and threw up gold and emerald streamers. No one knew what caused these arches, mostly appearing in the north. Douglas believed they represented a concentration of ions in the upper atmosphere—a bombardment of magnetic rays from the sun. Webb and Bage, the two magneticians, had established a connection between the aurora and the earth's magnetic field: with each strong display the magnetic needle oscillated wildly.

Again the sky mutated, this time into curtains—two, three, four velvet drapes laid one upon the other, suspended from the heavens as if from an invisible clasp. For seconds they hung motionless, as though before a silent stage, flounces and folds unperturbed by wind that blasted the men's backs as they huffed vapoured breath and stamped throbbing feet.

The curtains lifted through the sky, each drape swaying to a soundless rhythm, shimmering lilac, rose pink, heliotrope—floral light winding through each fold. Along the edges of the upper curtain, filaments charged towards the zenith, their hue accelerating from green to crimson, their brightness continually fading then revivifying.

Douglas scribbled furiously in the notebook as Cecil Madigan sang the time displayed on the half-chronometer watch. 'Twenty-one twenty.'

> 21-20 Four brilliant curtains with very rapid streamer movement to the E. Display becoming much more brilliant and rising toward the zenith. One curtain almost to the zenith.

> 21-21-1/2 Very rapid streamer travel in the zenith curtain.

Douglas took responsibility for the recording during the day, and would assiduously check the nightwatchman's log. The men had deemed the aurora *the nightwatchman's terror* for the hours the recording swallowed up, robbing the nightwatchman of the job's favourite perk: a hot bath followed by a hurried load of laundry before the bath water froze. Each did their best but some of the non-scientific

party failed to understand the importance of correct termi-
nology and systematic notations. *Many trembling and
glittering pencils of rays moved in all directions,* Mertz would
write. *The eyes could hardly find the time to admire them all.*
X refused to believe that even in one hundred years' time an
aurora could be explained by science.

The travel of excitation along the streamers grew so
rapid—Bage and Webb later calculated sixty-six miles per
second—that light rippled and flickered like sparkling
waves. Objects on the surrounding landscape lit up a mile
away and when Douglas looked across at the reflection
from the eastern ice barrier he saw a lyrebird's tail. If he
could only package the moment, send it to Paquita across
the sky.

21-23 Now a great mass of nebulous bands and curtains from the
N. horizon to the zenith.

The sky turned into an ocean of breaking waves with crests
tipped rhodamine red. Directly above the hut filaments
raced past the zenith, constellating into the most
astonishing corona he had ever seen.

21-26 A vortex of colour and motion crossed the zenith from the
W.N.W. to S.E. This corona was quite obviously due to the
perspective affect of looking at a convolution of the curtain from
directly below.

'My eyes are full,' said X, turning in circles, his arms open to the sky.

Ninnis giggled like a girl. 'I used to think stories of auroras were exaggerated.'

Douglas turned to them. 'I doubt something this grand has been seen anywhere else in the world.'

'Not even at the famous Cape Royds?' Madigan said mockingly. Someone alongside stifled a laugh.

Douglas's intention had not been to brag. He'd been asked about the 1907–09 expedition with Shackleton time and again, quizzed by the men on the volume of science achieved, the tireless hours put in every day without complaint; he'd been asked to speak about the vast tracts of ice they had sledged. If Madigan chose to ridicule those accomplishments to make light of their own lack of progress that was entirely up to him.

The aurora had waned and several men raced towards the hut, teeth chattering, the sky's hypnotic lure broken by a fresh blanket of stars and the overwhelming cold.

Douglas, X and Ninnis climbed up the snow bank leading to the roof. How quickly it had become the norm to enter one's home via trapdoor and ladder. Hurley was balanced precariously on the roof's apex, one leg stretched to match his tripod, his camera tilted skyward.

'This time last year,' Ninnis panted, 'X and I were still in London, as busy as fleas and preparing to venture out onto the high seas in the dear old *Aurora*. Our thoughts were full of what we would be doing in a year's time. This time next year we shall look back and remember that on this July night of nineteen hundred and twelve, in this little-known corner of the globe, we polar men of the AAE stood witness to a spectacle of nature the likes of which have never before been seen by man and might never again in the history of the world—'

Frank Hurley broke into a comic howl, and who could blame his display of agony? Ninnis was inclined to prattle when given free rein. Hurley devoted hours to photographing the auroras, experimenting with different exposures and using up a frightful quantity of glass plates and photographic material. So far his efforts had resulted in nothing more distinct than a nebulous haze, though it didn't stop him scoffing at X who believed *the supernatural* could never be captured by a photograph.

Douglas, as much as Hurley, wanted to bring home an aurora and show it to the world. Privately, though, he savoured the notion that the aurora could render powerless a photographic wizard armed with the latest gadgetry. Aurora—the Goddess of Dawn—refused to be tamed.

ZOLATOV
ISLAND

CHAD BARRELS OVER THE SEA ice, the quad's engine spitting as he sweeps around a melt pool. With each pass before the camera he stretches out to one side and curls the bike, wheels skating across the glassy slick. He rights his course and glances back. The groundsheet trails from his bike like a purse seine flung from a trawler, waves of green rippling over ice.

He loops a figure of eight to bring the bike alongside her. 'How was I that time?'

Freya slowly shakes her head and looks around. 'I'm trying to capture the movement of colour going by.' She unwinds the camera from her tripod and paces. 'It still isn't right,' she says. She kneels, she stands, she angles the lens to one side. Whatever result she's after, she seems reluctant to share. 'It's just an experiment,' she offers, an experiment to which she devotes a morning's work and a fearful amount of oversized film. It puzzles Chad, this coyness; a guard against what? Not that he's complaining. He would happily spend the rest of the day hooning over this traction-less playground of ice with a coloured tarp billowing in his wake. It's the closest he'll ever come to starring in the movies.

He readies the bike, but still she wanders back and forth. She stops to stand beside him, dappled by filaments of cirrus that skate across the sun and play tricks with the light. She turns to look away, she glances back, this woman of mismatched halves. The loveliness of her left profile accentuates her other, blemished side. What hardships linger in the birthmark that gathers at her throat and spills across her cheek? The contrasts in her face draw Chad to wonder if her childhood, like his, was divided into happiness and want. A fleeting memory escapes his hold: not a wave of a hand, not even a glance in the rear-view mirror as the ute pulled away. For all anyone knew the old man could have fallen off the perch years ago, abandoned life as quietly as he had fatherhood. The whole show fell apart after Ma.

The drone of propellers has him scanning the sky to see one of the Casa planes forming a silhouette against the sun. *Ginger* and *Gadget* are the future, the bigwigs claim. 'No namesake will outclass the sledging dogs,' he says, realising too late he's spoken aloud.

Freya gives him a confused look. 'Pardon?'

'Talking to myself.'

The Casa passes overhead, its span of wings merging into cloud. He has to admit, it's a neat-looking plane.

'It must have been a different era, the dog days,' Freya says.

'That's for sure.' These days you can't fart until you've filed a report.

'You miss it?'

'Seems a lifetime ago now. Like they say, nothing stays the same.'

'It can't be all bad. You keep coming down here.'

'It's not bad at all,' he corrects her. 'I'd go so far as to say that on days like this, out here on the ice, there's nowhere else I'd rather be.'

'Well, that's nice to hear, and something of a relief.' She beams at him then kneels on the ice, immediately intent on the view through her camera. 'Could we try making the groundsheet billow more?' she says with a rippling of her hand. 'Perhaps slow down on the turn.'

She lies flat on the ice and rests her camera on its case. Her iceberg-blue eyes twinkle. 'Ready when you are, McGonigal, Queen of the Ice.'

SHE SEEMS HAPPY ENOUGH BY the time they move on. There are no shortage of landmarks as they drive down the seaward side of Hawker Island; still she grips her personal GPS, inspecting it like a hawk.

'Hey.' He waves her to a stop. 'Put that thing in your pocket.'

'Why?'

'You have a map, don't you?'

Her face drops. 'Please don't try to make me use a compass. We could end up anywhere. Macquarie Island, ahoy.'

He grins at the thought. 'Freya, on a clear day like this, out here on the sea ice, the only compass you need alongside your map are your eyes. You want to *see* what's around you, not spend the whole time driving with one arm held out like you're holding a lance while you study a screen.'

'I'm not that good with directions,' she protests.

'You're just out of practice, been driving down freeways too long.' He pulls out his map and indicates features along the coastline, then gets her to locate the nearest islands. 'Two things you need to know: where you are now and where you're going. You've already figured out a few milestones to help you along your way; now trust what's in front of you.'

She sighs. 'I'll give it a shot.'

The sea ice runs in a corridor beside open sea. They stop to photograph an elephant seal heaving itself along the ice at a pace that belies its tonnage of rolling blubber. Chad sniffs on the wind the unmistakable trace of an elephant seal wallow.

'We won't see ele seals hauled out near the station until after the sea ice breaks out. Want to check 'em out?'

'Absolutely,' she says, collecting her camera. 'I have a little-known fact for you,' she announces as they walk towards their bikes. She looks childlike, eager to share.

'Hit me with it.'

'Did you know that just one half of an elephant seal tongue is enough to feed eighteen men?'

He smiles at this unexpected gem. 'Who told you that tale?' The moment he utters the words they sound like a challenge. His lack of social grace is confirmed by a flash of her eyes.

'My husband,' she says quietly, the bubble surrounding them burst. 'Douglas Mawson's men shot an elephant seal at Commonwealth Bay, according to the journals Marcus is reading.'

Shyness returns to thread him in a knot. 'Your husband got the raw part of the deal.'

She stacks her camera case and tripod on the bike rack. 'How's that, Chad?'

'You're down here having all the fun while he's stuck at home reading about the place.'

He sees her bristle. 'Marcus isn't *stuck at home*. It's what he chooses to do. And this,' she ties down her bag with a mangled knot, 'is what I do for a living. It might seem like nothing much, but it's what I've spent years training for, in the same way you have with your trade.'

Chad registers her distress as she squeezes the bike helmet over her head. 'I wasn't saying—'

'Onward!' She points at the island in the distance, snapping her visor closed and roaring away in a clatter of gears.

WALLOW, FREYA DECIDES, IS A fitting word for a gathering of malodorous elephant seals. Amid a squeeze of girths and press of bellies, these gargantuan blubber bags literally wallow in a mire of urine and foul-smelling sludge. One stretches the end of its flipper like a hand and nimbly pares off casts of its russet-coloured skin. The surrounding rocks are littered with sun-leathered, freeze-dried sheaths. Another elephant seal gapes a colossal pink mouth in a yawn, its jowls wobbling as it sneezes a voluminous spray of mucus in Freya's direction. That chore squared away, it slumps its bulk across a neighbouring back and returns to sonorous sleep. The wallow resounds with a cacophony of belches and farts. A bull's outrageously oversized snout acts as a foghorn, reverberating off the cliffs. Is it a *come hither*, Freya wonders, to the new arrival they watched slop across the ice?

Freya skirts the perimeter of the wallow, springing across rocks and over spongy hillocks of dried, compacted sludge, surely representing decades of faecal waste. She takes a shortcut to where Chad sits watching, stopping herself short from jumping onto an apparent boulder that suddenly rises and blinks at her with soft brown eyes. The seal snorts, its quivering nostrils spluttering strings of snot across her boots. Quickly she retreats, noting the seal's jowls are scarred with a cross-hatching of wounds.

Chad defends their graceless ways. 'Eles are highly social. During the summer moult they'll use one another as rubbing boards. The urea in the urine soothes their itchy skin.'

Two bulls rise up to full height and chest-butt in a rippling of blubber. They growl as they biff one another, the larger pressing the smaller backward with each thrust. The big bull, sporting a mountainous proboscis, buries its canines into the flesh of the other, wrestling the smaller challenger and dragging it from side to side like a dog tearing at a bone. The smaller bull soon retreats.

'Beachmaster versus wannabe,' Chad says. 'Not ready to surrender his fiefdom this season.'

AT ZOLATOV ISLAND, THEIR FINAL destination for the afternoon, a pair of skuas settle on a nearby rock, as bold as you please, sizing up Freya and Chad as they share sandwiches and thermos tea. The birds, feathers ruffling in the wind, appear perfectly at ease in human company. This pair seems less interested in the contents of a packed lunch than in observing two strangers. Freya wonders who is entertaining whom.

'They're not as feisty as people make out.' She takes her camera from her pack and composes the bird's face full-frame in her viewfinder. 'I think they're regal and proud.'

'They're sharp-looking birds.' Chad nods. 'Smart as a whip.'

The skuas shift their focus towards the glacier in the distance, tilting their heads at the deep rumbles and explosions that issue from the ice. By the time Freya looks up at the frozen precipice, the ice has calved; all she catches is a billow of spray rising from the base where the ice has plunged into the water, the swell washing against the white cliff before the ocean subsides.

She turns to Chad. 'Marcus—my husband. I asked him. He didn't want to come.'

'Fair enough,' he says. 'It's not to everybody's liking. How about you? Why Antarctica?'

She thinks for a while. 'I guess it began when my father took me to see the *Fram*, Roald Amundsen's Antarctic ship, before we came out to Australia. I would have been only seven, but it made a huge impression on me. And then I saw Frank Hurley's photos. That was it. Hook, line and sinker. I had to find a way to come here for myself.'

'So, here we are.'

'Here we are.'

What if Marcus had decided to come? How would he have coped? Or she, if he were here with her? He'd balk at the menial chores, socialising with the throng of people at the station; even today, out here, he'd quickly tire of the place. Marcus avoids social gatherings, even the monthly market days Freya loves. It's not that her husband isn't giving. When they're home alone, he smothers her with affection. When it's just the two of them he can be funny and playful. And quick; ask any of his students. Marcus can outsmart any mystery novel you hand him; he will, during Freya's favourite movies, spot gaps in plot and slips in continuity that are simply beyond her scope. But here? Forced to converse with people, some of whom he might otherwise scorn? She thinks of the times she had invited people to their home: it wasn't worth the angst, her husband visibly bored and drawing on his wit to belittle her before her friends. One excruciating evening he selectively derided their guests—people from the magazine she worked for. The sting in his barbs. Furtive glances of disbelief.

Focus on the good things, Mama says. And isn't every marriage a contract of concessions? She had freely given Marcus her pledge before they married, *no children*, never imagining the difference a decade would make. Perhaps she has Sophie to thank for changing her outlook: the unexpected joy in watching her niece grow from a tiny girl to a teenager, the flood of warmth she feels in being part of Sophie's life, entrusted with her secrets, in loving and being loved in return.

I'm forty-seven years old, Marcus had silenced her. *I don't intend slaving for the next twenty-some years to support an iGeneration brat.*

Marcus, she reminds herself, makes up for it in other ways. He dedicates hours to this project, encourages her career, not once has he objected to her wanderings. The man Freya married is rock-solid, never has he left one of his student's despairing, or made them wonder, should they give it all away? Of course she returns. She owes it to him, to them both, to bring home the perfect picture.

THE BEST OF THE DAY has gone, a freshening wind and the sky thick with cloud. Freya zips up her Ventile jacket past her neck warmer, grateful for the extra layers she has brought along to shield out the chill. As they pick their way over rocks towards the bikes, the lunchtime skuas swoop into view and circle above. They hover, perfectly balanced, their wings daubed with flashes of white.

'Farewell, skuas,' Freya calls. The birds shriek. 'What's wrong with them?'

'We must be near their nest.' Chad looks around. 'Watch where you step.'

Freya is jolted by a sudden knock to the back of her skull. The force of the blow pushes her against the rocks. She wonders, momentarily, if she's been stoned. She rubs her wounded head and sees her fingers smeared with blood. A skua spirals above.

She scrambles up off the rocks and tries to make a run for it but the birds dive at her from opposite directions. Chad manoeuvres to the left to avoid them. The skuas shriek fearsomely, swooping again and again, a pair of maniacal demons in perfect formation. Freya cowers back against the rocks and drops to her knees. 'Why do they keep coming for me?' she cries.

She sees him stifle a smirk. 'I guess they like you the best.' If she were not so terrified she would very much like to thump him.

'Walk in this direction.' He beckons. 'Hold your tripod above your head. They'll aim for the tallest part of you. Don't be scared.'

Freya edges towards him but can't help cowering each time she senses a movement. The sharp beak comes straight at her again and she hears herself whimper. The clawed feet drop like the landing gear of a stealth bomber. She ducks and runs after Chad, wielding her tripod like a white flag. The titanium legs jar in her grip with each new strike.

'There's the nest down there.' Chad points to a scrape of gravel, indistinguishable from the surrounding rock except for the two large speckled eggs resting there. One of the adult skuas lands at the nest and paces, clucking its distress.

'A month away from hatching,' he says. 'You wait till you see the chicks. Little grey fluff balls.'

She takes up position behind Chad, thankful for a substantial shield, suddenly seized with the urge to laugh at how she must have looked. She is pulled up short by the sight of a penguin flipper and loops of fresh entrails that lie strewn around the nest.

'The adélie would have been injured.' Chad senses her disgust. 'They wouldn't take on an adult otherwise.'

Freya grimaces. 'That doesn't make it less revolting.'

'A skua's got to eat. This is a tough place to stay alive.' He inspects the back of her poor head. 'Man,' he remarks, clearly shocked by what must be a large lump sprouting from her skull. 'They copped you a beauty. Your induction to Antarctica; now you'll have something to write home about.'

He scans the clouds scudding by and gestures at their bikes. 'That's enough fun for one day. Time to drive the huskies home.'

AS FREYA STEERS HER QUAD, the cold wind whistling through her helmet, she holds in her mind an image, not of Hurley but of Xavier Mertz kneeling in the snow with his camera as the dog team thundered toward him. *Time to drive the huskies home.*

Soft focus, atmospheric lighting, shadows from the dogs spilled across the snow—a Hurleyesque impression of nature.

*Belgrave Ninnis and the
dogs taking a load of stores to
Aladdin's Cave.
Photographer Xavier Mertz,
1912.*

Aladdin's Cave 1
August 1912

DOUGLAS, MADIGAN AND NINNIS SPENT two days excavating an ice cave five and a half miles south of winter quarters, a sledging depot protected from weather, and a portal to the plateau. The crystalline walls glittered as though with a wealth of diamonds and within the magical cavern the three men discovered anew a world replete with silence. In the blizzard outside, the sledging dogs curled in on themselves, their matted hair frozen down, eight dark snouts barely visible above the snow.

Inside Aladdin's Cave, as Madigan and Ninnis dubbed it, colours looked dreamlike to Douglas, the luminescence in the ice casting an eerie veil of blue. The three ate quietly, unaccustomed to such a small company after living for so long with a hutful of eighteen, absorbing the absence of wind; in its place, though, their ears reverberated with an endless peal of ringing.

Douglas abhorred waste, but not even he could finish the boil-up of hoosh, so rich was the sledging porridge of dehydrated beef and lard pemmican, ground plasmon biscuit and glaxo milk powder all mixed to a slurry with boiling water.

A REPORT BOOMED FROM DEEP within the surrounding ice. Douglas lay facing Cecil Madigan's back in the three-man bag. The meteorologist's body was folded to a crook, his limbs awkward and muscles taut from unwanted intimacy. The heat generated by three bodies swaddled and lulled, rhyming breath soon giving way to sleep. Madigan's head sank back against Douglas's forearm, his hair coarse and dank against the silken reindeer pelt which exuded a trace of the Arctic tundra's earthy scent. Douglas wondered if the smell of a flesh-eating animal differed from that of a herbivore, if his own skin, like the others, oozed a disagreeable odour from a diet of penguin and seal.

A CANOPY OF MORNING CLOUD diffused the light and reduced the surface definition so at times he would step awkwardly into a trough, or catch his foot on a crest of sastrugi. Wind on the plateau had scoured the snow to concrete. He and Madigan took turns at running alongside the sledge, keeping on course dogs that loathed running into the bite of the wind. Before this trip the sum of dog sledging had been training circuits taken by Ninnis and Mertz. Now, on an uphill gradient and patches of slippery blue ice, the three men—badly out of condition after a winter cooped up indoors—struggled to keep pace with the dog team. Douglas called for a rest and Ninnis, riding on the back of the sledge, planted his foot to push the brake's steel jaws into the snow. Dogs eased to a halt in snorts of steam.

Douglas had hoped to run three days to the south to explore but he read the southern sky well enough to know that its blanket of stratus would soon be upon them, that snowdrift, even blizzard, could force them to hole up for days.

Ninnis and Madigan gaped with disappointment at his decision to turn back. Madigan's subversion of his leadership was artful enough to be mere inflection, a shift in tone too subtle to object to. Now his voice, tinged with disdain, reported the sledge meter's meagre record of eight miles and two hundred yards from the hut—Douglas heard the unstated inference, that they were turning tail because of his lack of pluck. Confused, Ninnis looked from Douglas to his Hyde-Park-Corner compatriot, his allegiance wavering. Douglas thought of sea elephant bulls sparring along the shoreline at Macquarie Island, the master continually having to defend his realm against contenders.

'Bear in mind, if we're holed up in bad weather we've only brought three days' rations of dog pemmican. After that the dogs will go without.' He addressed himself to Ninnis, who fretted over the dogs' welfare and imagined ailments. Ninnis and Mertz had formed a 'secret' Kennel Club, extending membership only to those who smuggled the dogs tidbits from the kitchen. Small chance Douglas would be invited to join. Bad enough to know it was going on behind his back.

His hope that they would make winter quarters by dark was dashed by a maze of small crevasses, and a sixty-mile-an-hour tail wind that blew the sledge into the dogs and sent them skittling in a tangle of traces. When they unharnessed the team, to take over hauling the load themselves, Pavlova was the one dog that stayed by their side. Grandmother, who was in fact a grandfather, shot away the moment he was loosened, and with the innate sense of direction unique to sledging dogs, the other miscreants ran hot on his heels back towards Aladdin's Cave.

The following day the three men spent bored and fidgety inside Aladdin's Cave while outside, in pea-soup drift, the dogs hunkered down, their bodies succumbing to occasional bouts of shivering. The drift was almost as thick the next day, and Ninnis joined Madigan in trying to persuade Douglas that they should attempt the five and a half miles to the hut.

'Experience,' Douglas said, 'has proven that it is usually best to wait until the drift eases.' But he finally acquiesced, reasoning that as they had a sound knowledge of the direction of the hut, they couldn't stray too far off course. Just the same, he hoped the drift would clear before they reached the coast.

They had travelled half a mile when Ninnis cried out that the dogs weren't following. 'They'll be back at the cave buried in snow.'

'I'll run back,' Madigan said, unharnessing himself from the sledge.

'No.' Douglas motioned to the drift. 'I don't want anyone going off in this alone.'

'We'll all go,' Ninnis suggested.

Before Douglas could respond, Madigan said in a patronising tone, 'You're being overcautious, Mawson. I'm faster than either of you. I'll be back in no time,' as if it were he, Madigan, who had the Antarctic know-how to decide what was best.

'No!' Douglas ordered, tired of having his authority challenged. 'The damned dogs can catch up on their own. We've wasted enough time.'

Together Douglas and Ninnis hauled the sledge downhill towards the hut. Madigan stayed at the rear of the sledge holding a guy rope taut in case the load started to slip away down the slope.

'You wait and see.' Douglas nudged Ninnis. 'As soon as the dogs get hungry they'll bolt for the hut. Chances are they'll be home before we are.'

DOUGLAS LAY ON HIS BUNK at winter quarters, the candle's feeble light flickering over the pages of his journal. He read back over the last fortnight's events, wincing as he recalled his certainty that the dogs would make their own way home.

> 15 *August: Got to the Hut at lunchtime—heard that bergs had calved from the cliffs some 2 days previously. During our absence the top of the south mast had been put up. They had two calm spells for a few hours each . . . Arranged for Bage, Mertz and Hurley to start first thing in morning for dogs.*

> 16 *August: Drifting heavily and strong wind, so they cannot get away . . .*

Nor had they left the following day. The wind howled at eighty-five miles an hour, and they spent another day confined to the hut, sewing harnesses, and weighing and packing provisions ready for sledging.

> 19 *August: Still drifting and heavy wind. The dogs will be in a bad way.*
> 20 *August: Thick drift, heavy wind—poor dogs . . .*

They finally got away on the twenty-first; the dogs had been stranded six full days. Bage, Hurley and Mertz had set off in early morning twilight; *a mere zephyr*, Hurley, dismissing the sixty-mile-an-hour wind. A bank of heavy cloud was blowing in from the north.

August 24 and no sign of them. Douglas had spent the day scraping the build-up of ice from the roof of his cabin, imagining the worst. He would go tomorrow himself. Drift poured into the store and outhouses. It took a group with shovels all day to clear it.

25 August: Sunday: Service 10.30. Weather better today but drift fair; strong wind. We clear up outside. Rather expect the return of Bage's party. At 2 pm they appear, all well, but Grandmother dead.

Hurley had come into his cabin breathless and weatherworn and sat on the edge of his desk. 'Castor must have got wind of us,' he said. 'We saw her jumping about when we got within sight of the cave.'

'Had they broken into the provisions?'

'Not one. They'd curled up in the snow as if they were waiting for us. Basilisk and Castor were the only two not frozen down. All the dogs were listless and wouldn't eat a mouthful until we cut them free and took them into the cave. Pavlova was in the best nick, Grandmother was as good as dead. X said Grandmother had missed out on a meal the day before you left the hut.'

'That's true,' Douglas recalled, 'and we rewarded Pavlova with extra food. She was the only dog that stayed with us after we unharnessed them.' He shook his head in amazement. 'Seven days in wind and drift without a scrap of food.'

'I doubt they'd have lasted another day. All gone in the hind legs. Could barely hold themselves up.'

Hurley's voice quietened when he told how Mertz handfed pieces of pemmican to the weakest dogs.

'Grandmother took only a few mouthfuls before he fitted, pawing at the air like the dogs on the ship coming down. Poor old X was beside himself,' Hurley said. 'For more than an hour he held Grandmother in his arms, murmuring to him in German, trying to warm him, and all the while Grandmother was barely breathing, just staring ahead with glassy eyes.'

HERE IT WAS THE END of August 1912 and their knowledge of Adélie Land extended a princely eight miles, two hundred yards magnetic south. Another dog had died and the rest had come dangerously close to death for no greater cause than that he wanted to assert authority over Madigan. On the opposite side of his cabin wall, Ninnis, Mertz and Madigan would be sitting on their bunks in Hyde Park Corner as sombre as mourners.

When Douglas closed his journal it occurred to him, not as a new concern but as the twisting of a knife, that the Australasian Antarctic Expedition could easily finish up an unremarkable failure. He pictured the ignomy of bringing home only meteorological and magnetic recordings, as well as a few caseloads of skins, birds and geological specimens. He cringed at the prospect of facing sponsors, government officials, the Australasian Association for the Advancement of Science, who had collectively vested forty thousand pounds in his ability to explore new tracts of land in the name of science. He thought of those he'd be letting down: particularly John King Davis, captain of the *Aurora*, his second-in-command—his friend—who had believed in his vision from the start. They had stood on a London street corner and gripped hands in a compact before they had even ten pounds to put towards a ship—*We'll sail to Antarctica come what may*, Davis had said.

In a cutter, Douglas had seconded, *without a scrap of equipment if it comes to it*. He could hear his father in those words, a scholar with no head for business, soliciting investors for his latest get-rich-quick scheme.

Would Paquita think less of him if he failed, as he did his father?

You and your little hutful of men have done your utmost, he could hear her say, sounding, at times, a lifetime older than her twenty years.

He wished he could enwrap himself with Paquita's warmth, just for an hour, touch the lace of her dress, rest his head upon her lap and hear—without properly listening to her talk of homely things—the lilt of her voice, the lingering trace of Holland in the clip of her words.

A twig of memory, a snap of remembrance; he turned back the page of his journal, ashamed to realise he had let the date slip by unnoticed.

19 August: Still drifting and heavy wind. The dogs will be in a bad way.
20 August: Thick drift, heavy wind—poor dogs . . .

He took up his pencil and, as if to make amends, crammed another line under 19 August, recording Paquita's twenty-first birthday—the day he had pledged her all of his thoughts: *Angel, it will be you all day long*—between two miserable entries devoted to the dogs.

ROOKERY
LAKE

CHAD SEES FREYA CROUCH DOWN over her handlebars as intently as a rally-car driver, the headland in her sights, anxious to reach Rookery Lake in time for the best of the afternoon light. Without her GPS to hold her back, she bounds across the surface—fearless or feckless, Chad can't decide which. Either way, she pays precious little heed as she crosses a series of leads—thin channels of water where sea ice has split and eased apart.

Other than these rifts, the stretch of blue ice forms a perfect highway, smooth as a newly sealed road. Chad is mindful of the variations in cycles of freeze and thaw. Some years he has watched ice choke Prydz Bay through January; in others it has blown out of the harbour before summer begins. These stretches of sea ice and frozen fjords are fragile bridges linking islands and shores. He is reminded, with each open seam they cross, of their vulnerability on these frangible roads. Each fracture merits inspection, each rift a caution to those who cross.

Many rivers to cross is the title of the CD that Elisia Hood, fellow winterer, has put together and presented him this morning for his forty-second birthday. Lis, who has a phenomenal number of songs in her collection, has gone all out with his birthday compilation, including not only the Toni Childs version of the title song he always sings along to, but that of every other artist who's performed it.

Freya suddenly appears beside him with her head tilted quizzically, wondering, he supposes, what the lunatic alongside is mouthing. He gives her a nod and she pushes ahead, wheels reeling, engine drumming. The music in his earphones pulls his thoughts away. Chad is drawn towards wistful songs and this, with its rivers and crossings and wanderings lost, swamps him with melancholy, dredging up a memory so palpable that even now his leg feels dull and sluggish, heavy with pain.

Sunday, 5 January 1975, the night the Tasman Bridge was felled by a ship, was the Sunday his bedroom at the bay came alive with the crazy-making drone of mozzies enraged by each squirt of the can his father brandished above his bedhead. Too preoccupied with pain to cover his face with his pillow, to care about the rain of pyrethrum falling about, Chad lay on his sheet, venom spreading from his blackening calf to glands tender as a bruise in the pit of his groin. He has never since experienced pain so engulfing as that inflicted by the razor-sharp tail of a stingray thrashing to free itself from a net. The discomfort of the six blue stitches threaded up his leg by the neighbouring veterinarian were nothing compared to the throb of poison coursing through his veins.

It was not until the following day that he first heard news of the bridge. Outside, the sunless sky matched his mood. Still shaky and weak, Chad had fallen into a sulk listening to splashes rising from the rocks where other boys were doing bombies off the breakwater. All morning he was confined to bed, impatient for Ma's return from Hobart. Was she still at home watering the lawn, fussing over her hanging baskets that lined the porch? From there, you could look straight out at the bridge. Perhaps she'd been held up at Nan and Pop's, yakking non-stop as usual. Ma had promised to return with apricots ripe from Pop's tree, along with the antibiotics the vet had prescribed—*on the off-chance of infection*, old Mr Macey had said, scratching Chad behind the ears.

He remembers his father scoffing at the prescription: *For Chrissakes, Sal, Knowles Macey is a* vet *who should have retired ten years ago. They give these warnings as a matter of course, to cover themselves*—words even Chad knew were guaranteed to needle a will like Ma's; a woman with plenty of spongy cushioning but innards packed tight as a fist.

AT ROOKERY LAKE CHAD HAULS the esky and a large tub of provisions into the Apple field hut, so named for its red domed fibreglass structure. Freya has brought enough food from the station kitchen for a club of skuas to feast on for a week, never mind two people on a two-night stay.

If Chad were here with another man he wouldn't bother with a toilet tent, but as things stand he quietly pieces together aluminium poles and collects large stones to weigh down the tent's valance in case the weather turns bad. The polar pyramid has hardly changed design since the early explorer days, except that Goretex has replaced burberry, and aluminium poles are used instead of bamboo. He gives Freya a hoy to lend a hand. Try getting one of these forty-kilo babies up on your own.

CHAD POINTS OUT THE LOCATIONS of the three adélie colonies in the vicinity, the furthest an easy thirty-minute walk ordinarily, but something of an ordeal, he fears, if they have to lug her heavy camera gear. He gives a silent *yes!* when she chooses the closest colony to photograph; its feathered residents are visible from the Apple, close enough to pick up their acrid odour.

They trundle over snow-covered rock laden with her cases and packs. She carries more than her fair share and he's surprised at the weight she manages; but how she thought she would do this project alone is beyond him—with her swag of cameras—digital, 35-millimetre, large and panoramic format—as well as lenses, film and tripod, she has more in her kit than any one person can carry.

The rookery is all brays and bustle, the to-ing and fro-ing as frenetic as any mainland city rush hour.

'If you're sure you don't need my help,' he says, 'I thought I'd take a wander across the rocks, check out the other two colonies. You still have your VHF?'

Freya pats the radio in her pocket. 'I'll leave it on channel eight, same as last time.'

'Call me if you need a hand?'

'Promise.' She shouts after him above the din: 'What time do you want to meet for dinner?'

'Eight-thirty at the Apple give you enough time?'

'Eight-thirty it is.' She gives a businesslike nod.

The middle colony Chad treks to is a hurly-burly of nest building, stone-stealing, dustups and full-on flipper-smacking, beak-battering brawls. At the same time, however, first-time couples, and new arrivals reunited after a winter apart stand together in a swoon, displaying the distinctive adélie breeding ritual: chests swelling, necks extending like concertinas, eyes rolled down and a hypnotic swaying of heads as they bray. Established pairs take turns at egg sitting, one mate taking custody of the nest until the other returns from foraging at sea.

Stones may be gold to an adélie, but to a south polar skua the bounty of a penguin's nest lies within. Chad sees two skuas strategically positioned on the perimeter of the rookery. A third does a flyover, scrutinising the colony. The skuas bide their time, waiting for a squabble to break out and a tasty penguin egg to lie exposed or inadvertently tumble from a nest. Sure enough, within minutes the skua in the air swoops down amid the throng and rises again with an egg clutched in its beak. The area directly under siege shrieks; neighbouring penguins hunker down.

Chad ambles over the rocky hill towards the third and furthest colony, skirting around a fresh scrape of rocks when he hears the *kek, kek, kek* warning from a skua hovering overhead. Most people hold skuas in low esteem, repulsed by their practice of snatching live penguin chicks as well as eggs to feed their young. But Chad regards the feisty birds with quiet admiration. Skua parents will tackle any intruder—feathered or human—who encroaches on their territory. They will dive bomb the unwary, or fly straight at you, a formidable beak and a murderous glint in their eyes, dropping their feet in readiness to thwack your skull and unhinge your frontal lobe. They'll hammer you with their beak while you cringe and cower, shadowing you even as you run for dear life. Only then, once you have reached a respectable distance and found a place to recover while your heart stops pounding, will they settle down two metres away to let you admire the view. They'll plump their coffee-coloured feathers, tuck in their wings and blink at you adoringly, as docile as doves.

An adélie versus a skua? Give him a skua any day. Such vehement protectiveness could measure up to that of any doting matriarch; could even rival Ma's.

Chad remembers counting the hours until her expected return. His father had initially proven a poor second in fulfilling his requests for special treats. Dad couldn't whip up a plate of chocolate crackles festive in paper patty cases; nor could he produce, as Ma would magically have done, a brand-new comic book or even a choo-choo bar set aside for just such a crisis. His stitches aching, Chad had lain in bed bored and morose, his stack of *Richie Rich*, *Phantom* and *Casper* comics reread too many times.

But his father's one startling effort was compensation for any lack of matriarchal wizardry: he had given Chad the transistor radio to put next to his bed. The reception, his father warned, twisting the aerial this way and that, would be weaker during the day than at night. Chad would have to settle—*I don't want any grizzling*—for whatever they could raise on the dial. Still, to be entrusted with his father's prized possession had made an eleven-year-old feel grown up, almost a teenager.

Yet the glow soon wore off. No matter how he wound the dial or wiggled the aerial, Chad failed to pick up above the static anything more audible than the ABC's agricultural report. Not a single cricket test, no songs, no serials, just the announcer's posh and proper voice droning away about Tasmania's fruit export industry being on the verge of extinction.

The rhythmic monotony of the report was suddenly interrupted by *an important news bulletin*. The reporter's voice had a new edge to it:

> Repeating earlier headlines of the Tasman Bridge disaster. At nine-thirty last night, the *Lake Illawarra*, an 11,000-tonne bulk ore carrier transporting a load of zinc concentrates from Port Pirie, lost steerage in the Derwent River and struck the Tasman Bridge. The ship collided with two sets of pylons near the eastern end of the bridge, causing the collapse of three deck spans. At first light, divers . . .

A collapse of the bridge? The Tasman Bridge. *Their* bridge. *Dad!*

A hail of roadway above the impact point guaranteed the same fate for the ship as the ship brought to the bridge: tonnes of concrete and girders of steel rained down upon the *Lake Illawarra* along with a brief cascade of cars that plunged through the blackened chasm, carrying motorists to watery tombs. Within minutes the blighted ship had sounded like a whale, straight down to the river bed with its cargo of Broken Hill zinc and seven crewmen mustered in the smoke room with no prospect of escape.

IT IS CLOSE TO DINNER time when Chad approaches the Apple, its red dome aglow in evening light. He sees no sign of Freya returning; she must still be lingering at the rookery with her camera, soaking up the light. He walks by the shallow tarn and sits down on a rock. For as long as he's visited the area this lake has been the venue of a skua club: dozens of birds congregate here to bathe and socialise. Their gregariousness is a little-known endearing side of an otherwise maligned disposition. Outside their individual territories, neighbouring birds will sit together at the edge of the tarn, preening their feathers and clucking like old pals kicking back at the baths.

Freya's camera gear sits heaped on the hidden side of the Apple and it strikes Chad that she would have made two trips to ferry it back on her own. Three adélies confer around the assorted gear, their pea-sized brains entranced by the array of shapes and stone-like shades. When Chad tries the hut door he finds the handle locked; he can hear Freya rustling about inside.

'Who is it?' she answers his knock.

He shakes his head, looks around wryly. 'Who were you expecting?' There is a discord of squawks from the three musketeers.

It takes him a moment to register that the girlish laugh from within the Apple is hers. 'Just a minute,' she calls.

The door soon opens to a billow of steam and a delectable aroma wafting from the stove. The inside of the Apple is adorned with party balloons and a birthday banner. There's beer, wine, cake, candles to blow out, even fancy Swiss chocolates sent down by her husband, Marcus, *to tide me over.* There's a birthday gift wrapped in paper serviettes and tied with twine— two chocolate cherry bars and a packet of his favourite gingernuts.

He cradles his plate on his knees, sipping wine from an insulated mug, assailed by balloons; the gas heater is glowing, door ajar, penguins pad past. He feels ten years old again, indulged and special, a birthday boy as tipsy with pleasure as he's growing from wine.

After dinner he reclines on his bunk beneath the Apple's porthole window, completing his journal entry.

November 25. Rookery Lake. 42nd birthday (you old bugger). Clear sky, wind nil. Assistant to Freya. Adélies on eggs. Plenty of skua action at middle and northern rookery. Slap-up dinner.

Curled in her sleeping bag opposite, Freya turns the pages of her book, her elbow propped on a pillow.

'How's Mawson's diary coming along?'

'Okay,' she says half-heartedly. 'He can be a little dull.'

'Dull?' Chad bellows, past caring that he's three sheets to the wind. 'I heard you and Malcolm singing his praises the other day. Now you don't like him.'

'Oh, stop.' She laughs. 'It isn't that I don't like him. He's just a hard person to know; there's so much he doesn't say.'

She should talk. 'Like what?'

'Well, now Captain Davis, he tells it straight, no holds barred. But with Mawson, there's so little emotion. It's all so rational and stoic. It's hard to imagine there's a real person with feelings beneath the words.' She responds to Chad's puzzled expression. 'Like this,' she says, leafing back through the pages. 'Since we're onto birthdays.'

19 August: Still drifting and heavy wind. The dogs will be in a bad way. This is Paquita's birthday.

Chad blinks, fearing he's missed the point.

'Three measly snippets,' Freya looks across at him with a trace of exasperation. 'It doesn't say a thing about what's happening around him in the hut, the seventeen other men, what they did, who said what, not a word of what he's thinking. And his fiancée—it's practically his first mention of Paquita Delprat in the eight months he's been at Commonwealth Bay. It's as if she's a postscript, tacked on after the weather and the dogs.' Freya stretches the ribbon marker down the spine. 'My husband says if you only relied on his journal you could easily think him unfeeling.'

Chad thinks it unwise to admit he'd prefer that to the tripe some people fill their diaries with. 'Why persevere with it?'

'Research for the exhibition.' She sighs. 'Besides, it's good to make up your own mind about these things.'

'Big Douggie may not have been Prince Charming but I guarantee he never would have expected that one century on Freya Jorgensen would be critiquing his personal journal.'

Freya smiles. 'You have a point there.' She snaps the book shut and yawns. 'But he's not going to beat me. I'm determined to figure out why everyone thinks he's such a big hero.'

Chad won't let that one past the keeper. 'For a start, Freya, if it weren't for Douglas Mawson and John King Davis, you and I wouldn't be here. There'd *be* no Australian territory in Antarctica.'

Freya rolls onto her back and gives a gurgled groan. 'You sound like my husband.'

'And secondly,' he says, wondering if he's just been insulted, 'they were all heroes. Not just Mawson and Davis—every one of their men and crew.'

Freya rolls her eyes at his outburst.

'They came down to Antarctica in an old Dundee whaler that leaked like a wicker basket, with gear and equipment up to the gunnels—Mawson even brought down a plane he used as a tractor sledge. If the plane hadn't pranged before they left, it might have made the first Antarctic flight. It took weeks to find a rocky site to build a base on, and even then it was miles further west than they'd planned. Commonwealth Bay is nothing like the Vestfolds. It's a wind bowl with a few ridges of rock surrounded by mile after mile of ice cliff. Mawson had no way of knowing he'd chosen the windiest place on earth to build his hut. They had no contact with the outside world. For all they knew, the ship could have broken up in pack-ice and never even made it back to Australia. Then no one would have known where to find them.'

Chad gestures out the window towards the ice cap. 'We're in our heated hut within radio contact of the station. When they left winter quarters all they had was an ice cave plugged with a covering of canvas. In those days, if something went wrong when you were sledging, there was no rescue. No radio. No aircraft. You were entirely on your own.' He draws a deep breath.

'I had no idea you felt so strongly. Or knew so much about it,' she says quietly.

He knocks at his skull. 'Some things seep into the grey matter. At least, you'd hope so after spending eight weeks at the joint.'

She sits upright in her sleeping bag. 'You've *been* to Commonwealth Bay?'

'A few years ago now. Did some work on the hut with a restoration team. I can tell you one thing, Freya. Read all the books you like, but nothing compares with being there. Even Hurley's photos seem different afterwards.'

'In what way?'

'Every way. Take winter quarters—it's tiny. Photos don't give the scale. When you're inside the hut it's hard to imagine how eighteen men could have existed in such confinement—and for the most part got along. They would have been on top of each other, working, sleeping, eating, socialising.' He pauses. 'All I'm saying is, heroes like Mawson are everyday people. As flawed and as capable of stuff-ups as the rest of us.'

Freya gives him a haughty look. 'Speak for yourself.'

Chad returns to his journal and reads back over today's record. He retrieves his pencil and adds, *Top day*, not wishing to be thought of as dull.

He reads the last weeks' entries, staggered at how rapidly summer is passing. He has taken to working on the new accommodation module half the week, leaving the remaining time free to help Freya in the field. Touch wood, there's been no serious gripes yet from his fellow chippies, although Adam Singer, the only tradie he can't seem to warm to, makes a point of winding him up. This morning Adam stopped him on his way out: *Watch her*, he said, *I can tell you firsthand she's a prick teaser.*

He catches her studying him.

'Have you seen many auroras?' she asks.

'*Seen many auroras?*' he crows, setting down his journal. 'You happen to be speaking to the man who's clocked up nine winters in Antarctica.'

She looks at him earnestly. 'Is nine a lot?'

'Is nine a lot!' He flounders until he catches the teasing in her smile.

She demands he tell her everything: colours, form, how an aurora travels across the sky, even how it makes him feel. The last question gives him pause for thought. 'What's all this in aid of?' he asks.

She hesitates. 'It's for a series of photos. These shots I've been taking of you and the bikes—and the others—out on the sea ice.'

'Spill the beans, then.'

'It will probably sound bizarre.'

'Try me.'

'I'm wanting to "create",' she draws the quote marks with her fingers, 'a summer aurora—bold, vivid colours swirling through the ice as they might in the night sky.'

'Sounds alright,' he says. 'You know there's as many auroras going on in summer as in winter.'

'There are?'

'We can't see them in summer because of the perpetual daylight. But they're there, in both hemispheres—the southern and northern lights are all part of the same loop.' He turns to his trusty journal. 'Well then, in the cause of research and the Arts, let's see what we have in here.'

He flicks back through the pages to the winter months. 'Here we go. June nine. Auroral arch from north to northeast, visible 7.15 pm. Curtains changed to form a luminous green band. A ball of light travelled east and west.'

He looks for something more impressive. 'August seven. A deep red arch rose and broadened from the northeast, then folded back. At its eastern end, long streamers of turquoise. So bright it lit up the sea ice with reflected colours.'

'August eight—' He looks across at her. 'You awake?'

'Mmm,' she replies without opening her eyes. 'I'm listening. Visualising. It's wonderful. Keep going.'

'August eight. Lovely green and silver curtains. Curved fragments of bright yellow to the east. Pulses of light. Luminosity tracked to the east. Western end faded out.'

Chad turns over several pages. 'This one was a beauty. September one. You'll like this: brilliant red aurora like a Japanese fan opening and closing. Spread out to the east. Colours from bright green and purple to a deep red around the ruffles. Continued . . . through . . . Freya?

'Freya?' he whispers.

She answers with a snuffle and rolls over to face the wall.

Chad sighs and rests his journal on the floor beside his bunk.

Through the window of the Apple, he can see two adélies sleeping on their feet, their beaks tucked down into the crook of their wings. The evening light is velvet soft. For twenty years, now, summers and winters, this world of light and dark has been a part of him, each day of it on record in his journal. *Is nine winters a lot?* Five hundred and fifteen days he'll have been here by the end of summer; more than once a long-standing member of the 500 Club, he could have skited.

He turned down the last offer to summer at Mawson Station in favour of spending time at home. A balls-up he'd made of that: half of November moping at the bay pondering the end of another decade.

The day he turned forty he'd had a gutful of himself; he was dressed and in the car before the morning chorus brought the bay to life. He'd belted down the east coast highway like a bat out of hell, motored past Hobart before mist had fully lifted from the hills, and was waiting at the gates for the mill yard in Huonville to open. He picked up a trailer load of King Billy pine, celery-top and sassafras, some choice birds-eye Huon pine that had been put aside for him. Back in town he whiled away an hour at the Chandler stores down by the docks, talking himself out of a pair of topnotch binoculars that would have swallowed every cent of profit from the sale of one of his dinghies. Face it, he thinks, the old man and his prudence will always be a part of you. Then down to the river for lunch, as always settling on a bench in full view of the bridge.

The rusting hulk of the *Lake Illawarra* still rests on the Derwent River bed. Twenty-four metres beneath the surface, the broken vessel lies too deep to be a hazard to ships passing above.

When he left after lunch he should have driven straight back to the bay, but instead he pulled off at a phone box; stale smoke lingered in the mouthpiece. *I leave for work at six*, Jocelyn told him in a voice absent of emotion. Every time was to be the last; but like a moth to the light, once again he found himself merging the Jackaroo into the eastbound lane, its trailer load of timber brandishing a red rag, the pit of his stomach churning to lustful desire by the time he'd reached the rise of the bridge. He fancied he could feel when his tyres crossed the join where the new span of bridge abuts the old.

Chad can't remember when they abandoned the foreplay of a meal out, when each put away the last dressed-up vestige of social masquerade. Did she ever speak of him as her boyfriend? Whatever hopes she might once have held for him had long since been discarded, the promise he saw in her unfulfilled, the lees of their relationship a cojoining of bodies parched for touch and lacking the prospect of a different kind of joy.

The sex was containment and release, a scrambling of buttons and zips, a belt unbuckled, a top pulled free, shoes pushed aside and socks left on, a stripping of straps, a tearing at clasps, the freeing of breasts too large for the gaunt frame that carried them. Ill-fitting bodies kneeling on scuffed wooden floorboards against a creaking bed, and the rough and tumble entry into an oblivion of fleshly warmth. It was his belly pumping against the angular fall of her buttocks with a stark reminder of his bulk in contrast to a rib cage pushing through the lining of its skeletal back. Lovemaking; hardly, there was none of the exploring and caressing or the slow, rising heat he dreams of with a different woman. Both were silenced by the tawdry afterglow.

A benumbed mind and body carried him from the broken screen door to his vehicle in the lane. The same stupor navigated him back out to the highway. In a fug he made the turnoff to the coast. Only when he shifted down gears and began the rise into forested hills, passing beneath canopies of wattle and gum, did he think to wind down the window and draw in lungfuls of crisp bush air. And only once he reached the meandering downhill run to Triabunna and caught the familiar coastal comfort of kelp—on a full moon night he could trace the silhouette of Maria Island filling the bay—did dullness leave and feeling creep back in. He stopped at the Orford store for hot salted chips and a pastie with sauce, but not until he had wolfed them down and brushed salt from his shirt did he wonder at the gaping chasm in the base of his gut.

He drove in wretched silence along the coast, window down, the orb of moon as white as quartz in the apex of the night. The moon lit up nuggets of granite glinting with mica at the side of the road. The moon scattered shadows through the bush. The moon cast a bridge of seclusion wider than a mile across water at ebb in Great Oyster Bay.

*An ice cavern carved from
the sea*

THE REAL
THING

WIND RATTLES THE STUDIO. SNOWDRIFT blinds the bay. Freya sits at her desk cradling her drink, buoyed up by digital previews of her summer aurora. If her large format shots should prove as strong . . . She clings to the thought, trying not to fret about the quantity of large format film she has already used. She feels thankful for a day of poor weather to spend catching up in her studio; photos taken at Rookery Lake a fortnight ago are still waiting to be sorted.

Chad McGonigal had spoken more in those two days than in all their previous outings combined. She had woken early in the Apple to see lying loose on the floor beside his journal a clue to his past, a tiny dog-eared print with *1974* pencilled on the back, the polaroid coating so bleached of colour that the woman's beaming face, dappled with shade by her sunhat, looked otherworldly.

You have your mother's smile. She had returned the portrait when he awoke, her urge to ask questions subdued by the weight of his silence.

Her laptop chimes with incoming mail. *Breaking news: Hurley's ice cavern.* A knot tightens across Freya's shoulders before she even clicks on the image. Her computer processor grinds, the timer icon asserting her husband's effort and devotion with each circuit. Frank Hurley's ice cavern bursts onto the screen, an ethereal figure wound in light. The photographic wizard who conjured this image into existence almost a century ago would have revelled in seeing it shining silvery on the screen, every bit as wondrous in pixelised glow. *An ice cavern carved from the sea.*

>> Forget what I emailed you yesterday. I see this as a much
stronger image for the catalogue cover, the other we'll keep as a
promo piece.

Freya shrinks at her husband's fervour. What began as suggestions has morphed into decrees; email by email, her project sequestered away. She slumps before her laptop, an upwelling of tears veiling the screen, frustrated not at Marcus, who has always been like this, but at her own submissiveness, at years of being swept along unresisting, dragged down, held too long.

Freya had tried to leave Marcus once; late one night she drove to her parents' house. In the morning, after Papa left for work, her mother dismissed her complaints of his overbearingness, scolding her like a child being marched back to school. *Look at how he provided for you all those years, the studio, the kind and generous things he's done to make you happy. You have a good husband, a lovely home.*

It ought to be enough. She should be grateful and happy. It feels churlish, then, to single out the patio—a birthday surprise from Marcus, the sky blocked out with sky-blue bonded steel, transformed from a sanctuary to a cell. Or the wall he built soon after, *all under wraps until you got home*—her husband brimming with such pride as he showed off all that planning and expense, rendered bricks the breadth of the block, a graceful curve around the largest gum tree. *For privacy*—he wound his arm around her and held her tight, smothered her with kisses—*no more strangers on the street peering in.* Freya couldn't bring herself to injure him, seeing, beneath all that intellect and apparent confidence, a boyish need to be praised, revered—a man in constant need of bolstering. Is her husband's vulnerability so different from her own, a disfigured woman needing to be cherished, wanting to be loved? She had smiled then, praised her husband for his triumph. Only on her morning walks, looking out across the escarpment to the Swan Coastal Plain, could she grieve for what she'd lost: lush expanses and aged, unfettered trees, views that stretched forever. She wept for a house that had once captured her heart with its balmy sense of space. She cried for herself. Ten years beholden, not to misguided acts of love, but to her own passivity, her own lack of fortitude. It was as much her own doing—their *lovely home* had been reduced to a suffocating cocoon moulded for two, and she felt a growing urge to take on more and more projects that took her away from it.

She returns to Marcus's email:

>> Hurley had recently returned from a rescue mission to retrieve some sledging dogs from Aladdin's Cave, and was inspired by the quality of light that filtered through the cave's walls. On the last day of August, he and the surgeon, Leslie Whetter, set off from the hut with some alpine rope and scaled down the ice cliffs to the frozen sea below. There, they entered this magnificent cave where Hurley secured a series of five images. Whatever will the purists say to that? Not a fake at all.

Freya scans the icy enclosure, the foreground canopy that for years was thought to have come from a separate negative, merged by Hurley in the darkroom to form a seamless composite. Art critics believed the image 'fudged', declaring it too dangerous for Hurley to have entered an unstable ice cave from an equally unstable platform of sea ice. They underestimated the lengths Frank Hurley would go to. Now Marcus writes that the photo has been re-examined and deemed *the real thing*, the new assessment verified by several of the diaries.

It is Freya who is a fake. She conceals her growing discontent, keeps from Mama, from them all, her sorrow for a life that will never hear the squeals of children darting beneath a garden sprinkler, or even a dog panting at the flywire door. *Focus on the good things.*

>> Hey you, not a word from the Frozen South this past week. Have I lost my wife to the wiles of the wild?

Freya jumps at the banging on the door. Hot chocolate scalds her hand.

Chad stands on the landing, his yellow jacket slapping like a sail in the wind.

'Come in,' she yells above the noise, but he keeps his distance, fishing a battered notebook from his overalls.

'You've probably seen this.'

'Come in out of the weather.'

'Can't stay.' He turns his back to a squall to flick through calculations, notations, diagrams. 'You asked what else I remembered from Commonwealth Bay. Here, for what it's worth.' He tears off a page and hands it to her. 'I found this written on Hurley's darkroom wall at winter quarters.'

Chad is halfway down the stairs when she calls after him, touched by his offering. The words on the page send a tingle down her spine. *Near enough is not good enough.* Her thanks are snatched by a fresh blast of wind.

The *Adélie Blizzard*
October 1912

DOUGLAS RETURNED FROM THE ROUNDHOUSE to a stifling
pall of pipe smoke. Those seated at the dinner table cackled
like a gathering of crones, Archie McLean fit for the part
with his cheeks and lips sporting the remnants of rouge
from Saturday's theatricals.

The odour of tinned fish and cayenne pepper lingered
from dinner, mingling with the stink from the slops bucket
where tea-leaves floated on a fatty scum. The bucket also
held the remains of the morning's culinary debacle—*Grab
them while they're hot, boys!*, a futile cry; the nightwatchman's scones, hot or cold, were as palatable as pumice stone.

Douglas groped through a wilderness of long johns and
woollen socks, cardigans and burberries—clothing provided
at great expense to the expedition, now heedlessly slung
onto nails. Finnesko boots lay higgledy-piggledy around
bunks, their sennegrass liners kicked off and thrown onto
desks mounted with sewing machines and microscopes. One

good whiff of eighteen fur sleeping bags infused with the aroma of unwashed bodies would send a weaker man to his knees. He scowled at the most indolent pair—eight hundred applications from young men all around Australia who'd have given their right arm to be part of the expedition and here was John Close, their 'physical culture expert', forty if he was a day, snoring on his bunk at 7.30 pm, *The Strenuous Life* laid open on his chest. Reserving energy for his own interests was their illustrious surgeon, Dr Whetter, brazenly swotting for his final medical examinations on expedition time.

Walter Hannam sat alone with his journal. The wireless man had been a portrait of misery since yesterday evening— Black Sunday as he named it, the date that one of the masts crashed down. The puff anemometer had recorded the limit of its capacity: two hundred and two miles an hour. Douglas was blown off his feet retrieving the instrument from the hill. Hurley, outside to record the phenomenal conditions, had been lifted off the ground with his cinematograph, photographer and eighty-pound camera deposited in an unruly heap on the rocks. The remaining mast they had lowered this morning for fear it might be blown down onto the hut. All hope of communicating with the outside world dashed. One more notch to failure.

Ninnis, the day's rostered cook, stood at the end of the dining table clutching a wooden spoon as he relived, scene by tedious scene, the latest version of his recurring dream. 'The entire hut was transformed into a theatre.' He wielded the spoon like a baton. 'The Doc's room was the actresses' dressing room and while the play was going on our fellows were constantly coming in and out of it in polar kit. In the next breath I was arriving home at Paddington Station. Or was it Victoria? Let me think. No, no, I'm almost certain it was Paddington. I say that because—'

'Moving along, Cherub!' Hurley roared.

'No matter,' Ninnis continued, undeterred by a chorus of jeers. 'After I arrived home and had my bath, the first thing I asked my mother was whether Captain Scott had reached the South Pole and she said yes, then duly proceeded to weep.'

'First to the pole *and* to show the Norskies the honour and glory of man hauling.' Bickerton, their patriotic Brit, licked his spoon clean, ready for pudding.

Hurley thumped the table. 'Dogs over man hauling. My wager's still on Roald Amundsen and his team of dogs.'

'Five squares of chocolate says you're wrong!'

'Raise you five,' another rallied.

'In all my dreams about returning home,' Ninnis wheeled on, 'no one seems the least interested in the expedition. Last night, for instance, I knew we hadn't sledged a yard, and I kept on pointing out that our work was not finished, that I was home only briefly.'

Ninnis's ceaseless recitations of failed sledging and thwarted homecomings irked Douglas immeasurably. At the start of September they had all been hoodwinked by three perfect days of calm. *A change in our fortune*, he'd declared like a fool. They all raced outside, eighteen lunatics leaping about in the snow and hooting like residents of Bedlam. Hurley had added twelve dozen plates and half a mile of cinematograph film to his collection. Douglas had spent every daylight hour helping to dredge the bay, at one point breaking through thin ice beside an open lead, immersed to his armpits in a bath of ice. Johnny Hunter's eyes stood out on stalks at the sight of his benches and workshop floor and the dinner table piled high with treasures from the deep. In those three serene days they had done as much scientific research as in nine and a half months at this wind-ravaged site. On the fourth day of dredging he had looked up to see a wall of drift billowing down the ice slopes and tumbling helter skelter across the bay towards them. Within seconds the first squall hit, followed by a devil's onslaught of wind that sent them racing shoreward, the sea ice splintering dangerously beneath their feet. A minute's delay and they'd have blown out with it. And not a break in the weather since—their hopes of early spring sledging dimming with each new blast of wind.

Conversation lulled when Douglas sat back down at the table and watched Ninnis scrape a shameful quantity of uneaten salmon kedgeree back into the pot.

Ninnis threw him a defiant look, flushing like a schoolboy. 'I shouldn't expect the bow-wows will complain. We're all of us human, we all make mistakes.'

Every mistake a *Championship*, in the local vernacular, Ninnis nominated a *Crook Cook* for another evening meal made inedible by him misreading Mrs Beeton's recipe: tonight *1 oz of butter, finely-chopped parsley, salt and pepper, grated nutmeg* had become two ounces of salt, two ounces of pepper, a spoonful of red-hot cayenne pepper and never mind what else.

After the first few mouthfuls, Bob Bage's face turned puce and Walter Hannam launched into a sneezing fit. Douglas had pushed his plate aside with a few choice words for both the cook and his messman. Their genial Swiss had gallantly finished his serving, all the while dabbing at his forehead. 'Englishmen like their food spicy.'

Ninnis lifted his pot of discards. 'Mrs Beeton, Mrs Beeton,' he began. 'Since we eighteen fellows of Commonwealth Bay first tiptoed over the threshold of the female domain and embraced the fair sex's noble work, has any other lady's name reached such giddying heights as that of Mrs B? Why, Mrs Beeton's heavenly image presides over our wee kitchen like a ship's figurehead, a bibbed apron over her gown and in her saintly grasp a wooden spoon.'

Douglas halted the babble. 'Do we have any words of sense written for the *Blizzard*?'

'Joe finished his.'

'Let's hear it then.'

Joe protested, claiming his article for the *Adélie Blizzard* newspaper needed a lot more work.

'Let us be the judge of that.'

Madigan brought the loose pages from Joe's bunk. '*Genus Homo. Sub-Genus Blizzardia*,' he read out. '*Blizzardia dropemalli*. In the vernacular known as *X*, this species is noted for the number and vigour of its championships. Size medium, nature excitable, perpetually hurried.'

The crowd broke into a fresh round of cackles as Mertz went to take a bow and knocked a mug from the table.

Madigan turned to Ninnis. '*Blizzardia cherubis*,' he read. 'Form very elongated and angular, posterior regions feebly developed. Elegant in appearance, this species is very particular in regard to hair arrangement, this being usually parted exactly in the centre. It lives chiefly on the prospect of accruing medals.'

'But doesn't care for fish,' Douglas muttered, at which the men erupted into such raucous laughter that John Close woke in his bunk with a start.

Madigan continued. 'Another characteristic is that of speech, which is typically of the La-de-da type.'

'Wretched lies!' Ninnis clutched his chest. 'Yet another dagger through my heart.'

Madigan turned the page. 'Here's one for the Chief. *Blizzardia dux ipse.*'

Joe, the author of the piece, mumbled and scratched his head. Silence fell like a blanket over the table.

'*Dux ipse*,' Madigan repeated, 'leader of himself.' He eyed Douglas mockingly. 'General form elongated. Aspect austere, occasionally relaxing. It is somewhat dreaded by other species, particularly cooks, though it is not so ferocious as its appearance sometimes suggests. Amongst its more particular idiosyncrasies, it is extremely critical in culinary matters.'

Hurley snorted, breaking the silence.

'Hear, hear,' Ninnis cried. 'And lives mainly on the grilled bones of mere mortal chefs.' He gave a dramatic flick of the head and strutted out to the dogs' verandah with his pot of salmon kedgeree.

Bob Bage at the sewing machine inside winter quarters

DRESSED
TO KILL

'THE GUYS HAVE BEEN HERE.' Freya hears Elisia at the other end of the dress rack, searching through the larger sizes.

In preparation for tonight's *Dressed to kill* party, Kittie, Freya's closest friend at the station, has mounted an expedition to the dress-up room.

Freya holds up a pair of false breasts covered with scraps of a beige slip, hand stitched and edged with lace. Good grief.

'This, girl, is you.' Kittie pulls out a glittering, powder-blue gown. 'This would sell for a mint in a Sydney retro store.'

Freya takes the dress, measuring the split against her thigh. 'You must be joking.'

'Try it on,' Kittie urges. 'You can never tell till you have it on.'

'I wish it was my size.' Elisia takes a second, hopeless look along the rack.

Freya manoeuvres her head and arms through the openings, then Kittie clips together a tackle-box worth of hooks and eyes.

'I can't breathe,' Freya moans.

'Shush. You don't have to breathe.'

'It's too tight. I can't stand tight clothes.'

'Stop complaining and turn around,' Elisia says. 'It'll loosen up.'

'What did I tell you?' Kittie beams. 'It was made for you.'

Elisia tips her head to one side and frowns.

'What's the matter?'

'The bust.' Elisia wiggles the bodice. 'She could do with some boobs.'

'Couldn't we all.' Kittie sighs. Seized suddenly with the same idea, they grab the hand-sewn set of fake breasts and stuff them down the front of Freya's dress.

Elisia and Kittie cheer when she does a little twirl and shows off the thigh-high split. Kittie claps and Elisia chortles as she struts up and down the dress-up room, her sparkling décolletage flaunting a lopsided cleavage.

'PLENTY OF GLITZ AND GLITTER around the traps tonight.' Malcolm turned aka Count Dracula, eyes Freya's shimmering blue gown.

Charlie gives her a whistle as she walks through the foyer; he has her spin around. 'Very swish.'

'You scrub up alright.' A sparkie raises his beer in a toast when she walks into the lounge.

'You look lovely for a change,' says one of the scientists. *Thank you* to the evening's gold medallist of backhanded compliments.

Even the best-looking man on the station, Adam Singer, sets down his gun and bows. 'Freya, you look sensational. Good on you for dressing up.'

Freya curtsies in return. 'You look quite suave yourself, 007,' and in that exchange she feels an unspoken tension ebb and wash away. As she walks past him she senses the lightest touch on her bare back, so fleeting she wonders if she's imagined it.

The only one who doesn't offer comment is Chad, standing fixed to the floor, a sight to behold in his crocheted shawl and tatted bonnet, a basket of treats clutched between his paws.

'What big ears you have.' Taking a sweet, Freya has to sidle past his bulk, treading on his tail on her way to the bar.

The room soon fills up with the usual suspects: Frankenstein's monster, wicked witches, pirates with home-made cutlasses, Darth Vader, an applaudable Frankenfurter—the shaven legs of Anastagio, an engineer, accentuated by stiletto heels and fishnet stockings, are voted the shapeliest of the night. Women slink through the door in black, Charlie and his Angels make an entrance in white. And no gathering steeped in a century of cross-dressing peculiar to Commonwealth bases could be authentically Antarctic without a gaudy array of hirsute, ruby-lipped maidens in fishnet tights and little lacy numbers.

Freya sees Malcolm nab the walking sandwich board by the frame of his placard, which is illustrated with a skull and cross bones and the words *Tommo's Tired Stew*. He ushers the sandwich board, along with a male field assistant clad only in a G-string and wielding a whip, towards the door. 'Exit right, you clowns. I didn't see cruel or lewd written on the noticeboard. Back up the stairs and rethink your wardrobe.'

The windows have been masked to block out the sun; a disco ball and strobe light spins a mosaic of silver mirrors around the walls, and Elisia cues an evening's worth of dance music.

First away is Ian the physicist, so often preoccupied in a cloud of atmospherics, who steps onto the dance floor with his colleague, Becky, wowing the crowd with a command performance of the Rumba.

Freya tells herself to stop after the first bottle of champagne—Marcus abhors drunk or raucous women—but Kittie keeps pouring and Elisia keeps toasting; soon the three cavort their way to the dance floor. Elisia entices Chad to join them—a circle of four emboldened by costume and wine, dappled by mirrors streaming lazily by.

The floor becomes a press of bodies, Tommo the chef and Frankenfurter escaping the crowd to dance an intimate tango off to one side. The music slows, bodies sway; the lights swirl around Freya until the horizon becomes a blur of shoulders and heads. She turns to Chad, who has abandoned his costume keeping only the tail, which continues to cause havoc each time a passing shoe pins its tip. She doubts she can stay upright without someone to steady her, each turn of the floor giddier than the last, the room aglitter with flashing lights. Freya props her head against Chad's arm but still the room weaves by. Within its arc, eclipsed by the strobe, she sees a menacing beak and glinting eyes fixed upon her. When she lifts her head she realises she was foolish to flinch. All that stands before her is a slightly out of focus 007, Adam Singer's arm outstretched, the barrel of his gun searching out her head. A mocking wink. Kapow.

FREYA NURSES A HANGOVER THAT four tablets, a litre of water and a slow Sunday morning in her studio have been unable to shake.

Forty-five years after the expedition, Marcus writes, *'Joe' Laseron, the biological collector, looked back*:

>> One phase of our expedition is indelibly impressed on my memory. When eighteen men are herded together in a space twenty-four feet square for over a year, in a climate so severe that the greater part of the time must be spent indoors, and when these limited quarters must serve for sleeping, cooking, eating, and for the pursuit of many specialised callings, [this] indeed is the test of true comradeship. It was in these trying circumstances that the expedition can, I believe, make an almost unique claim.

Hurley's photo of Bob Bage at the sewing machine inside winter quarters shows an orderly chaos, the close-packed living Chad had spoken of.

Freya pings a quick reply, ignoring her throbbing head and whatever mistakes are bound to catch her husband's eye. She shuts down her laptop and reaches gingerly for her pack.

Glasses. Gloves. Lights. Door. *Thud.*

She's joining Chad to hike to Lake Stinear then on to the lookout. Freya has limited herself to one digital camera and she paces down the hill grateful for her feather-light pack and the rest day. *Sunday.* No Saturday chores, no backlog of films to catalogue, no images to burn. A day of play all over the polar world. When Chad phoned her studio an hour ago to ask whether she was fit enough to take a walk she'd responded in a rush of enthusiasm, *no worries*, flattered he would choose to invite her on this, his free day, her bravado belying a pounding head.

She watches a GP glide south along the coast—and laughs when she realises she's used the Antarctic acronym for giant petrels. Next she'll be spouting *blows* and *blizzes*, loading the bike with a *rat pack*, sorting recyclables to be *RTA*'d to Hobart on the *AA*, answering *roger* and *copy that* without a moment's pause.

After an ambivalent introduction to Australia, years of her childhood spent struggling to unpick a new country's jargon, it still puzzles Freya how the vernacular, through some invisible process of osmosis, became a part of her. These days, to Mama's disdain, Freya struggles to recall her mother tongue. Apparently it is not all lost; Marcus says he loves the trace of Norway in her speech, that the quaint expressions she used in the year he taught her at college were what first tweaked his heart.

It's worth remembering, he'll invariably segue, *that the written impression you make on your photographic clients also counts for a lot.* And off he'll go correcting her spelling and grammar.

A quick pitstop at the dark and dingy expiries container. Freya digs through the plastic bins, looking for a glint of purple foil in the piles of out-of-date food. Right now her lowest priority is the station-wide contest to find the oldest chocolate bar; any chocolate will do. Not yet halfway through December and her new monthly rations are gone. Despairing, she throws herself across sacks of packaged rice to reach the unsorted supplies pushed against the back wall. She riffles through dehydrated dinners and instant potato, waterproof matches, miniature jams. She digs through an entire seam of Vegemite, stacks tins of butter and plum puddings to one side, perks up at a rustle, only to deflate at the sight of packet after packet of silver-wrapped sledging biscuits. Finally she grasps a rectangular wedge, hard, tessellated; more are buried beside it. She extricates two precious blocks of chocolate, drawing a mental map of where to find them next time, and rolls onto her back to proffer thanks.

On closer inspection, however, the old-fashioned white wrapper of the fruit-and-nut bar is as foxed as the pages of one of Marcus's first editions. She relinquishes the antiquated bar and pockets only the fresher one—still well past its best. Everyone has their limits.

She bolts the rest of the way, bursting into the foyer of the living quarters to find that Chad has already turned over his tag and marked their expected return time on the whiteboard. She feels an unexpected sting to see a third name listed, and quickly reprimands herself. Elisia Hood, she reminds herself as she enters the lounge to greet them, is a treat to have around.

THEY TRUDGE THROUGH KNEE-HIGH SNOW to reach the shoreline of the lake. Freya has never seen Chad so relaxed; he and Elisia are reminiscing about their winter months. Elisia came to Davis Station as the wintering dieso and, like Chad, opted to stay a second summer to help out with the planes. They try to include her and she does her best to join in. *Which one was Beacon? Three days straight as slushy during winter!*

Freya finds herself trailing, has to quickstep to match their thundering pace as Elisia tells her about their winter crossing of the Sørsdal Glacier to the Rauer Islands. Eight of them, half the station, had set off in two Haggs and struck bad weather, the poor visibility obscuring the cane line—bamboo wands staked along the ice to mark a safe route. 'Chad, Beacon and I drove twenty hours without stopping; pea-soup conditions all the way.'

Chad slows to match Freya's pace, to describe how they made ten days worth of pre-cooked dinners ready to zap in a microwave oven that they carted along in the back of their Hagg.

'Meals on wheels!' Elisia cries.

Chad grins. 'In the case of the Hagg, snacks on tracks. How about Beacon's laksa, Lis? How good was that?'

Elisia hits him. 'What about my lasagna?' and off they forge, reliving each meal.

Then Elisia throws her arms to the sky. 'The ice was here, the ice was there, the ice was—minus-fucking-forty on the way home. Remember, Chad?'

'Who could forget?'

'We pitched the tents in a circle like a small tepee village,' Elisia says. 'Microwave beeping in the Hagg. I brought my sound system. The Waifs, Keb Mo, wafting over ice. And both nights, *both nights*, auroras to die for.'

Chad moves back to Freya's side. 'It's true.' He lights up, as animated as she's seen him. 'The sky was unbelievable. Intense pink, blue, the white so strong it blotted out the stars. You would have been in seventh heaven.'

'Wow,' Freya says. Really, she's impressed. What she would give to see just one good aurora. She feels a prickling awareness of her lower status as a summerer—one of the lightweights who blow in and blow out at the end of the season. She lets herself drop back, in a huff at God knows what.

At the far end of Lake Stinear, Elisia waits for her to catch up. 'How'd you fare this morning? As green around the gills as I was?'

'Biliously green.' Freya confesses, vowing never again to drink champagne. She hesitates. 'Last night, Lis, did I do anything . . . stupid?'

'Do you mean, was I the only one to notice you and that man over there looking cosy on the dance floor?' Elisia turns to her. 'Can I say something to you, as a friend?'

'Of course you can.'

'Chad's been very good to me. He's one of the most genuine, honourable people I know. I'd hate to see him hurt.'

Freya blinks. 'He's hardly interested in me! And I'm certainly not out—I'm married, Elisia.'

'Yes,' is all she says.

'Lis!' Chad beckons her over to the ridge where he is rummaging through a collection of rocks.

'Gotta go. He could be on to Lasseter's Reef.'

Freya stews over Elisia's words, distressed that the very act of speech carries the momentum to make something out of nothing. It unsettles Freya to find herself lured into even imagining the idea.

She watches Elisia striding across the ice, her plait of fair hair bouncing on her back. Freya thinks Elisia radiates more natural beauty than any other woman on the station. She exudes an aura of calm. She never wears a scrap of makeup, even on Saturday nights when the station dresses up for dinner. Elisia is taller than Chad, her build as athletic as it is strong. She has proven photogenic too: as part of Freya's portrait series, she set up lights in the workshop and photographed Elisia welding, sparks showering her overalls and safety glasses. Freya envies Elisia her sense of place, her practical knowledge and skill at mending broken things.

Is there a place in Antarctica for artists like herself? Except for Chad, she can hardly align herself with the trades. Nor would the sciences claim her as their own—which is probably as well: just walking through the laboratories makes Freya tingle with unease, sends her clamouring for a breath of untainted air.

She senses that some on station think her project frivolous, her title of artist-in-residence a sham. Freya can guess at some of the opinions expressed: *The way the government wastes public money on the arts.*

One way of cadging a free ride south.

Malcolm, she is sure, would give short shrift to any whisper of elitism. *God forbid Frank Hurley or Herbert Ponting hadn't gone along to photograph the early expeditions. Freya is adding a twenty-first-century account to the layers of Antarctic history.*

Meanwhile some from the workshops refuse to believe that photography rates as work. *Come to get your playmate?* Adam and the other chippies gibe when she goes to meet Chad.

Freya waves back when Chad beckons from the brow of the hill. She races to catch up but when she reaches the crest they have already bounded ahead, snatches of their laughter scudding by on the wind.

At the lookout Chad produces mugs from his pack. 'Tea.' He extracts the first thermos. 'And coffee, strong for those who need it.'

Freya sips her coffee, resting against her pack while Chad and Elisia fossick among the rocks below. Through Chad's binoculars she can make out the Sørsdal Glacier's scintillating diamonds of light. To the east the repeater mast of Tarbuck Crag glints in the sun. She has never questioned the phone in her studio, or that she can hook up to the internet any time she likes, but suddenly it strikes her that it all began a century ago in a tiny wooden hut. None of the men at winter quarters, Marcus told her in an email, were even aware that in late September 1912, a few weeks before wind felled and smashed one of their masts, they had made history—the Macquarie

Island relay station picked up snippets of morse code from the radio officer at Commonwealth Bay: *Having a hell of a time waiting for calm weather to put up more masts.*

Sheltered from the breeze, wrapped in her jacket, hat pulled low, she feels the sun's glow radiating warmth through her.

Freya stirs to Chad nudging her. 'Wake up, sleepyhead. You've been out for nearly an hour.'

Dozy, she reaches for his outstretched hand so he can help her up but fails to grasp it firmly. She reels backwards, leaving her glove behind in his grip.

Chad winces as she lands on her pack. 'Ouch.'

'I'm okay. I'm officially awake.'

'Sorry, sorry.' He returns her glove. 'I was born under the sign of slapstick.'

Only then does she register the band of waxen skin on her finger. Furtively she retrieves the wedding ring from inside her glove and hides it in her hand. 'I'm the careless one.'

As Marcus likes to remind her. She marvels now at a ring's capacity to enact its marriage vows and dominion, the circle of wedding-white as good as a brand upon her skin.

My very dear Paquita

This is the first occasion since landing in Antarctica that I have addressed myself to you in writing, though daily a warm glow of life feels to have crept in to me coming from the far distant civilised world, and of course it can be from none but you.

I have concluded, once again, that it is nice to be in love, even here in Antarctica with the focus of the heart strings far far away.

Here in a primitive world, in its most rigid aspect with an expanse of tempest tossed ocean between come warm messages straight from your heart, born in earlier days when you and I were together.

Although not writing, daily I feel to hold communion with you in dreaming reverie of all our former happiness. You see I have been reaping comfort for having spoken to you on that quiet dark evening at El Rincon, now nearly 2 years ago. (How the time flies!) How I sometimes think that you are paying compound interest on my life loaned to the 'Wild'.

The non-fulfilment of the expected wireless messages will have been attended with anxiety and then the Aurora might have been caught in the pack or sunk after leaving us. All is so doubtful that I know my true love must have been harrassed by a multitude of doubts and I hope never to incurr such in future. Indeed, I even look forward to making up for this offence.

Down here, things are different. I feel that you are in the best keeping and I only hope that you are passing the time as pleasantly as may be.

Dear Paquita I am writing this note in case anything may happen which will prevent me reaching you as soon as the mail from here, which is expected to be picked up next January. So many things may intervene for truly one lives from day to day here and then our sledging journey is about to commence.

How terribly disappointing this land has been. Our only consolation is that we feel that everything has been done that could be done and that on account of the rigour of the climate the information that we have obtained will be of special value.

Since the ship left in Jan. last, we have had but a few days of calm weather and the wind has blown with such terrific force as to completely eclipse anything previously known elsewhere in the world. Some of the men have done such remarkably good work in the hurricane wind as to call for admiration from anybody. I trust & hope that better conditions will be given us during the coming weeks.

10 November 1912

The weather is fine this morning though the wind still blows—we shall get away in an hours time. I have two good companions Dr Mertz and Lieut Ninnis. It is unlikely that any harm will happen to us but should I not return to you in Australia please know that I truly loved you from an admiration of your spirit. And should we meet under other circumstances please know and love me as a brother.

In case of my non-return my total assets come to somewhere about £2000 including of course salary at the rate of £400 per annum from the expedition which is paid in lieu of my University salary. Accounts in the Bank of Australasia. I have told you of the other things including all my photos and private belongings at the University. Take what you want of all and if any remains you can give to my Mother if alive in lieu to my brother.

I must be closing now as the others are waiting—give my admiration and love to all the Delprats, each one separately . . .

Good Bye my Darling may God keep and Bless and Protect you.

Your Douglas

CURLICUES
OF FILM

THE IMAGE OF THE WEDDELL seal spills from the edges of the baseboard and sprawls across the darkroom bench. Freya takes time adjusting the lens of the enlarger until she is quite certain the focus is sharp. She slides a sheet of photographic paper from the drawer and rests it square upon the platen. With the photosensitive sheet protected by the safelight's coloured filter, the seal's eyes gleam, his coat sleek with the tangerine glow. Below his whiskered snout he wears a perpetual grin.

Freya fires up the enlarger's soft light that slowly floods the emulsion with life. She lifts the photographic sheet by its two brittle edges, carries it carefully to the sink and rests it in the first tray. A fragile thing, this future she holds in her hands.

As she rocks the print through the liquid, the developing agent laps mesmerisingly from corner to corner. The jowls of the weddell seal rise through the emulsion as if rolled with washes of ink. Freya works beneath the fruity glow of light unfazed by the cramped quarters. She feels a familial comfort—the vapour of developer, the constancy of warm air on her skin, curlicues of film suspended from an overhead line of clips. When she pictures her father it is not the heavy-set, suit-and-tie man he was at the end, his darkroom business powered by a bank of employees, but a younger man in a home-built darkroom no larger than this, his shirt sleeves rolled up past his elbows, the fair hair of his arms tinged red by the safelight's glow.

Freya lifts the softened paper with rubber tongs and slides it into the stop bath. She winds the timer to thirty seconds, each ratcheted click a fraction of time waiting to pass. As an eight-year-old, a newcomer to a continent where seasons came topsy-turvy, Freya would linger in the darkroom after her father finished his work. She would stand on the footstool and wind the timer forward, the orbit of iridescent lines glowing in her hand. Clickety-click, clickety-click, watching right down to the last moments, her fingers halting the dial just before the jingle of the alarm tickled her ears. So long as she kept winding the dial forward, never allowing it to complete a full circuit, Freya could keep the future on hold.

She transfers the print into the fixing solution to rid the emulsion of undeveloped salts. Freya eases the handle of the tap to open and lays the hose of running water in the rinse tray.

The darkroom is where she first fell in love with the magic of image. When she grew tall enough to reach the developing sink she was allowed to rinse the prints, careful not to scratch the surface of the fragile paper with *sharp little nails*, mindful not to wind the tap too fast *in case the water sprays*. By the time she was eleven she had learned each darkroom process from mixing chemicals, to black and white printing, to developing film, to cibachrome colour, until she acquired her very first camera. From behind boxes on the top shelf of the closet she pulled out a Leicaflex SL, *J. Jorgensen* stamped in gold leaf on the leather case. The flourish of her father's *J*, she thought, could as easily be read as an *F*. At twelve, printing her own black and white photographs, she happened upon her first composite through an error of double-exposure. She rocked a print in a tray of developer, waiting for the texture of granite to appear, and spied, through the pattern of rock, the faintest image of her sister's eyes. Astrid's face looked moulded from stone—as if the granite was the keeper of an ancient secret only the darkroom's sorcery held the power to reveal.

Freya flicks on the main light and surveys the black and white print. She is pleased with the density in the shadows, the spread of midtones, double highlights gleaming life into the weddell seal's eyes.

She pulls on cotton gloves and removes the negative from the enlarger's carrier. She runs a lupe over the remaining strips of film spread across the lightbox. Already two and a half Antarctic months have clicked past; Christmas is only a week away, the tree brought out of storage and dressed. The kitchen has taken on a festive feel, bringing forth an uncanny cheerfulness in Tommo, the older chef. Sandy, too, stands at the large mixer whistling a tune as he breaks dozens of eggs into an oversized bowl. The kitchen exudes the buttery richness of baking. Slushies box Christmas treats to be flown out to science parties working in the field. The station is alive with the fervour of gift making. Each evening a trail is blazed to the workshops by amateur craftsmen and -women. Latecomers scour the off-cut bins for workable lengths. The carpentry shop buzzes with the grinding of the router; the belt sander whines, wood shavings coat the floor around the lathe. In the plumbers' shop, scrap metal has been picked over, and someone has gathered ribbons of copper sheeting into a posy with sculptural intent. Beads of melted solder drip to the floor, the arc of a welding gun sparks like a green flash at sunset. Gift-makers shield their projects from the keen eyes of passers-by. Freya, too, took her turn at reaching into the Kris Kringle hat and drawing out a name; she immediately decided to print out this photo of the weddell seal to give to Radio Officer Charlie.

That Davis Station still maintains a darkroom is tribute to a bygone time. In the last decade, with the uprise of digital, Freya has seen all but one of Perth's darkrooms reinvent itself or close its doors. What would have become of her father's business had he lived long enough to see the full impact of digital photography? She likes to imagine he would have seized it as a chance to return to his first love, to the viewfinder of a camera, and for no other gain than pleasure. And what of her, had she followed the path her parents mapped out?

At nineteen, she resisted a career that would have limited her to developing other photographers' work. She didn't care how good the prospects were for her father's business. When her mother's voice rose in pitch, reminding her of the hundreds, *hundreds*, of aspiring artists waitressing in restaurants, she wouldn't be swayed. Instead she watched her father's downcast stare while her mother's voice slid into a whiny litany of professional photographers having to serve at petrol bowsers weekends and nights simply to put food on the table. Finally Papa pushed back his chair and left the room as silent as a stone.

Why? Freya would ask her father if she had a second chance. *How could you throw it all away?*

She had determined never to relinquish her camera as he had done. She would go to Melbourne to study at the photography college—adding with all the bravado she could muster, *whether you help me or not.* Couldn't they understand? *Can't you see, Papa?* It was the same driving want that had once emboldened him to cross hemispheres and turn seasons upside down.

Freya chooses two negatives, the first of Chad at Rookery Lake, the second *a study of the photographer* he insisted on taking with her camera.

Gone are the weighted silences. They spend their days in a pattern of easy quiet, broken by bursts of chatter. Chad makes her laugh. She laughs at herself. Freya has her gear ready the night before, but it still takes an age—three times longer than it would at home—to get ready in the morning to leave. Those who have been south before are resigned to this aspect of Antarctic life. She likens the time in a day spent dressing, lacing boots, pulling at velcrose and zips—all to venture outdoors—to an armoured warrior preparing for battle. Out in the field, Chad seems content to wander off and leave her to her work, checking in with her by radio from time to time. After twice inadvertently jettisoning her emergency pack from her bike rack—spare socks and thermals sodden thanks to a broken thermos, her chocolate smashed to smithereens—she has taught herself to tie a clove hitch over the good old granny knot. Thankfully he has gained some faith in her abilities while she, in turn, better understands the map, can read contour lines and pinpoint corresponding hills. She trusts herself to find the way. Down here she is not, as Marcus would have her, *a girl in need of rescue*.

These last weeks they have driven hundreds of kilometres over sea ice, following the coast, returning weary-bodied to the station late at night, their faces raw. Clear sky or cloud, nothing short of an impervious foundation of white zinc cream—disagreeably claustrophobic—can protect skin from the glare thrown up by snow and ice. However, in a few more weeks, Chad says, the sea ice will be gone.

The shape of his crooked smile emerges through the developing agent. Freya has not before examined him so blatantly: tawny hair tied back in a ponytail, straight white teeth beneath a crooked nose. She gauges the mildness in his eyes—gentle eyes, flecked with the sadness of an unspoken past. Never married, no partner, an only child—parents and grandparents, all his family, gone.

Freya wonders why she feels compelled to print the portrait of herself. She won't give it to Marcus. Lord knows it will not be one her mother would show—Mama is forever encouraging Freya to pose with her *best side* before the camera's unforgiving eye. Only Papa believed his daughter's mark of birth a blessing. He saw it as a charm. Didn't she share her name with the Norse goddess Freya, Chief of the Valkyrie, *our own little Daughter of Time?* One day, he'd said, she too would fly in the image of a bird and sprinkle summer sunlight, *your shining armour sparking the aurora's lights.*

Freya places the image in the enlarger. For the most part she is resigned to the stain on her face that brands her, but it still jars to see her birthmark inky black beneath the darkroom's coloured light. She steps back from the face projected on the baseboard to assess its repugnance, surely why strangers turn and stare.

She tried explaining to Chad why she shies away from the face of her lens. *I take photographs because they let me be part of a world that's as beautiful as I care to make it. Why would I,* she touched her cheek, *or anyone else, choose to be reminded of this?*

Chad stood silently until she finished speaking, then extracted her camera from her hands as if not a word had sunken in.

How is it, he said, *that someone with so much courage has so little faith?* He knelt on the ice and framed her face against the sky. *You can't begin to know what other people see.* Chad stayed quiet for a time, intent on composing the image.

What do you see? she asked, her voice steadier than she felt.

I see someone who's been holding herself down for too long.

He made it sound as simple as a choice.

Here I am looking through the camera at a woman who tells me she's sensitive to beauty—he stopped.

He kept his finger depressed on the shutter, photo after photo. *Stay exactly like that.*

The portrait stares at her from the baseboard of the enlarger. She forces herself to look away from her birthmark to the unruly shock of fair hair turned orange in the darkroom's light. It maddens her, this tangled mess across her face. She isn't beautiful, not by a long shot, yet there's truth in this portrait, her face flooded with joy. And something more. She has disciplined her feelings for so long now, used her camera as a shield from disappointment, from every kind of want. The face before her, caught unguarded, reaches through her camera's eye. It jolts her to recognise her own desire, to be exposed in such a way.

Wind, Drift, Drift, Wind
December 1912

THE INCESSANT FLAPPING OF THE tent, burberry canvas
slapping against three reindeer fur bags; the smarting of his
eyes from air thick with smoke—the Far Eastern Sledging
Party were camped two hundred and sixty miles east of
winter quarters, one month out, now holed up in the
blizzard for a third dreary night.

Propped in bags on either side of Douglas, Ninnis and
Mertz drew on pipes, their faces as wizened from cold and
wind as those of the sealers they'd encountered at
Macquarie Island on the voyage south. Ninnis's fingernails
were embedded with grime, his hands the texture of hide.
His cheeks bore a ring of raw, frostbitten skin. At winter
quarters Ninnis would not have let a day go by without
standing before the mirror and parting his hair down the
centre, just so, before combing it back in a slick. Now it
hung around his face like a helmet, lank and oily in contrast
to the russet frizz sprouting from his chin.

Both men looked as stiff-backed and sore-buttocked as Douglas felt from lying cramped too long on an unyielding bed of ice. Neuralgia coursed an electrical charge across his left cheek and down the side of his throat. The pain felt fire-poker red, eclipsing the pulsing of a lip swollen and burst from exposure to the wind. To add to his discomfort, he needed to visit outside.

Ninnis dealt with his own suffering by remaining uncharacteristically quiet, though not even the torment of two fingers so red and swollen with whitlows they looked as though they had been slammed in a door could deter Cherub from his daily ritual of journal writing. Even with his cack-handed grip of a pencil he still managed fine penmanship—with his theatrical mannerisms and epicene sensibilities Ninnis should have trained as an architect or calligrapher, anything but a soldier. Douglas knew that Cherub shuddered at the prospect of returning to his battalion in a few months' time.

The phrases Douglas saw scribed on the open page of Ninnis's journal prompted a glimmer of a smile that set his lip smarting anew: *Verily I say unto you . . . the great and glorious fact must occupy a line by itself . . . Mertz, needless to recount, was like iron . . . alas and alack, our dearly departed bow-wows (a ghastly business) . . .*

Gadget, Jappy, Fusilier, Blizzard. Douglas had carried out the first *ghastly* deed.

Gadget simply cannot keep up; *she's entirely unfit to pull*, he'd felt compelled to remind his two companions when

179

her ladyship, not content with riding atop the sledge, took to chewing through the leather straps holding fast the cooker box.

Ninnis and Mertz had conveniently busied themselves with other duties when they saw him drag the rifle from the sledge. They needn't have feared. He'd not ask another man to undertake such a task.

Just the same, Mertz had helped butcher Gadget and her unborn pups into twenty-four rations, all wolfed down by the other dogs except Shackleton, who gave her entrails one guarded sniff then turned up his nose. Ninnis had paced to the far side of the sledge to puke in the snow.

Douglas had never known such an odd, endearing fellow. In early 1911 Ninnis had sashayed into their London office trussed up like a turkey in his fancy suit and bowler hat, volunteering to help with the expedition and might he come along? Ninnis had proven his worth through trying months of fundraising and again at winter quarters. Although Douglas had made a public show of stacking away copious volumes of Ninnis's *London Illustrated* magazines (page upon page of drivel the roundhouse could have put to better use), and Ninnis's clothes boxes, buried beneath a verandah-ful of snow, contained more finery than Douglas had owned in his life, when it came to mucking out the dog verandah, bringing in the daily ice, or emptying the roundhouse drum, Ninnis was an ever-willing volunteer. In spite of his comical affectations and a wit that could wound, every man warmed to Ninnis—with the possible exception of big Walter

Hannam, who dubbed the hut alcove *Snyde* Park Corner. (On the occasion Hannam took to his bunk, groaning and bilious, after bolting down two tins of sardines before realising they were spoiled, Ninnis had cried, *For mercy's sake, Hannam, if you really are going to die, best you toddle off inland as far as you can so we can make a dog food depot out of you for Dr Mawson's sledging journey.* Poor Hannam, doubly aggrieved.)

Mertz lay propped on his elbow on a pillow of burberries, his charcoal beard covering his throat like an overgrown hedge. X apparently felt less inspired by these idle hours to fill his journal with brilliant literature. English openers punctuated each line of German:

> 6. *Dezember: Drift, Wind, Wind, Drift . . .*
> 7. *Dezember: Wind, Drift, Drift, Wind . . .*
> 8. *Dezember: Wind, Drift, Drift, Wind . . .*

Douglas felt momentarily contrite when Mertz caught him looking. X smiled and laid his journal open on his lap, as if to show he didn't mind.

'I rehearsed in my head the dramatic part.' He pronounced it *dwamatic* and began to recite, entirely from memory, another passage from Sherlock Holmes. 'A hound it was,' Mertz boomed in his thick accent, drowning out the flapping of canvas, 'an enormous coal-black hound, but not as mortal eyes has ever seen. Fire breaks from its open jaws, the eyes they glow with a smouldy glare. Muzzle and hackles light up with flames.'

Neither Douglas nor Ninnis corrected Mertz's English, instead Ninnis howled with such comic effect that Douglas forgot his neuralgia and joined in.

'Never,' Mertz went on, 'never in the strangest dreams of the disordered brain can a thing more hellish be imagined than a dark form and savage face that breaks from the wall of fog . . .'

Douglas marvelled at X. The Swiss had adapted without complaint to an Australian diet laden with meat. Coached by Ninnis and Madigan, his English vocabulary had exceeded expectation. X had begun his apprenticeship in the vernacular with a shock of seaman's curses learnt from *Aurora*'s crew on the voyage out to Hobart; then at winter quarters had added a further swag of idioms to his repertoire. These days X could rival Walter Hannam with his *Gee whizz*es and *Up the bloody spout* and *Didn't 'alf come a cropper*, all delivered with a European flavour which sent the crowd into hysterics.

Douglas squirmed, unable to delay the moment any longer.

'Rears.' He nudged Mertz apologetically.

'As sooner we deliver,' X sprang from his bag and reached for his burberries, 'as quickest we return.'

In easier conditions Douglas would have left the tent on his own, kept private the act of squatting into the wind, a rag or sheet of sanitary paper at hand, or if nothing else a fistful of snow. But when the wind-chill of a seventy-miler plummeted the temperature below zero degrees Fahrenheit, with the force of air eddying and spiralling anything in its path upward around the body, taking a crap—the most personal of bodily functions—became one more act of brotherhood.

The atmosphere was bright with midnight sun but in the howling drift they could see less than three yards ahead. X kneeled in the snow on the leeward side of the sledge with a canvas sheet gripped in his outstretched mitts and the lower edge of the cloth pinned to the snow with his knees. The screen had naught to do with modesty. Douglas squatted before Mertz, the rounds of his moon-white buttocks in full view of his comrade. Moulded together, Mertz looped his arms around Douglas to close the skirt of canvas about him and save bare flesh from frostbite.

One saving grace of a slurry-in, slurry-out diet of greasy hoosh: the motion was quick.

On hands and knees Douglas followed Mertz, two cavemen groping their way back through the tent's flapping vestibule. He drew off his gloves to toggle off the burberry chute.

Douglas changed his socks and stuffed the damp pair into his armpits to dry. Not a trace of warmth remained inside the moulting reindeer bag, whose hair found its way into every mug of tea they drank.

The hopeful anticipation of summer sledging had slid to frustration by early November. Douglas half-expected the stir-crazed crowd at winter quarters to run a Calcutta sweep on the makeup of the six sledging parties that would fan out from winter quarters to explore the hinterland and coast. He spent hours in his cabin juggling names and abilities: the trio led by Frank Bickerton, the Western Party, would make use of the defunct aeroplane converted to a tractor-sledge and explore the coastal highlands west of the hut. Cecil Madigan was the clear choice to head an Eastern Coastal Party which would investigate the coastline in the opposite direction—leadership became Madigan more naturally than it did Douglas himself. He paired brute physical force with scientific expertise, choosing large, robust Frank Hurley to bolster magneticians Bob Bage and Eric Webb on an extensive man-hauling journey to the south magnetic pole; this Southern Party was to record magnetic observations en route. Smaller, lighter men in the form of Herbert Murphy, Johnny Hunter and Joe Laseron would act as the Southern Support and accompany Hurley and the magneticians as far as practicable. A second support group, the Near-Eastern Party, would assist Madigan's trio, then undertake mapping the coastline from winter quarters east to the large glacial tongue.

A charge of neuralgia made him wince and he toggled up the bag around his chin.

Ludicrous to ever have imagined big Walter Hannam squeezing into a fur bag sized for the body of an Eskimo; and Hannam had seemed relieved, almost chuffed, to be left in charge of the hut and daily recordings.

Ninnis packed away his journal and eased down into his bag, his face ragged with pain.

'Your fingers still troubling you?'

Ninnis nodded.

'Try to get some sleep. We'll look at them in the morning.'

'Night, night,' Ninnis said.

'Sleep tight,' X cooed.

Douglas hoped it would be so, thinking how pain could scramble the unconscious mind. These last nights he and Ninnis had been taunted by dreams vivid and bizarre. Douglas's father had appeared before him, filled with scholarly wisdom, delivering a warning that Douglas couldn't make out, his father's face so sad and real that when Douglas woke he searched the tent. Ninnis frequently dreamed of arriving home and being unable to stay there, of needing to return to the ice to finish his work. His latest recurring dream was of Captain Scott and his party returning from the pole, all dressed in new furs, thundering by with a vast team of dogs. Ninnis woke Douglas, shouting, 'Hike! Hike!' as if to spur on his own dogs. Both Ninnis and Douglas envied Mertz the way his dreams satisfied his waking cravings, replete with soufflé and mountain berry pie.

The fifteenth of January, he had instructed each party leader, *the fifteenth at the latest*. Captain Davis and *Aurora* were expected back in the first half of January to relieve them, and even then they'd be in for a mad dash west to retrieve Frank Wild's ancillary base before a new season's ice hemmed them in. *How far along the coast will Wild's party be?* someone asked the unanswerable question; only Providence knew if *Aurora* had even made it safely home last summer. If any team should be late returning, Douglas warned, God help them for he would not be answerable for his actions. They had neither ship's coal nor surplus funds to cover delays, and the wellbeing of Wild's party and the success of the expedition all hinged upon prompt timing. Each set of eyes in the hut—sixteen of them blue-eyed, Mertz once noted—absorbed the grim prospect of being left behind in this frozen Godless site.

There had been no question that the sixth and final team, his own Far Eastern Sledging Party, would travel the longest and potentially most hazardous route with the dog teams and include the two dogmen to tend to them. He acquiesced to Mertz's request that his skiing expertise could be employed to front-run the dogs—if and when the terrain allowed.

Douglas told himself he had chosen Ninnis and Mertz for their skill with the dogs—and why not also choose a pair who worked hard and made his life easy? But in truth he chose them because he enjoyed their company and had come to care for them as brothers. He chose Ninnis and Mertz because there was no Ninnis without Mertz, no Mertz without Ninnis; they came as one inseparable unit.

SUMMER
SOLSTICE

BEYOND TURNER AND MAGNETIC ISLANDS, too close now to ignore, a line of ocean rests as quietly as a lake. Two weeks ago he and Freya could have driven their bikes beyond that line; then, the sea ice stretched to the horizon.

Chad sits in silence at the high point of the island, looking out past Freya and her camera. The adélie rookery is alive with new-born chicks that crane their beaks towards the parent at the nest. When they hear their parents call, the chicks peep beseechingly, frantic to be fed.

A homeward-bound parent lumbers up the hill with a swaying gait, its belly bulbous with krill. The jet coat gleams, the white-feathered chest pristine after days spent flying through the sea.

Freya looks up from her camera. 'Is everything okay, Chad?'

'Yep.'

She shrugs. 'You seem quiet, that's all.'

He watches the greeting ritual of the adélie pair as they exchange guardianship, the swaying and bobbing of heads, the press of feathered bodies. Freya's camera drive whirrs. His morning confrontation at the workshop is still raw as a graze.

Before leaving this morning he'd defended himself like a man on trial. *I was asked to help her*, he told his workmates. *Talk to Malcolm if you have a problem with it.* Chad can't decide which irks him the most, Adam Singer's inference that he's no longer needed, or the prospect of giving this away.

Freya leaves her camera and joins him for a time, sits hugging her knees. 'They may smell bad,' she surveys the rookery, 'but there's nowhere else I'd rather be.'

The newly arrived parent turns its attention to its young, leaning down to open its beak. The siblings vie with one another, each craning to be foremost in the receipt of food.

You're hardly first prize in anyone's raffle, matey, Adam had hissed plenty loud enough for Chad to hear.

'It seems like a good system,' Freya says. 'Both parents taking equal responsibility for rearing their young.'

'That's the way it ought to be,' he mutters.

Freya rises, props her tripod against her shoulder and waits. 'You ready?' she says gently.

'You go on. I'll stay here a while.'

'Shall I stay here with you?'

'Nope.'

He registers the huff in her response: 'Suit yourself, then.'

Suit yourself. Stay or go. Would it matter to anyone but himself?

He gives a nod and away she marches, heading over to the island's sunny side.

FREYA SITS SURROUNDED BY THE wonder of new life. She refuses to let anyone's doleful mood prevent her from revelling in the delights of hundreds of adélie chicks, none older than a week, soft, fragile things so small she could cup a pair in her hands. She watches a parent tend its baby, another pair reuniting. Freya is struck by the penguins' dedication in caring for their young, by each parent's reliance upon its mate. When they return to Antarctica to breed, they navigate south through hundreds of kilometres of open water and across sea ice, relying on some internal GPS to reach the same site on the same island where they nested the year before. There's extraordinary skill, she thinks, in finding your way across difficult terrain; in trusting that your mate will be there waiting for you.

Today is her first summer solstice in Antarctica—the longest day of the year, she'd reminded Chad, who, throughout the morning, has been pensive and quiet. *I don't need reminding of dates*, he had snapped at her.

She tumbles the rock she has found, twists it so it glints like a semaphore mirroring the sun. Her hands carry in their shape the hands of her father—narrow fingers curved in an outward sway, speckled fingernails above rising keratin moons. *Snap!* Freya likes to imagine her father walking the Vestfolds beside her, well pleased by the name an early Norwegian captain chose in honour of his home province.

She has a memory, the Indian Ocean, glittering with the colours of a new vocabulary as their ship approached port. Her father had pointed to a sign: *Welcome to Western Australia.* *Vestfold*, he'd squeezed Freya's hand, *the west side.*

The duplex they moved to, long since knocked down, perched on a hill a stone's throw from the beach, within sight of a city skyline punctuated with building cranes. If they were to cross the escarpment and keep driving east, Papa said, they would watch earth turn red and bush grow sparse, see where scrub gave way to an endless expanse.

Her father brimmed with talent, yet his photographs of everything he found majestic about this vast western state met rejections from dealers in Norway and Europe where his work was shipped. A man not easily deterred, he produced new, larger landscapes for galleries in the city, and sent them to the eastern states as well. Each prospective buyer shook his head doubtfully at a Norwegian wedding photographer turned artist; even the best-known photographers failed to sell their work as art. *Who but a foreigner*, the string of nos and sorries implied, *would put creative passion and their life savings into the back of beyond?*

Freya remembers her parents arguing over money, her mother's distress that her father poured *the last of our savings* into film and paper, chemicals for the darkroom, photographic trips away.

Three more months, Solgunn. Just three more months.

Her mother pleaded, *Think of your girls.*

Once, when her father was away, Mr Madsen, his agent in the city, called in to their home at Floreat Park to return the unsold photos. *Girls, say hello to Lars*, their mother said. *Lars*, she called him, all aflutter. Mr Madsen greeted Freya and Astrid with a little bow, *How do you do, little lady? How do you do?* Her mother's laugh, strange and girlish at things he said: *real coffee!*, and *my word* to a second slice of kromkake.

When Freya found the boxes in her parents' attic filled with her father's early landscape prints—beautiful compositions alive and lustrous with light—she asked her mother, *How could Papa give up something he loved this much?*

Mama wound her cardigan around her waist. *Your father chose to put his family first. We were new to this country. You can't begin to understand.*

She didn't want to understand Mama's sobs behind closed doors, her father's voice as sharp as steel. Enough to watch as joy and laughter leached from her father. Papa no longer stretched on the grass beside her to help count the stars. He stopped his morning swims and runs along the beach. He never sang his old college songs, and spoke to her in English all of the time, even at home. He talked of leaving the coast, moving away from the *stinking city*, up into Perth's foothills; as if an escarpment, a rise of several metres, would somehow change their lives.

Freya stops mid step, removes her tinted sun glass to register the colour. Close to shore, adélies torpedo out through the lead, some landing squarely on their feet, others skidding on their belly and easing to a stop. Their feathers glisten as they march towards the rookery, pausing only to pass the time of day with those outbound. Freya sees Chad in the distance down by the rocks, staring at a sea that even the midsummer sun seems unable to penetrate, a band of indigo ink abutting the impossible blue of the Antarctic sky. *A world of colour*, Douglas Mawson wrote, *brilliant and intensely pure.* She pictures her father marvelling at the layers of colour through the ice, the hues of the evening sky. She thinks of him finding the same peace that she feels in this timeless expanse.

Papa hardly used his new Leica, but packed it away in its leather case and shoved it to the back of a high cupboard that would be opened once or twice a year. In two years he had outgrown his home darkroom business and purchased a building and adjacent land in a rundown part of town, four blocks east of Perth's only other commercial darkroom. At the end of the third year he hired a girl to keep the books and a technician to run the printing and processing. He removed himself to the opposite side of the darkroom door, his focus honed on making profits grow.

He left this world as he'd lived in it; a life arrested, a career that culminated in a toast of wine with his accountant and darkroom manager, celebrating a successful bid to take over the business of his biggest competitor. And yet there would have been enough work for both of them—her father had said as much himself. As if refusing to be party to soulless gains, her father's heart attacked this last betrayal of his spirit.

FREYA SEES CHAD STRETCHED OUT on the rocks near the bikes, his head resting on his pack. She scrambles down to sit beside him, breathless, certain he will love the treasure she has brought him.

'Close your eyes,' she says. 'Hold out your hand.'

Reluctantly he plays along. She lays the rock plain side up and presses his hand closed around it. She watches as he unfolds his fingers to reveal an unremarkable stone striated with rust and a few lines of grey.

'Turn it over,' she prompts. 'Turn it to the light.'

She sees his surprise at the swathe of miniature garnets studded across its face. He smiles for the first time all day, bedazzled by the band of glittering gems.

'You like it?'

'Very, very much.'

He turns the cluster so it glisters in the light. 'Lovely.' he smiles, flashing it at her eyes. He tries to pass it back.

'No.' She beams. 'It's yours to keep.'

Chad examines the stone in his hand. 'Freya,' he says quietly, 'it isn't yours to give. It belongs here in Antarctica, where you found it.'

She feels her face flush. 'It's just a rock. You like rocks.'

He returns the stone to the palm of her hand and just as she did to him, wraps her fingers around it.

'I'll keep it myself, then.' Even to her own ears she sounds like a pouting child. She wishes she'd never picked it up at all.

He glowers at her. 'Does anything I say or care about mean anything to you?' He runs his hands through his hair and turns away. 'Why would it? Do whatever the fuck you want with it.'

'Of course it does. Of course I care. What's wrong with you today? You're like a bear with a sore head.'

He rests back against his pack. 'I've had a gutful of trying to work things out.'

'What things? What are you talking about?'

Freya waits until finally he speaks. 'Malcolm wants a carpenter to go to Mawson Station to work the second half of summer.'

'You can't go!' She surprises herself with her outburst.

'No one else wants to. The others say they've done the lion's share of work since they got here, that I should be the one to raise my hand. It's fair enough.'

'It's certainly not fair. Speak to Adam. I know he'd listen—' She halts at Chad's odd look.

'Trust me, Freya, you don't know. Anyway, it's no big deal.'

She's almost afraid to ask. 'You don't mind going?'

He glances from the stone up to her face. 'Is there a reason to stay?'

'There's a trillion reasons.' Freya plows on, not daring to acknowledge the undercurrent: 'Anyway, you should have first say. The Division asked *you* to stay on an extra summer because they needed you here at Davis Station. Not at Mawson.'

He offers her a crooked smile. 'You needn't be concerned about your project. There's a score of people who'd be itching

194

to help you out. Adam Singer, for one. You can finally choose who you want.'

She rolls the stone in her hands. 'I have exactly who I want.'

The words hang in the air between them.

'My best mate Barney Foot is over at Mawson. Our Antarctic days go back to the eighties.'

Freya struggles not to sound aggrieved. 'What sort of person, other than maybe a Flintstone, has *Barney Foot* for a name?'

Chad smiles. 'The Feet, they're known as back in Tassie. He and his two boys live just an hour's drive from my place. You'd like Barney. You would have loved his wife. Maggie was a wonderful woman. An artist.'

'What happened to her?'

'Killed in a car accident a few years back.'

'I'm very sorry,' she says quietly. 'Chad, you have heaps of good friends here, too. We don't want you to go.'

'Are you representing the entire station now?'

'I'm speaking for myself. I like being out here with you. Sharing all this with someone—with you.'

He pats her shoulder paternally. 'Nothing's decided. The Casas won't leave for Mawson until after New Year. There's time to figure something out.'

Freya slumps on her pack, eyes fixed on the rift that angles out across the sea ice towards the line of ocean. She ought to get up off the ground, fetch her other camera from the bike. She ought to photograph this vastness, this day, sea ice yielding to the ocean. She remains motionless, detached from the surrounds.

Chad points to the horizon. 'Sea ice will soon be gone.'

She can see that for herself.

'We've had a good run with the bikes,' he adds, to which she musters a *yes*.

He says he is pleased, for her sake, the ice has held so long.

He turns to her. 'You think I should stay then? See out the project together.'

She answers carefully. 'You have to do what's right for you, Chad, nobody else.'

'What's the right thing for *you*, Freya? What do you want?'

'It doesn't matter what I want,' she says, suddenly frightened. 'This is about you, not me.'

'Have it your way.' He gestures at the garnet stone. 'What will you do with it?'

She turns the rock again in her hand, summoning a round of courage. 'Is it so very wrong to want something, knowing it's wrong, wanting it anyway? What if it were just for a while?'

Chad hesitates. He meets her gaze. 'You're the one holding the stone,' he says quietly. 'I think that's for you to decide.'

Furthest East
December 1912

THE SNOW PETREL CIRCLED HIGH above Ninnis's sledge, tracing the parhelion that circled the sun and seared through cloud. Too soon their tiny visitor flew northward, its wings a flutter of farewell. How was it that the lingering impression of such a beautiful thing—the first living creature they'd seen outside their own circle in weeks—could gladden the heart, quieten the soul, turn Douglas's thoughts homeward?

Packed on Ninnis's sledge were two of the dilly bags Paquita and her mother had stitched by hand. Before leaving Hobart he had opened her parting gift to find one dozen calico bags in the boldest shades imaginable—*vibrant colours*, she had written, *to remind you and your little hutful of men of the goodness and warmth of home.*

A quarter-mile ahead, breaking trail for the little pilgrimage, Mertz glided on skis. He belted out one of his student songs with such patriotic fervour that any moment now Ninnis would launch into a yodel to set the dogs howling too.

Mertz had made it his mission to bear out the worthiness of skis in Antarctica. Every so often he made a show of halting and gazing back, hand on hip—an exaggerated yawn, do you mind—while Douglas, Ninnis and the dog teams clambered in his wake through patches of knee-deep snow.

Ninnis had woken this morning his old jolly self, prattling *this time last year . . .* , *this time next year . . .*, rough-housing with Mertz and playing the giddy goat as they harnessed the dogs. Cherub had done himself a disservice by remaining stoic for so long; when Douglas finally lanced his whitlows, his fingertips were purple and bulbous with pus.

Douglas reached a stretch of névé—old, compacted snow indicative of a snow bridge—and stepped onto the sledge to spread his weight. Back on fresh snow, he flicked the whip and shouted, 'Look out behind you, X. I'm hot on your tail!'

Thirty feet behind Douglas, Ninnis called to his team of dogs. Douglas turned to see him jump off the back of his sledge and run alongside the dogs to give old Franklin a hasten-along.

They were a jolly team trundling east in only a whisper of breeze, a balmy fifteen degrees Fahrenheit, the dogs pulling eagerly with their brushes flicked towards the sky.

Until yesterday a third sledge had carried the heaviest load to save the runners of the other two. Discarding it represented more than their imminent approach of the halfway mark. Men and dogs had slogged unyieldingly, traversing two crevassed rivers of ice so large that Douglas pictured their tongues slicking out across the ocean for fifty miles. Yesterday's ritual of redistributing the load equally between his sledge and Ninnis's was affirmation that they were fairly humming along; for once the expedition was all harmony and order.

Forgotten was the calamity of Tuesday's broken bottle of primus spirit, though for two pins Douglas could have throttled Mertz for his wild, clumsy ways. Fading too was the tedious zigzagging at the glacier's headwaters to detour around filled-in crevasses one hundred feet across. They had skirted pie crusts of ice whose frozen depths boomed as ominously as cannon fire. He'd lost count of the detours to avoid yawning mouths of ice with jaws hinged open.

The dogs slowed to a languid pace and today he didn't mind. Sledging was rarely the relaxing pastime some imagined—most hours were spent heaving the load across waves of sastrugi, or untangling brawling beasts, or loping alongside to keep their bearing true. Tracts of glorious smooth terrain that allowed one to actually ride the sledge and relax for a time—well, moments like these were pure gold.

'I still have my eye on you, George,' he growled. George might be solid ivory between the ears but he was cunning enough to put just enough weight on the trace to feign the effort of pulling. Ninnis's rear team comprised the pick of the dogs, while his front team—at greater risk of encountering a crevasse—boasted a motley collection of loafers, wasters and mischief-makers. If Haldane—named by Ninnis after the bigwig in Whitehall who had objected to his secondment from the army—ranked as the ugliest dog, then Johnson wore the medal for foulest odour. Mary and Pavlova worked only for as long as their ladyships were of the predilection, while Ginger, having recently dropped a litter of pups, pulled her little heart out but simply lacked the power of the larger dogs.

Douglas took the almanac from his kitbag to calculate the noon observations. He saw X raise his ski stock in caution then glide on. When his dogs reached the same place Douglas saw no sign of hazard and eased back on the sledge. The dogs trotted over a patch of névé marked with a hint of a depression, similar to many they'd crossed before. Still, Douglas turned back and called a warning to Ninnis who paced alongside his team. Ninnis's reaction—swinging the dogs to face the névé straight on—was practice honed to instinct. The Far Eastern Sledging Party was a cracking *A-One* team.

Douglas returned to his sums, savouring air gentle with the slick of wooden runners over ice, crunches of snow beneath dogs' paws, a faint whimper from one of the team at the rear who was likely feeling the lick of Ninnis's whip.

'Hear that, Georgey boy?' Douglas called. 'You'll be in for some of that if you don't pull your socks up.'

Latitude 68°, 53', 53" south; longitude 151°, 39', 46": three hundred miles east of winter quarters. The hour was nigh to depot the bulk of food and gear from Ninnis's sledge, make one final dash and stake the Union Jack at the furthest east. *In the name of King George the Fifth.*

Douglas glanced up and saw Mertz had halted, his head canted in puzzlement as he peered back along their tracks.

Douglas turned, stung to see nothing behind him but a single set of tracks. He rolled off the still-moving sledge and raced back, thinking a rise in the terrain had hampered his view of Ninnis and his team. Even then, part of him knew. Too late, he knew.

A CHILL BELCH FROM THE crevasse.

The contorted mouth of the smashed ice lid exposing an abyss too wide to bridge. His frantic wave to Mertz to bring the sledge and rope. The echo of their calls bouncing shrill and alien off walls as sheer as glass and a piercing iris blue. The stygian gloom below.

A pathetic cry and struggle of a dying dog, its back broken, caught on a ledge so impossibly far down the animal looked as small as a mite. The futile farce of spooling out one hundred and fifty feet of fishing line to estimate the distance to the shelf below. They might as well splice all their lengths of alpine rope and try climbing to the moon.

Only with field glasses could he make out broken pieces of the sledge littered over the shelf: the remains of the tent, and a canvas food tank—the fortnight's rations representing a fraction of man and dog food swallowed by the crevasse.

No sign of human life.

The hoarseness of their voices ragged from three hours of calling; another onset of neuralgia that skewed Douglas's face into a grimace and seized him by the throat when Mertz began to weep—what should he do? What could he do but take action, however inane, and walk X away, *Come, Xavier*; support his arm and steer him to the rise; go through the mechanics of recording a bearing with trembling fingers and the tic of an eye.

One last pitiful hour sounding with a weight and bawling into the crevasse, *Ninnis! Ninnis! Cherub!*, as if refusal to relinquish hope might resurrect an angel.

Fallen comrade . . . Supreme sacrifice.

Words of his own to ease Mertz away, for no bible's prayer would save the two of them.

*Frank Hurley's Southern
Sledging Party and the
Southern Support Party
camped on the plateau,
December 1912*

CHRISTMAS
DAY

>> Merry Christmas, sweetheart. The wee hours here in Perth, the
night too hot and sultry to contemplate bed. The temperature still
hasn't dropped below 30. Ghastly. I'm trying to conjure images of
ice and picturing you sound asleep . . .

Two am at Davis Station, in front of her computer and too
wired for sleep, Freya's mind is aswirl with replays and
imaginings. Flakes of snow catch on her studio window only
to be whisked away by the next flurry of wind. She watches
the last of her images download. Those she took tonight could
as easily belong to Hurley's time—the evening sunlight diffused
by falling snow, the distant glow of Davis Station, and
everything around them sepia soft.

She opens the photo that Marcus attached to his email:
two tents staked upon the plateau. In nine weeks of sledging
south across the ice cap, how did Frank Hurley, restricted to
a single camera and a handful of glass plates, determine which

of the prime times to preserve on film? She pictures him standing at a distance, absorbing the meagre camp amid the endless expanse. He captured this moment for the same pictorial qualities she sees in her own evening's images of the sea ice—low atmospheric light, everything soft-edged with low scudding drift, sky aglow.

How did you become so enthralled by Hurley? Chad had said tonight as they returned across the ice to their bikes.

I love his passion for photography, that he saw it as art, that he strived to be good and taught himself all he knew. I think he was adventurous and good-humoured, and he loved nature.

Chad nudged her. *So many of my own fine qualities.*

That struck her as true, though she hadn't said.

On Hurley's man-hauling trek from winter quarters to the south magnetic pole, he kept a sledging journal. Calm conditions one day, the next, *frigid wind that parched and stung our faces*; the extract in Marcus's email brims with undiluted joy:

> >> In spite of these conditions there is something grand
> and inspiring in treading these virgin snows and breaking
> trail for the first time across the unknown.

Her own days are a joy, the place a meditation, riding across tracts of ice with the tireless help of a quietly self-assured man. In a different setting she might have overlooked such absence of pretence. In different circumstances, if she were free—Freya halts her thoughts.

You think you would have liked Hurley, as a person?

I know I would, she'd said to Chad tonight. *He was a bit of a showman, but that's okay. Marcus says he lived his whole life as an idealistic adventure, playing out his boyhood hero quest.*

There's a touch of the adventure hero in all of us, I'd like to think. Chad propped against her bike while she tied on her camera gear. *I wish you could see winter quarters. To some it's just an old wooden shell slowly filling up with ice and disintegrating by the year, but it stands for so much more. The final piece of the planet to be explored.*

The last great region of geographical mystery—so Marcus had written, revising her proposal to the Arts Council—*the first to be explored in conjunction with the camera.* Freya scrolls down the screen.

>> Call me this morning when you read this; I'll be heading over to your mother's around ten. I have your gifts ready to take.

Chad had glanced at his watch, *Midnight. It's Christmas Day.*

Freya placed her arm around his shoulder. She kissed him lightly. *Happy Christmas. I'm so glad you're here.*

He drew her towards him, held her gently, flakes of snow falling through the silence that closed around them and ushered in the day.

FREYA WAKES A FEW HOURS later, showers and dresses. She makes her way toward the living quarters, shunted along the road by an assault of wind that squeals and swirls through Davis Station. Gusts eddy around foundations of buildings, gathering up a mix of grit and snow that sprays against her hood and jacket.

A hardy few linger outside the main building: Freya sees their bodies turned from the onslaught of snow, clinging to railings, shielding their eyes as they wait for Santa and the traditional Christmas parade.

Hurrying indoors, she finds a seat at the window beside Kittie. Both of them watch the road for Santa through the blindness of white. From a corner of the room the choristers belt out a repertoire they've been practising for weeks. Big Davo, the strongest tenor, has been positioned at the back, but he still overpowers the singers in the front. Giant baubles hang from ceiling beams, bookcases are draped with fairy lights, and gifts form a rickety, unkempt pile around a disfigured plastic tree.

Through the window, four quad bikes emerge into view with an old sleigh in tow. Santa sits atop the wooden relic encircled by a huddle of shivering elves. Freya chortles when his elasticised beard blows up over his goggles and is scooped from his face by the wind. 'It's Malcolm!'

Cheers and applause herald Santa's entry to the room, his windblown elves prancing after him. Last to enter is a herd of blokey reindeers sauntering incognito behind reflector sunglasses and plastic noses, all the more photogenic, Freya takes up her camera, in their Hazmat suits and weather-beaten antlers.

Sixty people squeeze into a room designed for forty. Bodies spill into the foyer, congregate on stairs and line the walkway while the kitchen, with its promise of a banquet, remains strictly out of bounds.

Across the room, Chad returns her smile. He leans against a wall, his hair tied back, clean-shaven, wearing good trousers and a chambray shirt, a thorough contrast to his appearance last night.

Santa booms out names as vociferously as he does the fire drill roll call: 'Bertram.' *Here!* 'Morgan.' *Over here!* 'Jorgensen.' *Yes!* Elves leap over legs and sidle around chairs distributing Secret Santa gifts to those hemmed in at the back.

'Scott. Scott? Don't tell me bloody Charlie's still up at Comms.'

'Bugger off,' Charlie calls from the doorway, striding forward to collect his gift and plant an audible kiss on Malcolm's cheek.

'Seagram . . . Wazza . . . Davo.'

Secret Santas watch furtively as anonymous gifts are peeled of wrapping. Freya focuses on Charlie, her recipient, who unties the bow from bunting strapped around the photographic box. He slides reading glasses from his pocket to study the weddell seal print. 'That's a beauty,' she hears him say.

'One guess who gave you that.'

Charlie catches Freya's eye and sends her a nod.

The package on her lap is wrapped in a Saturday duties roster. She pulls from it a pre-owned book, *This Everlasting Silence, The Love Letters of Paquita Delprat and Douglas*

Mawson 1911–1914. On the title page the former owner's name has been neatly whited out and a message inscribed: TO FREYA. A NEW SIDE TO YOUR HERO. SECRET SANTA.

Did Chad wangle the draw to get her name?

She hugs the book and beams across the room to proffer thanks, however Chad is intent, not on her, but on Kittie beside her who unties the hessian sacking from her gift.

'Oh, my gosh,' Kittie says, showing off a turned wooden bowl.

The bowl is an extraordinary thing, an art piece, the grey-blond wood streaked naturally with green and inlaid with a spiral of burnished copper. The slip of paper resting inside reads SASSAFRAS. Kittie runs her finger around the bowl's wafer-thin lip. 'I love it. I adore it!'

Freya watches Chad, sees his unabashed delight.

A holler from the doorway. 'Call for Freya! Her husband's on the blower.'

Through the receiver, Freya hears corellas shrieking in the background. She tries to picture the line of sassy white cockatoos descending into the branches of their jarrah tree, gumnuts cascading on the roof. 'You're still at home.'

'No, I'm at your mother's place. Is everything alright, Freya?'

'Everything's fine.' It is more than physical distance. More than standing in the station foyer surrounded by other people's conversations. She feels utterly indifferent to the man at the end of the line. She barely recognises the timbre of her husband's voice.

'Hang on,' Marcus says. 'Sophie's about to bowl me over.'

Her niece's voice sounds shrill through the earpiece. 'Is it true,' Sophie launches in without preamble, 'that your fingers snap freeze if you go outside without your gloves?'

'Who says that?'

'I'm reading this raunchy novel set in Antarctica. The guys are so sex-starved that the women have to walk around in packs to protect themselves from being ravaged . . . ravished, whatever.' Freya can hear Mama in the background clucking disapproval at Sophie's talk of sex.

'Bestemor, hello?' Sophie outsquawks the corellas. 'I'm thirteen and a quarter!'

Freya steers them to safer ground. 'What's been happening there?'

Sophie falls into singsong mode. 'Everyone's here except you. I showed Uncle Marcus the photos you emailed.'

'Which were those?'

'You on the motorbike and the one of you standing in front of the blue iceberg. Uncle Marcus says you hate having your photo taken. Dad goes, *Apparently not, Marcus! I've never seen her look so radiant.*'

Freya winces at her own thoughtlessness.

'Is it freezing there? Are you having a *blizz*?'

'Not officially,' Freya says, thinking how, when speaking to her niece, so many topics are canvassed in so short a time. 'But it is blowing like crazy.'

'Wicked! Bestemor's doing the whole Nordic thing. She's cooked enough to feed an alpine village. She gave me some gold earrings that belonged to Great Aunt Ålsa.'

Freya privately bows to Sophie for showing more interest in their heritage than either Freya or Astrid ever have. Together, on Sophie's laptop, she and Mama are compiling a family tree.

Sophie crunches through the ear piece.

'Are you eating celery?' Freya hasn't eaten salad greens since the last of the station's perishable supplies wilted a month ago.

'Snow peas. Want one?' *Crunch.* 'Do people still get scurvy? Bestemor's worried about you. She had one of her psychic dreams.'

Freya hears her mother calling in the background, 'Let me speak to my precious baby girl.'

'Here's Bestemor. Ciao for now.'

A fresh round of cheers rises from the Davis Station lounge. Santa emerges clanging his bell and charges past, knocking Freya with his sack.

'. . . there, elskling?'

'Merry Christmas, Mama.'

'Has something happened? I saw you shivering. The sky was golden and pretty but you were *frozen white*. I saw your face as clearly as I see your father's. Are you eating enough red meat?'

Her mother's so-called clairvoyance always makes her smile. 'I've never eaten so much in my life. I'm too scared to stand on the scales. How's Marcus managing on his own?'

'Does the man helping you wear his hair in a ponytail?'

'What?'

211

'I saw him there beside you.' Her mother's voice trails off as it does when she knows she's struck a chord. 'Well, never mind. You're safe and well, that's the important thing. I have to check the duck and finish off the salads. Marcus is here now. He's picking up the phone in the other room. Take lots of good photos. We miss you. We love you, elskling. Merry Christmas.'

'I love you too,' Freya says, startled when she glances up to see Chad easing by. He gives her a hollow look and veers away, taking the steps two at a time.

'. . . waited an extra hour at home, expecting your call.'

'Marcus? I'm so sorry. I read your email and I planned to call you first thing but then I slept in and I was in a rush to get over here in time.'

'You read my email last night? What were you doing still up at that hour?'

She hesitates. 'Chad and I went over to one of the islands to get some shots.'

'That's odd. When I checked the Davis webcam it was snowing. It didn't look like any kind of night for photography.'

Freya feels herself bristle. 'Well, it was, and I managed to get what I think might be a wonderful series for the exhibition. The photographs are really coming together, Marcus. It feels like it's evolving in such a good way.'

'Didn't your donkey have anything better to do with his time on Christmas Eve?'

She hears her husband clearly now, the old familiar edge. 'His name is Chad McGonigal. Don't be mean.'

The double doors of the kitchen burst open. Sandy and Tommo emerge in full chef's regalia carrying platters of baked ham and salmon.

'What's the din?' Marcus says.

'They're about to serve lunch.'

'Then you'd best join them. We wouldn't want to keep you from your party pals.'

'Marcus, please don't do this. It's Christmas. Tell me how you are, what you've been doing. Have you opened the gifts I left for you?'

Silence. A great stream of disapproval reverberating through the ether. Freya's cue to rush in and fix things, be the dutiful wife. She can't do this anymore.

'Marcus, I'll email you tonight. Okay?'

She takes a breath, waits for a response—nothing—before returning the receiver to the cradle.

EACH PLACE SETTING IS ADORNED with a rolled gold-coloured napkin and a keepsake copy of the special menu. Candles flicker, stemmed glasses gleam ruby red with wine.

Three cheers for the chefs!

However exhausted Sandy and Tommo are from their four am start, their faces shine before the appreciative crowd and the sumptuous feast. Tasmanian trout, salmon, platters of crayfish, yabbies and prawns, honey-baked ham, roasted turkey, pork with crackling, baked pumpkin, onion and potato—the only vegetables left in cold storage—and not forgetting the vegetarian frittata, the vegan dishes, the specially made soy bread stuffing for the one coeliac on station. Who could have imagined such abundance? The applause grows louder. People rise from their seats to throw streamers. As celebrated as a pair of Olympians returning home with medals, the chefs pose victorious before their adélie ice sculpture.

Only when the clatter and clang of dining subsides does Malcolm, restored to officialdom by his navy blue jacket and ANARE tie, stand and chink fork to glass to bring the room to silence.

After the reading of faxes from Canberra politicians, emails from divisional heads, past expeditioners and well-wishers at home, Malcolm draws a slip of paper out of his jacket pocket.

'Here we go,' whispers the biologist opposite Freya. 'The Christmas pep talk.'

Kittie leans over from the next table. 'So long as he doesn't start rabble-rousing about Australia's allegiance to the monarchy.'

Malcolm takes a sip of water and begins. 'Now, every scientist in the room—and not forgetting those who are doing some real work out in the field today—understands the importance of symbiotic relationships. Here at Davis Station we have a working example of just such a mutually dependent and beneficial association, in the form of the trades and the sciences.'

A snort issues from the science laboratory manager.

'As we all know, one of our charters for being here in Antarctica, for maintaining an Australian presence begun by pioneers such as Douglas Mawson and John King Davis, in whose honour two of our three continental bases are named, is the advancement of science.'

Snickers and hisses rise from one of the far tables.

'At least we like to think so,' Malcolm says. 'This summer we have a record undertaking. Forty-two science projects and one arts project. All running smoothly—'

Apparently not, by the roar issuing from the seismology group.

'Settle down, settle down. One or two hiccups.' Malcolm flicks his hand dismissively. 'Seriously folks, here's the thing I want to say. Not one of these science projects—or arts project,' he nods to Freya, 'could be carried out safely or effectively—or at all—without the marvellous technical support we have here at the station: the expertise to construct equipment, operate plant machinery, service and repair vehicles, expand our living quarters and maintain an impressive infrastructure—this heated building whose comforts we enjoy today—that our tradeswomen and tradesmen provide.'

Kittie sighs. 'That's nice.'

'Could be worse,' the building supervisor concedes.

'The fact of the matter is that here in Antarctica, when it comes to the trades and the sciences, one would not and could not exist without the other.'

In spite of themselves the tradies scattered through the room look chuffed.

Freya turns to look for Chad at a far table. She knows he knows she is watching, but he won't meet her eye.

'Without any more carry-on from me,' says Malcolm, 'please raise your glass for our official Christmas toast.'

Freya holds her wineglass by its stem and looks through the red wine to the candle beyond. The flame flickers like a bird's wing bound by a teardrop of glass. Light shimmers in the wine.

Freya taps the glass and hears it ring.

'The trades and the sciences,' the station leader says.

'The trades and the sciences,' Freya whispers. Voices roar.

She brings the glass to her lips and drinks, mouthful after mouthful until the glass is empty and the bird has flown.

Christmas Day
1912

DOUGLAS ADDED AN OUNCE OF butter to give the paws a festive touch.

Mertz gripped his hand, tears welling up in his eyes. 'I hope to share many merry Christmases with my friend Mawson, if possible in the civilised world.'

'We will, Xavier. Next Christmas you and I will sit down and feast on the very best dishes. Stuffed turkey roasted until the skin sizzles, Yorkshire pudding with gravy, platters of baked vegetables, a Christmas pudding full of sixpences and drizzled with brandy sauce and so heavy it takes two of us to carry it to the table.'

'We'll finish with cream cakes drizzled in strawberry sauce.'

'And toast our good health with porto wine and a box each of your fancy Swiss biscuits.'

Every conversation, every dream, the sum of conscious thought, centred on this aching need for food.

In their makeshift camp fashioned from the tent cover which had been stored on Douglas's sledge, two sleeping bags obscured the floor of snow. Only one man could move about at a time, and neither could rise from sitting. It was impossible not to knock an elbow or crack a skull against the wooden frame Mertz had jigged from the legs of the theodolite, the instrument now set up on the cooker box to calculate their bearings.

One hundred and fifty-eight miles from Christmas camp back to winter quarters as the crow flies. If, and only if, they could keep up a daily march of eight, ten miles, continue supplementing the remaining food bags—the nine days' rations that were on Douglas's sledge—then it was an even race. Non-essential articles had been jettisoned to reduce the load: hypsometer, rifle, thermometers, camera and film discarded at the start of the stretch he had silently dubbed *Ninnis Glacier*.

26 December: I promised to do all I could for Xavier for him to see Australia and New Zealand.

Douglas had started out from winter quarters weighing two hundred and ten pounds, Xavier, one hundred and sixty. Even on full daily rations of thirty four and three-quarter ounces, they had dropped a substantial amount of weight. Now, with fourteen ounces allocated for each day, their strength was so reduced that the task of breaking camp took an inordinate length of time.

Cold and laborious the process of lacing the tent cover into a sail, one edge bound to Mertz's ski and lashed vertically as a mast, an adjacent edge secured to a second ski and lashed across the sledge as a boom. Even in fur mitts their fingers remained constantly numb.

The wild sky augured badly for the coming days. Douglas and Mertz flanked Ginger, their last, faithful dog, the troupe panting in unison as they hauled the sledge up a seemingly endless gradient.

When Ginger gave in Mertz carried her to the sledge as he had the others and gently strapped her on. They made a mournful procession through five uphill miles of ankle-deep snow.

GINGER RAISED HER HEAD WHEN Xavier took up the shovel. She laid back her ears when he knelt in the snow and stroked her head.

Giving to the end, she closed her eyes.

THE PAIN OF HUNGER GNAWED on the gut so violently that they were perpetually stooped with it. On Saturday evenings back at winter quarters—these images a poignant reminder of better days—Douglas had seen weekly rations of chocolate won and lost at a furious rate on the Huntoylette Wheel, a spinning jenny devised by Hurley and Johnny Hunter, whose cooperative had been dubbed 'the Chocolate Bank' for the spoils it amassed.

When the rest of the men ran their own auction of goods, a bidding frenzy had erupted over one of Mertz's ornate pipes, the article fetching an outrageous one hundred and fifty squares of chocolate—five weeks' rations. Few things stopped Douglas in his tracks, but X had humbled them all by presenting the pipe to the successful bidder free of charge.

Xavier sat before him now, the tent raining condensation from the heat of the primus, offering him the bone receptacle. 'I eat when you finish.'

'We eat together, X.'

The roughly carved spoon felt thick and coarse inside his mouth. They passed the skull back and forth between them, taking turns at scooping out Ginger's boiled brain, each eating to the middle line.

PIONEER
CROSSING

PIONEER CROSSING, A FINGER OF land bridging two fjords, will cut hours off their trip to the northern reaches of the Vestfolds. But along the edge of Long Fjord, jammed against the shoreline of the Crossing, lies the tide crack, a collision of ice compressed and crunched by tidal forces. These frozen waves and fractured troughs act as an obstacle course, making slow work of manoeuvering the bikes across the fjord to the bridge of land.

Chad heaves his weight against the back of Freya's bike. The chains on her tyres crunch into ice made slick by the midday sun. She leans alongside him, pushing hard, one arm outstretched, hand hovering over the brake, her other pumping the throttle. Finally the wheels grip and the bike stutters forward.

'Hard to the left.' He catches his breath as she walks the bike up the slippery blue ice.

He sees her quad round the crest and teeter. Undaunted, she springs to the seat of the bike as it starts to slide. It looks set to slip sideways, but Freya straightens the wheels and leans her weight back. How adept she has become, he thinks, watching her negotiate the last fissure of ice to bring the bike safely onto solid ground.

Chad's shoulders and arms throb from exertion. He returns her wave as he feels himself unravel. How easily it undoes him, this woman's smile.

Small wonder, Chad thinks when he tallies up the outings he's had with Freya, that the rumour mill on station has begun to grind. Even Tommo the chef threw him a nod this morning when he came to the kitchen to cut some sandwiches. *Another overnighter, McGonigal?*

Not a work trip but a *jolly*, says Adam Singer; since they reached a stand-off over who will leave for Mawson Station, Adam has been grousing to the others as staunchly as a unionist. Chad works to make up lost hours but still it grates on his sense of self-worth when he hears of Adam's remarks: *dead wood around the station*; *those who rest upon their laurels*.

Chad brings his own bike across the tide crack. 'Up for another detour?' he shouts above the engine.

'Do you really need to ask?' She smiles. 'Lead the way.'

THEY PARK ON THE ICE and tramp through a snowy gully to the lake. Freya stops to study flame-orange lichen smattered among the rock, minuscule beads of growth crusted along seams and crevices. The brilliant hue of the lichen belies its tenuous hold on life. Freya's wonderment brings back his own first summer, his surprise that vegetation could grow down here.

A graveyard of white disembodied wings litters their path. She collects a feather and runs it between her fingers. 'Angel wings.'

'Snow petrels,' he says. 'Sadly, no match for our skua friends.'

Lichen Lake sits frozen in a bowl-shaped valley girded by snow banks and rocky bluffs. He doubts the lake has seen a footprint since he came by last. On a clear day this has to be his favourite place among the Vestfolds—and today is an absolute pearler, a record nine degrees Celsius, not a hint of wind. Chad feels a boyish thrill in showing off the lake, as if it were his very own. Freya wheels in lazy circles, her arms held out, absorbing—he can see it mirrored in her glasses—the silhouette of surrounding hills, the shimmering rink that seals the lake, the stark contrast between snowline and thick blue sky. Her eyes follow a trail of snow petrels that dart from shadows in the rocks, a blink of white across the sky.

Chad takes time to pick with his axe through the lake's frozen seal, ascertaining the thickness and strength of ice, while Freya gives the frozen surface a few cursory whacks with the tip of her adze before striding out onto it. She beckons him across to where she kneels.

'Take a look through the viewfinder.'

Countless bubbles of oxygen are trapped in the lake ice amid crazes of starbursts and hairlines. 'Capsules of frozen time,' she says, wide-eyed. 'Who knows how long they've been here?' How long indeed: Chad has never seen the lake thaw.

He rests on his pack and adds to his journal the day's locations under a special section, LIST OF SITES. Chad McGonigal could look back through twenty years of note-taking and pinpoint the weather conditions of any trip, list the birds and mammals sighted, settle a debate with dates and names and times. He prides himself on being a dependable source of facts and shuns the notion of combing through his feelings to record sentiment. Why would he ever need reminding of how he feels today, with Freya on his favourite lake?

'Well, how about this?' he chimes. 'January second: it's a year to the day since I came here last. That was a far cry from today's heatwave.' He leafs through the pages. 'Half the month clapped out with bad weather.' He proceeds to report, line by line, the poor conditions, wind speed and temperature, his voice halting when he catches Freya lift her eyes from the camera and roll them at the sky.

Chad finds a fresh page in his journal and begins to sketch the outline of a snow petrel. He adds texture, shades the beak and eyes, smudges the curve of the feathers, imagining, as he draws, how it might be worked from wood.

Freya stands behind her tripod, her focus fixed on the viewfinder. 'Do you think about the summer finishing?' she asks. 'About going home?'

'Can't say I give comings and goings much thought.'

He's lying. The who-will-go-to-Mawson stalemate lingers in his mind. 'You? Counting the days already?'

Freya replaces her lens cap and collapses her tripod. Bird cries echo through the amphitheatre.

'Do you find it hard to settle down again?' she asks, her words clipped with the trace of a faraway land. 'After so long away?'

'Sometimes.' He stops short of confessing that some years he feels at the whim of a great tide, a vessel adrift, sustained only for a time by the familial memories his place on the beach holds. Not that he's unhappy at the bay. But he's never once known the anticipation—that sense of promise—homecoming brings others. 'I suppose home is what you make it,' he tells her, recognising it as the same quaint saying his grandparents would once have said to him.

'Does anyone ever get tired of Antarctica? *This*.' She holds out her arms. 'Do you ever think, been there, seen that, now I can give it all away?'

She's a font of unanswerable questions today. 'Some seasons are better than others. That's the nature of living at a station. For me, personally, the draw of the place never wanes.'

She waits for more and he struggles to explain. 'I feel different when I'm out here, Freya, away from the station. It's the one place I can be completely alone and feel no sense of loneliness. People say the size of Antarctica makes them feel small. It's never been that way for me.' He feels expanded by the place, as if he's breathed in everything around him. 'Look at it.' He scans the ice. 'The sheer power of all this. It's nature who's in charge here—at least until we fuck the planet up for good. I doubt I could ever grow tired of this.'

She scrutinises his face so intently he replays his words in his head. 'Am I talking gibberish?'

She shakes her head. 'I understand exactly what you mean.'

Chad slings Freya's camera pack over his free shoulder, surprised afresh at the weight she carries.

They retrace their steps across the frozen lake. 'What will Chad McGonigal do with his time when he gets home?'

'If he has any sense left he'll finish off a dinghy he should have delivered before he came south. Then he'll start on a new one, an eighteen-footer—his grandfather's design—for a family up the coast. He's rarely short of things to occupy his time.'

Her voice softens. 'One day I'd like to photograph a Chad McGonigal clinker dinghy. See the artisan at work.'

'Would you now?', his imagination careering off and playing silly buggers. 'Play your cards right and I'll let you row me around the bay.'

They scuff through a powdering of snow at the rim of the lake. The treads of her boots meander across his outbound tracks.

'I'm trying not to count,' she states, in that inscrutable way women chop and change a conversation.

'Count what?'

'The days we have left. Do you think anyone would notice if I stayed on for winter?'

'You have to go home sometime.'

'What if you don't want to?' she says. 'What if you've outgrown your home?'

'Then don't,' he says matter-of-factly, wishing he had the gumption to say, *Come home with me*, struck mute at the prospect of being shot down in flames. He waits, but she offers nothing more.

Chad unfolds the map and spreads it across the bike. 'We're here.' He points. 'Walkabout Rocks is up here. We'll do a dogleg at the top of Tryne Fjord, refuel at Bandits Hut and dump some of our gear, then head out to the ocean side of the coast. So long as the sea ice is in good condition we'll have a couple more hours of driving.'

To the east, gilded streaks are beginning to line the sky. He checks his watch: already gone five; at the rate they're progressing it's set to be their longest day on record. 'Still happy to press on?' he asks, knowing full well that nothing short of a sixty-knot gale could entice her to stop.

She gestures at the sky. 'It would be a monumental shame to miss out on that sunset.'

A trumpeting resonates through the fjord. The call of an emperor penguin is instantly recognisable, yet the closest emperor rookery is at Amanda Bay, miles further west along the coast.

'Wayward travellers. Now and again a small group without chicks to rear drops by over summer.' Chad cranes his neck and hoots his best emperor rendition. A call warbles in response.

Freya throws back her head and laughs. When she turns to face him he feels powerless to refuse the question in her eyes. 'Last detour, Freya. *Last*.' Their umpteenth for the day.

Three emperor penguins lie slumped on the ice, as barrel-shaped and listless as a poolside of corpulent bathers, the pads of their lizard-like feet turned skyward. By penguin standards today is a scorcher. A fourth emperor stands separate from the group, its head curved to one side, flippers held out in hopes of catching a whisper of cool air.

Twice the height of an adélie and a good thirty kilos, the emperor stands thigh-high to Freya. She crouches low as it waddles near, meeting it eye to eye. If she makes a sudden move or reaches out, the penguin will retreat. But she stays statue-still as the bird sidles close; when the emperor pecks her bootlace she turns and smiles up at Chad. He eases his point-and-shoot camera from his pocket. The trouble is he can't help how he feels: he's reduced to a starry-eyed teenager in the wash of her joy.

THE FROZEN HIGHWAY STRETCHES BEFORE him. The low-lit ice of Tryne Fjord feels strong and sound beneath his wheels, a welcome contrast to the conditions this morning. Before the station was awake, he and Freya had forged out onto the ice, picking their way through rotten ice and patches of slush—a slalom course to reach a safer footing on firmer ice to the north. He should have rethought this trip—Malcolm will close the sea ice for travel the minute he gets wind of how dodgy it is. Chad pushes back his visor and opens the throttle, losing himself to the rush of air and for once leaving his roving companion to dawdle in his wake.

If Chad were brought here blindfolded he would know with his first glance at these worn hills crisscrossed with igneous dykes where on the planet he was. The only thing to better tooling along on quads on such a summer's day would be to slide across the plateau on a sledge, the whine of motorbikes replaced by the slobbery panting of a trace of Greenland dogs.

The dogs were all called boys, he remembers, never mind their sex. *Ready boys. Mush!* to get them away. An angled haul up the Gwamm from Mawson Station, dogs snorting and farting like nobody's business, then the gradual uphill slog, sledging past the Russian aircraft wreck, hugging the bamboo canes that mark the route lest you or your dogs stray too close to the network of crevasses. The sheen of the plateau rising to a cobalt sky, the Masson Ranges and Rumdoodle Peak to your left, Fang Peak dead ahead. The solid thud of the sledge sliding over blue ice, teflon on the runners resonating through the wood, pinching yourself, *you lucky, lucky bastard.* Then as now.

The thought of time passing—evanescent, fleeting as a breath—jolts him at the very instant he swerves to miss an open seam running the breadth of the fjord, the rift in the ice invisible in the early evening light. He runs alongside the inky band of water until it narrows, then turns his bike to face the open lead straight on. He guns it over the break and raises his arm to caution behind.

Chad questions whether his first seasons in Antarctica offered an escape from the muddle of his twenties: Nan and Pop gone within a year of one another, any contact from the old man—never more than a Christmas card and twenty-dollar note at best—long since petered out; a time when his best mate had settled on a girl and was staking out his future like a bush block to be pegged. Now, at forty-two, Chad is as much an Antarctic veteran as the dogmen who taught the new boys how to drive—*old, bold and can't be told*, he'd thought of them then.

Even those who had never set foot in Antarctica mourned the departure of the sledging teams. The working dogs—deemed an introduced species by the 1990s Environmental Protocol—were the vestige of an age begun at a time when Antarctica stood as a frozen frontier, untrodden territory prime for enterprising heroes.

When the last Mawson dogs returned from their commemorative run out to Entrance Island and back into Horseshoe Harbour, the Mawson winterers of '93, waiting on the sea ice, must have looked as bereft as a funeral gathering. Chad held Morrie in a collar of arms, the dog's wet tongue lapping at his face; Morrie was no oil painting, one ear in pieces and the other torn off in a brawl, the greatest collar escape artist and harness chewer that ever was, but still Chad's favourite dog of all time. True to form, he evaded his leash and bolted back up the road like the young pup he imagined he was, pausing only long enough to leave his mark on each vehicle tyre and equipment box he chanced upon, ecstatic at the attention lavished on him by those in pursuit, and none the wiser that his sledging days on the great Antarctic trail had finally run their course.

The low-angle sun turns the fjord into a golden rink. As Chad rounds the corner towards Bandits Hut he lets the bike slide in a weightless arc of motion. He fans his bike across the ice in a great slithering curl and cuts the engine to wait for Freya.

The sudden silence of the fjord disquiets him. Minutes pass and still Freya fails to appear. Chad turns over the engine. He retraces his course, puttering at first, his gut tightening as the straight stretch of fjord eases into view. He pulls binoculars from his pack but can see nothing more than his own set of tyre tracks. His eyes smart from the glare but still he scans the breadth of the fjord until he catches a steely glint far away. He steadies his sights on the black curl of tyre hovering like a mirage above the ice, the chassis of an upturned bike. He waits, fruitlessly, for a sign of movement.

Before he closes the distance, he reasons that the open lead is where Freya's bike has come to grief. His mind refuses to remember if he turned around to check on her. Did she cross? Did he look back? They'd successfully negotiated a dozen such leads that day.

Mind and memory spin with imagined outcomes. A picture of the gaping chasm in Hobart's Tasman Bridge refracts from the ice. He sees Ma more clearly than he's pictured her in years, her ruddy face blanched with shock, her hands clenching the wheel of her Morris as it plunged through a blackened gap that moments before was bridge.

Splayed out before him, tumbled across the ice of the fjord, Chad makes out splashes of colour, the brilliant hue of lichen that is not lichen at all but the last of the station's fresh oranges, brought by Freya as a treat for him. In this surreal instant, he finally understands why the taste of apricot makes him gag when they once rated as his favourite fruit. The carton would have rested on the back seat of Ma's car, filled with fruit picked that afternoon from his grandparents' tree. Never once in his replay has he watched the box upend as it does now, fruit by the dozen dancing on the inside windscreen like a downpour of rain.

The channel of the Derwent River, cold and soupy dark beneath a blanket of Sunday night fog, would have folded in around her. Before, Chad has always halted his thoughts here. Part of him knows she was killed on impact, or knocked unconscious and drowned. But lurking at the edge of his vision is a ghosted image of her pawing at the window of every vehicle he's ever driven, willing him to picture her trapped in the river alive. He feels the weight of water bearing down upon her car, rising chill and briny around her feet no matter how hard she struggled with the door or tore at the window whose broken handle his father had never bothered to repair. Beyond the shuddering thought of her drowning he feels disdain for cause and effect, for chance, providence, for his own unwitting part—a vet's needless prescription, for pity's sake, to safeguard his sutured leg. When his father had dug in his heels and declared Ma *overanxious*, that *Chaddie will be fine*, that he, for one, wasn't driving an hour out to flaming Swansea for antibiotics they didn't need and couldn't afford, Chad had lain stock-still in his bed, in anguish at being the subject of their argument, momentarily forgetting his own painful leg.

'Suit yourself,' Ma had huffed. 'I'll take the Morris, *and* I'll make a proper job of it.' Not the hour's drive to Swansea but double the distance to Hobart, to prove a point.

Dad had growled, 'Don't be a bloody-minded fool, Sal.'

'Bloody fool yourself,' Ma snapped back. 'At least no one can call me a bone-idle fool.'

Don't go, Chad's eyes had pleaded when she'd leaned down to kiss him goodbye.

FREYA LIES IN A SHALLOW melt pool curdled with oil, beyond the open seam her wheels have clipped. Chad will not remember later how he lifted the bike to pull her leg free because his senses are swamped by her silence, by his own panic, by the aching cold of her skin on such a still and balmy night. He is alarmed at the limpness of her leg and checks for a break, squeezing and bending the limb without eliciting complaint. He feels a stronger wave of fright and orders, *Move your toes!*, which Freya does compliantly, speaking softly, *I'm alright, Chad; I'm very cold*, as if it were he in need of soothing. He leaves her only long enough to grab his sleeping bag and spare clothes, the medical kit buried in his pack. He peels off her sodden clothes and dresses her in his woollen shirt. He lifts her onto the sleeping bag and straps her leg as gently as he can.

He will remember, will covet the memory, below a sky giddied with gold, of holding the bundle of her against him, too roughly perhaps, wrapping an arm to envelop her with warmth, stroking her hair, resting his hand against her icy, blemished cheek and willing her to be still.

MIDNIGHT LIGHT SATURATES THE WALLS of Bandits Hut, varnishes the timbers of the bunks. Outside, the cry of snow petrels, inside a whirr of heat. She has missed her golden sunset, but he needs no camera to capture the night, to spool to memory the filmic quality of the room. The accident on the fjord has begun to fade, helped by the warmth of the hut, by a hot meal, by the feel of her skin as he winds a fresh bandage around her leg.

He sits silently at the edge of the bed, studying her face, aware of her hand weighted upon his arm. She reaches up to cup his face and in her touch he understands the question asked. He presses her fingers to his lips as proof of all he feels.

It drowns him, this want.

Stay, she whispers, drawing him down beside her.

Bowl of chaos
January 1913

TODAY WAS FINE WEATHER AND they had agreed to go on at all costs. But here they still were, cocooned inside their bags, cramped within the tent. Xavier continued to grunt and toss—sleep, delirium—the line between the body's need for rest and failure to survive spiralling to a blur, it seemed to Douglas.

He read back through his journal, trying to make sense of the past days.

30 December
Xavier off colour. We did 15 m, halting at about 9 am. He turned in—all his things very wet, chiefly on account of no burberry pants. The continuous drift does not give one a chance to dry things, and our gear is deplorable . . .

Xavier's waterproof pants and helmet were two of the many essentials on Ninnis's sledge to be swallowed by the crevasse.

Xavier wore an extra pair of under-trousers to compensate, but the wind froze his wet clothing and wicked heat from his body. Their sleeping bags were sodden and heavy from sleeping on a mattress of snow. The cold struck home as it never had before. Douglas had taken to wearing his burberries inside the bag, so wretched was the shivering that racked his malnourished body until sleep dulled the brain from feeling.

From the start Xavier had made hard work of digesting the dog meat. When had he crawled back into the tent complaining of dysentery, gripes in his stomach? Douglas had assumed the gnawing pains were no greater than his own. But then X almost kicked over the contents of the primus without his usual *sorry, sorry*, instead grizzling about the dripping tent and how it was that dog meat could boil for so long and still be repulsive and far too tough to chew.

Though nothing good could be said of the dog liver's foul tinny taste, it provided additional substance and could be demolished in an instant—a blessed relief after endless chewing on moistureless ropes of meat. And it was unlike X to complain, puzzling to see him out of sorts.

'We'll hoist the sail tomorrow,' Douglas said again to buoy him up, 'try for another splendid fifteen-mile march and really make some inroads.'

Xavier scowled. 'Tent. Sail. Tent. Sail. We lose eleven hours yesterday putting up and putting down, boil-ups of dog and tasks for nobody's real purpose.'

Douglas had been completely at a loss. They had to pull together—in every sense—if they were to survive.

31 December
Keeping off dog meat for a day or two as both upset by it.

'A new year, Xavier.' They had toasted 1913 with carefully husbanded perks: two and a half ounces of chocolate each, a minuscule helping of beef and lard pemmican, cocoa, three-quarters of a biscuit. Scarcely a feast for a doll, it had left them hungrier than before.

3 January
Mertz boiled a small cocoa and had biscuit, and I had a bit of liver . . .
   Did 5 miles but cold wind frost-bit Mertz's fingers, and he is generally in a very bad condition. Skin coming off legs, etc—so had to camp though going good.

Damp clothes added to the friction caused by walking and chafed their skin raw. Open sores on his fingers refused to heal. Skin shedding from their limbs and private parts. Peelings of it, and body hair, lined their underwear and socks. At one point Mertz had reached over from his bag and plucked a perfect skin cast from Douglas's ear. He could have done the same in return.

4 January
Mertz in bad condition so I doctored him part of day and rested . . .

Xavier's face had aged beyond his thirty years. His skin, stark against his jet beard, bore a sickly pallor with darkened rings around the eyes—likely a mirror image of Douglas's own. Their bodies were permanently cold and the skin around the hair follicles had pimpled like the hardened nodules of a nutmeg grater. Their alimentary systems were badly affected by short rations—Xavier's worse than his own. Surely lack of sustenance and continual exposure to the weather had brought on X's ailment.

5 January

I tried to get Xavier to start but he practically refused, saying it was suicide and that it much best for him to have the day in bag and dry it and get better, then do more on sun-shining day.

Douglas tried to persuade him, *Just three or four miles, even if we can't see through the drift properly.* Back and forth they argued, X refusing to be swayed. Finally, *We'll rest today, Xavier. But tomorrow, and every day after that . . .*

Xavier nodding through a veil of shame and tears.

6 January

Got off 10.30, Xavier not being able to help at all. Did not raise sail though favourable breeze—surface very good and downhill. Surface slippery, so occasional falls. Quite dizzy from long stay in bags, I felt weak from want of food. To my surprise Xavier soon caved in—he went 2 miles only in long halts and refused to go further. I did my best with him—offered to pull him on the sledge, then to set sail and sail him but he refused both after trial. We camped. I think he has a fever, he does not assimilate his food . . .

Xavier's heart seemed to have gone. This morning Douglas had found him in a pitiful state. Slow, so agonisingly slow the job of easing him out of his bag to remove his trousers and clean him. Xavier had grown so feeble that the best he could do to assist was kneel doglike on his bag with trembling limbs and his head hung low.

Rest, Xavier. Try to sleep now.

Douglas had toggled X up in his bag to warm him but he thrashed in a strange kind of fit, needing to be held down for fear he would damage the tent.

If they could not travel eight or ten miles each day, in a day or two they were doomed. Perhaps he could pull through on his own with the provisions at hand—but how could he possibly contemplate leaving his companion? And yet how could he abandon Paquita, lie idle and shivering in a makeshift tent—two sorry souls waiting for death? To be within a hundred miles of winter quarters and be faced with such a choice was awful.

Today was 7 January 1913; *Aurora* was due at winter quarters. They were expected back on the fifteenth, *the fifteenth at the latest*, he had instructed the others.

Douglas propped Xavier's head against his chest and supported his jaw. Beef tea dribbled from the spoon. *Come on, now. It will do you good. Small sips.*

Their chance was slipping away. It was not for himself that he minded, but for Paquita, his innocent girl who had no inkling of his fate. He imagined her spirit shattered after all these months of waiting, the despair of his non-return and the unanswerable *how? when?* She had a right to understand the fickle allure of ice that had snatched her mate away, to know the manner of her betrayal.

Ninnis had been running alongside his sledge when he crossed the crevasse, while Mertz's weight had been distributed across his skis, and Douglas's own along the length of the sledge. Douglas and Xavier had talked it through for days, nights, unable to sleep, certain now that the concentration of Ninnis's weight onto a single footstep had caused the snow bridge concealing the crevasse to collapse. Did Cherub have a sense, through his strange, recurring dreams, that he would not return?

The chance of a search party happening upon their bodies this far out was infinitesimal. They were separated from the hut by one hundred miles and another formidable glacier. The stories of their journey on the plateau—the telling of three lives—were held inside their diaries. Unthinkable that they might also be silenced, entombed within a cap of ice.

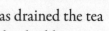

XAVIER WOULD DRINK NOTHING NOW. Douglas drained the tea himself and wrapped X in his arms to stem the shuddering.

While he felt sorrow and regret for himself, it was shame that racked his conscience at the prospect of letting down all those connected with the expedition—all who had believed in him. But as he supported Xavier and stroked his hair, his shame changed shape to guilt at the vehement wish that his companion would surrender quickly to death so that he might go on.

He prayed to God to help them both.

OUTSIDE A RISING WIND, DRIFT eddying around the tent, the atmosphere a bowl of chaos. Xavier fitted again, his jaw clenched in the strange, inexplicable way of the dogs on the ship. Again he fouled his trousers and Douglas cleaned him with handfuls of snow. Xavier was sliding deeper into delirium, his speech incoherent.

At eight in the evening he opened his eyes and glared unblinkingly at Douglas.

'What is it, X?'

Xavier gave a guttural cry and yanked himself to a sitting position by grabbing the tent poles. With an implausible strength he seized a leg of the wooden frame and snapped it from its apex. He struggled to escape the prison of his bag, the burberry tent slapping his face, his efforts as painful and pathetic to watch as a dog with a broken back. He flung out his arms at the tent, hit Douglas, punched at anything within his reach. Xavier moaned as he thrashed, *O Yen, O Yen*, over and over, the incantation to his God or his pain or whatever meaning lay within his words vying with the wind that wailed across the ice.

Douglas held him down—until he quietens, he told himself—*There, Xavier; hush, old friend*, a bodyweight of sorrow pressing down like a pillow on his face.

PAQUITA
DELPRAT

'McGONIGAL. RIGHT ON CUE.'

Malcolm beckons Chad into his office with his pinkie, the gesture a momentary diversion from scratching his newly trimmed beard. Freya sits at the corner of Malcolm's desk, her injured leg propped on a chair, staring, gloomily, through a window of white. The bay, normally in panoramic view from the station leader's office, remains obscured by driving snow.

'Perhaps you can explain to your cohort here the function of an incident report.' Malcolm turns to Freya. 'Chad's filed a few in his time.'

Chad pulls up a chair beside her. 'What's wrong, Freya?'

'What is wrong,' Malcolm enunciates to Chad, holding up a sheet of paper like a stray sock, 'is that here I have an incident report, signed by your partner in crime, that reads like an account of a Sunday picnic—all that's missing is the chicken and champagne. While here,' he grabs another page from the printer and snaps it, 'is a dieso's report advising that we have yet another bloody quad bike—let's see, *steering arm bent, suspension arm rooted*—to add to our growing inventory of equipment under repair. The diesos have enough work on their summer program without you blokes adding to the list.'

Chad takes a deep breath. 'The bikes got us home.'

'Not to mention our illustrious artist-in-residence here,' Malcolm continues, unbothered by squalls hammering the windows behind his head, 'who hobbled into my office this morning like a lame mule. What the bejesus happened out there?'

Before Chad has a chance to speak, Freya turns to face him. 'I told him I wasn't paying attention.' She looks and sounds jaded. 'The sun was in my eyes, the lead was wider than I thought. I was going too slow to cross it and too fast to stop.' She turns back to Malcolm and Chad guesses that she's repeated this story a dozen times before.

'She was unlucky,' Chad says. 'Her back tyres clipped the edge of the lead.'

'The bike toppled,' Freya says. 'It went over and slid, and I went with it.'

'What were you doing, McGonigal? Sitting back on your haunches watching the show?'

'Chad was right in front of me,' Freya lies. 'He pulled the bike off my leg.'

'Why didn't you radio in right away?' Malcolm looks as gruff as Chad's old headmaster, lacking only a cane. 'We could have got a helo out there.'

'We would have,' Chad said, 'if the VHF hadn't gone in the drink.'

'We were so near Bandits Hut. And when we got there, I didn't see the need to call it in.' She turns away from Malcolm to face Chad again but she doesn't meet his eyes. 'It was a mistake, Chad. The accident . . . I wasn't thinking properly when we were out there.'

'You're damned right on that count,' Malcolm snaps.

Chad feels his gut tighten. He turns to Malcolm. 'I don't understand the problem. We went on to the hut, re-strapped Freya's leg and elevated it. Nothing was broken. She seemed fine—' He glances in her direction, waiting for a confirmation that was not forthcoming. 'We stayed at Bandits overnight and the next morning Freya spoke to Charlie on the nine a.m. radio sked. Then we drove back to the station. End of story.'

End of story, Malcolm mouths.

'Freya, you did nothing wrong,' Chad begins, but she only looks away.

Malcolm wrinkles his brow in confusion. 'Don't take me for a turkey, McGonigal. Does she look fine to you? Does she?'

She looks decidedly overcast.

Malcolm scratches inside his thermal collar like a dog beset with fleas. 'Synthetics. Loathe them.' He scowls at Freya. 'I hope you have plenty of catch-up work to fill in your time.'

'Why?' she says, an edge in her voice.

'You won't be going out again until you're cleared by Dr Ev. She says you'll be out of action this week and most likely next.'

'No!' Freya cries. Chad has never seen her so upset. 'We're due to go out with the Casas before they leave for Mawson Station. You agreed.'

'I can't help unfortunate timing,' Malcolm pontificates, rocking in his chair. 'Antarctica is an unforgiving place, Freya. Especially for the novice. Now, we're all of us human, all fallible.'

Chad shakes his head: Malcolm on a pious roll.

'You had a close call this time,' Malcolm drones on. 'My advice is to consider this a valuable lesson for the future. If I were you—'

'You're not me, Malcolm, and I have all the valuable lessons I can stomach for now—an injured leg and your words to remind me of my *inexperience* and *poor judgment*.' She turns back to Chad. 'I didn't mean this to involve you,' she says quietly. 'I'm so sorry. I didn't mean for any of it to happen. It was all wrong.'

The underlying meaning kicks the breath from his chest.

Malcolm slides the incident report across the desk as though returning an article of dirty laundry. He looks with puzzlement at each of them. 'A new one by Friday, thank you, minus the creative writing.'

He dismisses Freya with a regal wave: 'Off you trot,' and Chad rises from his chair to follow. 'Stick around, McGonigal. You and I need to settle this Mawson Station issue.'

Freya limps across the room and gathers her crutch at the door.

Malcolm smirks. 'Or should I say, *off you hop*?'

Freya turns at the doorway, set to blow a gasket, by the look of her. 'At times, Malcolm, you can be a prize arsehole.'

Malcolm waits until she hobbles out of view. 'She seems to have eased into the swing of things. Hopping mad,' he chortles, his body racked with mirth.

FREYA DESPAIRS AT HER DIGITALS of Lichen Lake. She sits at her laptop, chin propped in her hand, while a gale buffets the studio. She scrolls through incorrect exposures, deletes amateurish errors of aperture and focus, sends to the trash a series of snow-white feathers, clusters of orange lichen, starbursts and bubbles trapped within the ice—all taken with a filter inadvertently left on. The best of her shots look under par, hardly worth keeping. Had she stayed at the station she would have saved herself no end of trouble. Saved them all.

Freya abandons the ruined images, shuts down her laptop and turns to *This Everlasting Silence*, her Christmas gift. She ponders the inscription on the opening page. TO FREYA. A NEW SIDE TO YOUR HERO. SECRET SANTA. Not from Chad at all. Another tick to reckless fancies. Going by the fastidious strip of corrector fluid obscuring the previous owner's name, the book of love letters has to be from Malcolm. Shipshape Malcolm. A new side to us all, she thinks wryly, shuddering as she recalls the morning's sermon.

She begins with the photo section, and is taken aback at the sight of an inked red stamp: DAVIS STATION. ANTARCTIC DIVISION LIBRARY. Freya thinks of the yearly library sales at home where Marcus picks up cartons of aged titles for a song. But this little paperback looks next to new. She turns back to the imprint page: published last year.

The preface explains the conditions under which Paquita and Mawson wrote:

> Their correspondence was not a conventional exchange of letters where one correspondent replies to the latest letter from the other. The extreme isolation of Antarctica in that era made such an exchange impossible . . .

How was it for Paquita, knowing her letters would not be delivered or read until the ship returned to Antarctica months later, and all the while receiving nothing in return?

Freya reads that soon after Douglas Mawson left for Antarctica, Paquita Delprat, along with her young brother Willy, was whisked away to Europe by her mother, to assemble her trousseau and ease the months of separation. Paquita collected Belgian linen and household fineries. Henrietta introduced her youngest daughter to the sophistication of European culture; they attended gala performances and met with her elder siblings and relatives in Holland.

How fanciful her benign, genteel world must have seemed to Douglas, her image an opiate against the ceaseless roar of wind.

9 Wagenaarweg

Haag

10 May 1912

My Douglas, mine.

I'm feeling so absolutely healthy and happy tonight despite the distance between us that I want to write to you. I wrote you a letter on your birthday but it wasn't a success. I know you thought of us thinking of you then. And we did. It was you all day long . . .

I hope you don't mind but I'm quite Dutch. I've never been so patriotic as now. I'm so awfully proud of my country and next year when we are together we must find time to come here . . .

I got your letters safely and just when I was wanting something from you. How different our lives are at present! My man, I wish I had been there to help you when you were so worried before you landed. What a lot we shall have to tell each other when we meet again. I want to come with you next year to Europe. I don't think anything will prevent it. You can't think how glad I am we came away this year. We seem to be in quite a different world altogether. I don't think I could ever live happily in Adelaide again as before—that is if it wasn't for you, of course. When we have a home of our own it will be quite different. I'm picking up such a lot of ideas! I've got a book for them. And houselinen is busy being picked! I've got some old Dutch brass already and have my eye on more. Our house will be the house in Adelaide, in Australia. Douglas dear, aren't

*you glad we've got each other? I'm feeling the fellow feeling so
very strongly tonight. No more boarding houses for my man.
No more nasty dinners and having to go away every night.
Always together—I'm a very jolly person to have about!*

*I hope everything goes well with you now. We aren't
worrying about not hearing per wireless yet. But I hope we do
soon hear. Scott will return about the same time as you. I hope
you come first. He will be disappointed at Amundsen getting to
the Pole first. How thankful we are that you aren't bound for
there. Don't you go and stay away another year! You're under
contract to return next year less than a year from now . . .*

*Willy is growing up. He fell in love on the boat and has
been repeating the experiment ever since. Unfortunately it
makes him sometimes grumpy. Leinte is also a duck. And as for
Mother I don't know how I shall ever leave her even for you.
Yes I do though. There is only one you. I'm sure you don't love
me as I do you. Women always love the most and miss the
most. Well I wouldn't like you to miss me as much as I do you.*

With my whole heart & my lips your Paquita.

The sparkle of words fits her portrait: the girlish roundness of
her face, tilted towards the photographer's light. Yet Paquita's
gaze, beneath her wide-brimmed hat, appears intent, evocative,
as one who is only now gaining the trappings of womanhood.

Freya turns to the editor's note:

Much later in life, Paquita confided to a friend
that, as her father had forbidden his family to

acquaint her with the facts-of-life, she had been
very afraid that some passionate kisses from
Douglas on the eve of his departure had rendered
her pregnant. When her medico sisters had learnt
of her distress, probably during Paquita's stay in
Europe during 1912, they had reassured their
young sister, gently educating her in the true
facts . . .

Freya understands, firsthand, how keen an impression Europe
would have made on a twenty-year-old girl, reawakening her
earliest memories, reminding her of forgotten textures, exotic
scents, turning her dazzled gaze to a spring brilliant with
colour, willows in bud, verdant fields. Freya feels a kinship
with this girl whose family left Europe for Australia when
Paquita was seven, just one year younger than Freya when her
family left Oslo. She marvels at Paquita's capacity to adapt—to
a new land and a new century, to the frontier town of Broken
Hill where her father was the newly appointed manager of the
fledgling Broken Hill Proprietary. Were they formidable years
for a child not fluent in English, a stranger to the language of
a new land? Did Paquita feel at odds with the upturned seasons,
the press of dusty heat?

Did the prospect of the new overwhelm her, confuse her,
make her want to turn and flee, clamouring for the comfort
of the old?

Freya's mother advocates, endlessly, the sanctity of family.
Listen to Mama and she'll convince you that commitment is

the universal salve for troubled times. Yet it was Papa who really swayed Freya into returning home to talk through her marriage with her husband.

The night she left Marcus and drove to her parents' house, Papa had appeared, flustered, beside her in the kitchen. *Is someone else involved?*, the accusation in his voice reducing her to tears—the idea of a lover the furthest thing from her mind.

Of course there is not! Mama cried as if in defence of them both, trying her hardest to shoo him away.

Freya?

She shook her head, too distressed for words.

Her father did a strange thing, a forgotten thing, taking her hand and placing his open palm against the mirror image of her own. *Not like this, tonight, all bitter and angry. Don't waste your life, choose as you will, but do it for yourself, without cause for shame or regret.*

Then Mama had started to weep.

THE GALE HAS PASSED, FLOUNCED and fallen, petered out to still. The lingering cast of grey does little to lighten her mood as she moves along the road late at night. The storm has left a residue of grit that coats windows and walls and dissuades her from lifting her eyes. She barely registers the absence of snow that yesterday sat in shadowed pockets at the edges of the road. That the station looks as grubby as a mining camp seems no more consequential than any other impression that crosses her mind, irked as she is by her tediously slow progress and the hindrance of a crutch.

It has to be the sound, a sweetness of rhythm, coastal, cajoling, that edges at Freya's thoughts. It has to be the moment of translation, realisation, that makes her stop to hear a sonance of water lapping the shore, a cyclic wash sliding over sand. She turns to face a view that sweeps her breath away. Islands no longer rise from ruffles of white. Evening light no longer pleats the ice with shadow. Before her breathes an ocean, an expanse of steely grey.

Three days ago she rode across this bay with no heed for its tenuous state. Capricious, the nature of ice; as impetuous as faithless deeds. How misguided her judgment—to have travelled with him, week after week, hazarding risk, spurning consequence. So easy to forget that sea ice is only a veneer, inherently flawed, skin-deep as desire, so transitory as to be scattered out to sea, displaced by ocean, dispersed by wind— gone in the lapse of a day.

Expedition sei ruiniert
January 1913

DOUGLAS ONCE TOLD PAQUITA HE was at his best upon a lonely trail; he said he felt with nature and revelled in the wilds. It was something entirely new to find himself alone and be racked with loneliness. The longing for another human voice made him open Xavier's sledging journal. Not a breach of privacy, he argued, when the sum of German words recollected from his Fort Street schooldays and the edition of *German Self Taught* at winter quarters amounted to rudimentary discourse.

SCHLITTENREISE mit Dr. Mawson und Lieut. Ninnis.
10 November 1912.

Wohl ein gutes Omen für unsere weite Reise . . .
A good omen for our journey . . .

Xavier had declared of the calm conditions on their first night at Aladdin's Cave.

Unsere Eskimohunde sind aber fröhlich immer . . .
Our Eskimo dogs are always happy.

Unerforschtes Land das noch kein menschliches Auge sah.
Unexplored land not yet seen by human eyes.

Douglas placed his hand upon the words and vowed to do all within his powers for those connected with the expedition, for everyone at home—especially, especially Paquita. His fate he would entrust to Providence, whose help he asked for in crossing the remaining glacier: *Mertz Glacier*, he would name the twenty-mile stretch if he returned to the hut alive. But he halted his thoughts, for if he let his mind look along the daunting expanse of plateau from the glacier to winter quarters he would be defeated. The goal he pictured instead was bittersweet: a high point above the glacier's western slopes where a snow cairn might catch the eye of a search party, where, beside his body, they would find the diaries cached.

Dux ipse, the men at winter quarters called him slyly; never had *leader of himself* been so unwanted a title. Rather he would call himself *custodian*, guardian to three sledging journals that in probability would amount to their lives' legacy.

He caught sight of his own name in Xavier's journal.

19 November.
Ich halte, denn das Tempo scheint mir für die Schlitten zu schnell.
I stopped, because I felt that the speed was too fast for the sledges.

Letzteres stimmt, denn 2 Schlitten sind bereits umgeflogen—
I was right, two sledges had turned over—

und Mawson jammert, da er wiedermal glaubt die ganze Expedition
sei ruiniert.
*Mawson yammered, again believing the whole expedition
was ruined.*

Douglas winced at the image of his snivelling through a
kind man's eyes.

HE FELT A CAMARADERIE IN cutting apart Xavier's burberry
jacket and sewing it to the canvas clothes bag to make a
ready sail—he liked to think that this patched old garment
somehow retained a part of X that would help ease the
sledge forward in favourable winds. He wrapped the two
journals inside their sledging flags—the red cross of
Switzerland and Ninnis's Order of Saint John. Surely the
souls of men could live on forever so long as there were
people in the world to remember.

The day was calm, sun-drenched, and he resolved to
march at least ten miles. Douglas leaned on his canvas
harness and instantly felt the difference in weight. He had
discarded every excess ounce, had even torn unused pages
from Xavier's diary and scattered them to the wind, then
dissevered the back half of the sledge to lighten the load.
With festering fingers it was a laborious task, and the only

tool he had was his Bonza pocket-knife. With the two sawn-off sledge runners he formed a cross to mark the head of Xavier's snow-covered grave.

The surface of the downhill grade to the glacier was good but his feet felt awkward and lumpy. He stopped to take a bearing, grateful for the brief rest but dismayed that his feet should trouble him after only one mile.

Through the second mile he grimaced with each step. When the pain grew needle sharp he sat on the sledge to inspect his feet. Perhaps the brain's capacity to register shock reached a limit after so many blows, for when he peeled off his sock and the sole of his foot came away, he studied it with scientific detachment. His other foot was in an equally deplorable state, the skin a loose glove of burst blisters and his sock soaked with watery leakage. *Grotesque* was the word that he uttered aloud; he could think of no better term to describe the state of human flesh rotting for want of nourishment.

He smeared the blistered skin and pads with lanolin from the medical kit, then bound the soles back in place with bandages. He pulled on all the socks he had—three pairs of his own and three of Xavier's—and bound his finnesko boots with soft leather crampons.

FOUR EXCRUCIATING MILES LATER HE was unable to carry on. Douglas sat on his jacket in the snow, naked but for shoes and socks, his trousers pushed down. With a deep intake of air that tore at the inflamed membranes lining his nose he surveyed the carcass of his body. He studied his cage of ribs and a sunken belly that gurgled like a wash-house drain. With swollen fingers he examined the excoriation of his scrotum, the flame-red skin a startling contrast to the snow.

Douglas stretched out on his back and closed his eyes, enveloped by silence and the sweet sensation of sun touching his body and tingling his skin. If he succumbed to sleep he would leave this racking hunger and dull his nerve-worn feet. He could rise from the wreckage of his body and surrender to everlasting sleep, absorbed into the radiance of light.

A voice inside his head slapped him awake. *Buck up!* it spat. The voice sneered, *Do your damndest and fight, you miserable wretch*, bastardising the words of *The Quitter*, his favourite Robert Service poem.

Douglas pulled himself to his knees and dragged his fingers through his hair; a clump came away in his hands. He'd turned into an old, worn-out man, kicked along by a yammering voice that droned on and on. *The plugging away will win you the day*, it sang, holier than thou, pushing him back to his red-raw feet, not caring that each step made him wince.

CRIMSON
BERGS

BENEATH A JANUARY EVENING SKY conspicuously dimmer than weeks ago, Freya climbs the steps to her studio landing. She stops awhile to look past the lights of the station, to trace the silhouette of two inflatable rubber boats scooting across an oily-calm sea towards the bergs. Malcolm's weekly sign-up sheet for evening cruises—FIRST PLACE TO THOSE WHO HAVE NOT YET BEEN OFF STATION—had been filled by morning smoko.

Her walk up the hill was no longer hindered by brace or crutch, though even after hours of strengthening at the station gym she still favours her stronger leg. *A few more days*, says Dr Ev. These ten days, confined to the station, have felt like ten years.

Kittie, perpetually sunny Kittie, says, *Lap it up, girl. Think of the sleeping in you get to do.* But Malcolm, bless his all-cotton socks, has, in the nick of time, conditionally agreed—*weather permitting, just up and back*—to let her join tomorrow's flight to Beaver Lake and the Amery Ice Shelf, the Casas' final run before they leave for Mawson Station. *Adam Singer has a request in*, Malcolm had added. *He'll be along for the ride.* No mention of Chad.

Waiting for a medical clearance to be let loose off the station feels an uneasy kind of swaddling. When she thinks of deceiving her husband she still feels remorse, but in the next moment Freya is befuddled by contrary feelings too strong to ignore. She misses the times with Chad more than she could have imagined.

She draws in the vastness of the view, scads of deepening sky and a glaze of mulberry ocean, and *look!*, out past the islands, crimson bergs unlocked from the sea ice and turning on a spindle of current, sliding with the will of the tide. Bergs whittled and gouged and etched and pared; beautiful, beautiful ice.

INSIDE THE CARPENTRY SHOP CHAD switches on the fluoro above his bench, conscious of the fall in evening light. He draws the mini grinder in an arc to finish roughing out the shape from a block of Huon pine—this single piece brought down with other, less scarce Tasmanian timbers. He takes a chisel to define the detail from lines he's drawn upon the wood. Though the shape is still crude, each stroke is measured, the pressure of the blade never once too firm or deep. He pauses to run his thumb over the coarse block of pine already honed to rest on the flat of his hand, conjuring as a blind man might an image from the flow of a curve and the texture of the grain. He draws in the fruity redolence; the Huon pine's perfume is unlike any other wood he has known. He drowns in the sorrow of the scent, as if such sweetness were his to savour for only the briefest time, unsure now that even the memory of it won't slip from his hold. He rounds his shoulders over his work and draws in to himself, shielded from the hurt and confusion of the last days, from distance kept, from the solitude of unuttered words. He has moved beyond the crazy-making angst of self-interrogation—recalling the mawkishness of all he said on the night they spent together, then burbling out childhood memories like a broken faucet. He has stopped berating himself for friendship gone wrong, the glow of something close to love as fleeting as a golden night. He replays the snatch of overheard phone conversation with her husband on Christmas Day; in her voice the same veracity once proffered, with touch, to him.

And still he loves.

He feels a returning sense of calm by whittling this piece of precious wood, returning as he always will to timber, the steadfast companion throughout his life. He chisels the wood instinctively, keeping the pencil sketch from his journal on the bench for reference. He pares the wood to free the deepest part of himself, to create with his hands what others seem able to express so eloquently with words.

In the time remaining he will finish the keepsake. Now he assesses the ruffle of a wing, considers how a needle of darker wood can be curved to form a beak. Once the bird is sanded and sealed, polished with beeswax and cut back to glassy smoothness, the honey-blond pine will gleam as it should. When the feathered breast of the snow petrel lustres, who but he will understand the leavings of his own heart etched through the lines?

My Douglas,

First of all I love you even more than when you left & there has not been a day—an hour almost—that you have not been in my thoughts. You will have a warm welcome on your return—my arms are open already as I think of it. Not only from your me but from our Mother and the others. I'm quite spoilt! They have tried to make up for your absence in vain but still it was & is angelic of them. But I had no idea I should miss you like this. Dearie, don't go away again. I'm longing to hear you say you've wanted me often . . .

We shall be very happy when you return with the separation behind us. Dear, I know you have done good work down there in the cold—you & your little hutfull of men. Things must have been hard now & then & perhaps you have not been able to do all you wish but remember that our aims must be the higher because we can never reach them, & you have done your best. We are all proud of you. Don't be disappointed if you haven't done all you wanted to. How often we have pictured you in your hut and sledging. I'm glad you don't feel the cold as last trip. Of course it is my love that does it. I warm you every night . . .

Oh how I hope it has done you nothing but good! You promised to come back fatter & better. It's no use telling you to rest on the Aurora on its return voyage. Your book & reports will fill your time. But when we are married then my turn will come and Paquita is going to look after, scold and cuddle her Dougelly just as much as she pleases & as is good for him. So come back resigned my dear, I shall never let you go again & you will have me for the rest of your days. Can you stand it? We are going to do heaps of good work in all sorts of ways.

I can't stop yet. Is four letters too much? I have so wanted to write more but it would be all the same song. Of how we here have thought of you & how interested all my aunts & things are. And how many pretty things I have for our home, the first home in Australasia just as the head of it will be the first in the world to the other half of the head. Rather involved but perhaps you can untangle it.

Now I shall stop. You are coming back to the warmest & lovingest heart that ever beat for its other half.

I can almost feel your arms round me & involuntarily as I write lift my face to yours. Seventeen months without one caress! One embrace. We shall have something to make up for.

With my hearts whole love to you my lover
from your Paquita . . .

Casket of ice
17 January 1913

THE SNOW BRIDGE GAVE WAY, the first hint of its existence
the sound of splintering glass. He plunged feet-first, a corpse
committed, his mind giddy in the vacuum of the fall. *So this
is the end.*

The rope jolted. A slap of shock reverberated through
spine and jaw and yanked taut his canvas harness. He waited
for the snap, the final letting go. In an instant sledge and
belongings would follow him over the edge, plummet
through the gaping mouth, crash down upon his head and
send him on his way. He saw man and crevasse as if through
a kaleidoscope: a discord of colour and shape, his emaciated
body spinning free, prisms of turquoise changing hue, the
rope that held him circling one way then the other. Below, a
nothingness of black yawned in wait. He would leave this
world without witness, without a trace. He reached for a
memory, a reference, a feeling with which to equate the
wonder of the crevasse, this casket of ice festooned with the

most beautiful crystals imaginable. How else could colour and light, the last impression of life, the brink of death, be fully absorbed? Countless times in the last days he had speculated on what the end would be like. He had not counted on this: sweetness, the surrender of control, light welling from his empty gut, inflating his chest, flooding his limbs, his fingers, his feet—a bolt of white replete with warmth. Below, the abyss held the promise of release from a living hell. Beyond, the great Unknown.

How long could his harness hold? He pictured the sledge fourteen feet above, its runners ground deep in snow. Would the slightest move on his part unbalance the load and set the sledge toppling? Or would the end be slow and cruel after all, snagged as a fish on a line?

Bile rose in his throat for want of solid food to retch. Not lost on him was the irony, after stinting himself as close to starvation as a man could go, of the remaining provisions sitting untouched on his sledge. These last days across the glacier, sumptuous images of food had haunted him in his dreams. He had woken drooling from fantasies of confectionary splendour, until his saliva glands, as if in protest at unrewarded titillation, refused duty altogether. Inflamed membranes lining his mouth and nose had turned as parched as paper. His entire body—boils erupting on his legs and face, skin shedding, the soles of his feet still an atrocious sight—was decomposing ahead of time, impatient for his spirit to surrender. To have culminated in this— failure and waste; to think that at any moment now he would plunge into the bowel of the crevasse, having left this life without one last proper meal . . .

He squinted upward into the glare of light. He could make out the overhang of ice, the rope from the sledge sawing the edge with each revolution. A deposit of snow broke from the lip and showered his face. His clothing was stuffed with snow from his plunge through the crevasse's fragile bridge. The sensation of warmth had vanished and his skin now felt damp and cold. The chances of climbing out seemed pitifully small yet he thought of Providence, his old ally—would it offer him a second chance? When he stretched up to grasp a knot in the rope, the blackened end of a finger burst. Beads of blood—as brilliant red as the dilly bags Paquita had sewn—seeped through the threads of sisal. With a lunge he clenched the knot in the rope and pulled his body up. His lungs felt set to burst. In ten weeks on the plateau he had lost a cruel amount of weight, his flesh now sapped of strength. His mind revolved in concert with the rope, swaying between the effort it would take to continue, and the ease of simply slipping from the harness.

He scanned the fathomless darkness below—if he fell on a ledge, he would linger in misery with broken bones. The words of Robert Service he had read in a rousing tone to his men at winter quarters (had he sounded self-righteous? a pompous ass?) mocked him. *Just have one more try—it's dead easy to die, It's the keeping-on-living that's hard.* He searched for a narrowing above where he might wedge his feet on either wall of the crevasse. He summoned the will to reach the next knot. His arms trembled as he pulled on his weight. He felt his throat bulge. He blanked out the blue above, and filled his mind with the sledge. If he made it to the top he would feast on food. If he reached the sledge he would gorge on dog and die a sated man.

THE BIRTHPLACE
OF BERGS

GINGER'S FUSELAGE IS LADEN WITH a conglomeration of equipment, a skidoo strapped down, boxes shuddering beneath their cover of webbing. Earplugs dull the shriek of the Casa's propellers, leaving Freya absorbed in the sphere of her camera. Adam Singer sits behind her in the plane's only other row of seats.

They leave the rocky hills of the Vestfolds for a vista of ice that runs as far along the coast as she can see.

Adam nudges her. 'Look.'

An enormous edifice of white looms from the ocean, eclipsing all that surrounds it. The top of the tabular berg is riven with a patterned weave so graphic it does not immediately dawn on Freya that the entire surface comprises a crevasse field. Each glistening fissure threads the ice with a ribbon of steely blue.

The plane banks to the left and leaves the coast behind, heading towards an icecap stretching south to the pole. The single interruption to the plateau is a nunatak, a mountain's once-lofty peak reduced by a millennium of ice to a dark crown above the white.

Adam slides an arm past Freya's face and gestures towards the cockpit. The pilot sits in his seat absorbed in a Sudoku puzzle, the page angled to the light. Freya cranes her neck to check that someone is actually flying the plane but the co-pilot remains out of view. She prays *Ginger* will not share the fate of its canine namesake.

THE CASA BEGINS A SHARP descent and Freya scans for where they could possibly land. Below lies a chaos of glacial ice. The plane veers and suddenly beneath them she can see Beaver Lake—frozen, limitless, aglitter.

Adam picks at her shoulder with a demand for attention that's as easy to ignore as the tap-tapping of a rock hammer.

'Fifty k's long!' he bawls above the engine.

'Huge!' she bellows back.

'. . . the fifties,' he yells.

'What did you say?'

'The old Beaver planes. Nineteen fifties they landed here.'

'Wow.'

Freya thinks it a mystery that a freshwater lake can exist so far inland from the coast and still be tidal. A curious linkage, that no one seems fully able to explain, binds the freshwater lake with ocean beneath the Amery Ice Shelf, two hundred and fifty kilometres away. The seal of ice keeps

Beaver Lake's upper layer of fresh water intact, while a vast distance below, an undercurrent of salty sea water ebbs and eddies in concert with the ocean's tides. Impossible to comprehend the Amery Ice Shelf as a floating platform, seventy thousand square kilometres of ice rising and falling with each new tide.

Antarctica, she thinks, is a place of perpetual layers where ice conceals all that it binds. An entire mountain range, all but its highest peak obscured by countless stratifications of ice, is reduced to a nunatak. Beneath an ice shelf hundreds of kilometres away, a channel of ocean runs so deep and far that it brines the base of a freshwater lake. To the west of Beaver Lake, the mountain peaks are the only glimmer of a continent locked beneath a fathomless crush of ice.

When Freya steps from the plane onto the crystal rink, she scans the huddle of Apple field huts perched near the edge of the lake. On the opposite shore, elevated above the hills, lies the icecap. Chad told her about a mate, one of the early ANARE guys, who, in the 1950s, dog-sledged all the way from Mawson Station and arrived to see this frozen lake edged with a moat. They say the lake has not been seen as open water since. Interred within the plateau are the remains of old sledges, abandoned belongings, the jetsam of expeditions and bygone lives. Frozen relics of history, Freya thinks, that inhabit a sliver of the plateau's overwhelming volume, the imprint of human spirit cached in one hundred years of ice.

THEY HAVE TWO HOURS BEFORE *Ginger* leaves for her next port of call. The map indicates a nearby lookout with a good view, Adam says. They'll see as far as Radok Lake, the deepest known in Antarctica.

Adam slides the map into his pack and rubs his hands. 'Two hours. The race is on. Sure your leg is up to it?'

'Lead on.' Freya smiles. He tries to take her pack. 'You have your own pack, Adam. I can carry this.'

He holds up his hands in retreat and gives her a wounded look. 'No offence intended. Cross my heart.'

'HOW ARE YOU ENJOYING DAVIS?' Freya asks as they pace across the lake ice.

'Between you and me,' he says, 'if it wasn't for the money I'd shoot through at the end of summer. Rejoin the human race.'

'Why?'

'I work my heart out and hold the place together while every other bastard goes out in the field whenever they feel like it.'

Freya wonders if he's referring to Chad. 'You're out in the field now,' she offers quietly.

'Whoopie doo.' He flaps his hands. 'Second time in three months.'

'Everyone says it's different during winter with the smaller group. You enjoyed Macquarie Island.'

'It won't be like that here.'

'No?'

'A winter with fifteen men?'

'And two women.'

'That would be Kittie the dyke and a middle-aged doctor with a butt the size of a volkswagen who's been stalking me half the summer.'

Freya has to smile at the assessment. 'I see.'

'A fucking freak show,' he says, walking on.

FREYA COMPOSES THE RANGE OF hills they call the Devil's Teeth, named for the flutings of snow that leave the rock face exposed in a line of Vs.

'It's fantastic. Would you like to take a look?' She offers Adam the viewfinder of her panorama camera.

But Adam is impatient to move on so they make their way to the edge of the gorge. Radok Lake has its own floating ice tongue but Freya can spy only a tip of ice.

Adam beckons her closer to the edge of the ravine. 'Come down. You can see it from here.'

Freya treads cautiously, stones around her dislodging and tumbling towards the precipice. She is suddenly afraid.

'Careful,' he says, reaching out to help her.

She accepts his hand but he grips it and pulls hard, feigning to send her over the edge. He steadies her and laughs, his arm fixed fast around her waist. Rocks bounce and fall and her knees threaten to buckle beneath her.

'What the . . .' Adam points overhead, seemingly oblivious to her distress.

Snow petrels flutter in and out of the shadow of the gorge; tiny birds hundreds of kilometres from the coast.

'What do they feed on?' She moves away, cautious of Adam now, her heart still thudding.

Adam shrugs. 'How does anything survive? The place is a wasteland.'

They find a navigable incline that takes them to the base of Pagodroma Gorge from where it's an easy one-kilometre walk to Beaver Lake. She can see the fire-engine-red wings of the Casa parked out on the lake. An icy wind funnels through the shadowed ravine.

'I'll catch up.' Freya slows, bemoaning the need to pee and the rigmarole involved.

She finds a ridge of ice along the tide crack that shields her from view and begins the chore of removing layers of clothing. She strips off her ventile jacket to access her overall straps beneath. Her bare hands ache with cold as she fumbles with zips and clips and tugs at buttons and velcro tabs. She peels down windproof trousers, her yellow overalls, her woollen work trousers, her long johns and finally her underwear. She crouches on the ice in the wind, her weak leg held out at an angle, trying to bunch loose clothes in one hand, gather her shirt-tails in the other. Cold stings her bare skin.

'I'll take your camera bag,' Adam calls from the other side of the ridge. 'I'm heading out to the plane.'

'Leave it,' she answers. 'I might still need it. You go on ahead.'

To her annoyance he's there when she emerges dishevelled, fumbling with clips. He has her camera bag propped on his shoulder.

'Adam, I like to have it with me so I can use it.'

'Come on,' he pleads. 'Let me feel useful. You might want to get used to it.' He nods to the plane parked on the ice, its paintwork gleaming. 'They're off to Mawson Station tomorrow, your alter ego with them.'

'What do you mean?'

'McGonigal's shooting through.'

Freya halts. 'Are you sure?'

'Positive. He surprised us all a few days ago. Said he's had a gutful of the people and the place.'

She feels Adam's eyes on her and does her best to hide dismay.

'These things are never easy,' he says kindly.

She remains silent, refusing to be coaxed into any conversation that could give herself, or Chad, away.

'You can't blame him, Freya.' Adam speaks gently, privy, it seems, to matters so intimate that it rocks her to think they've been shared. 'It might be best for both of you this way.'

Freya wills him to stop but he's like a dog with a bone. 'He was down here twelve months before you showed up. He would have been off his tree after spending a winter with twenty blokes. Twenty-one,' he winks, 'counting Elisia Hood.'

She nods, her head a world away.

'You probably stopped McGonigal going insane.'

THE CASA BANKS, TIPS ITS wing abruptly as if caught unawares by something below. Through the window, Freya catches sight of a tiny dark speck—impossible to tell whether it's a mountain or a stone. Perceptions of distance, size, perspective—a photographer's sphere—are shot to pieces against the infinite planar of ice.

As the plane descends, readying to land upon the ice shelf, objects on the ground sharpen and reveal themselves. Freya looks down upon a circle of tents faded to assorted shades of orange from their varying tours of duty. A larger Weatherhaven tent, its striped shell of blue and gold not yet bleached by sun or wind, looks as cheerful as a circus top. In the middle of the camp, plastic food bins sit in snow like the stones of a fire ring. At their centre, as if to mark this place, rises a cairn of ice topped with a bedraggled red star. Cairn and star hold fleeting claim upon the ice, staking a compass point, a grid reference, a name upon a map that is, for a time, the Amery Ice Shelf Summer Camp.

The co-pilot hauls boxes and bins from the body of the plane and passes them down to a chain of outstretched arms. From inside the fuselage Freya hears the splutter of an engine followed by a roar. The waiting group breaks into a cheer. The pilot ushers people clear as he reverses the overhauled skidoo brought out from the station, a carton of beer tethered to its back, down the plane's ramp and out across the snow. Slumped a distance away, sporting an ungainly lean, a second, wounded snowmobile—its frame warped and buckled—looks a sad and sorry sight. Just wait until Malcolm gets wind of it. Freya watches the broken skidoo being hooked and winched into the plane like a harpooned whale. The vehicle's fate will rest on a dieso's report, *skidoo knackered*, or a miracle cure by those same mechanical wizards.

Freya is directed to the big top, which accommodates a makeshift mess and field laboratory. The mail satchel she delivers from Davis is filled with printouts of incoming emails, letters from friends on station, old copies of newspapers emailed daily to the station.

Freya has to look twice to recognise Travis, the young field assistant she travelled down with on *Aurora Australis*. He gives her a wry smile. No longer the clean-shaven, baby-faced boy she remembers, his bearded face is sun-browned and lined, lips cracked, his hair hangs lank to his shoulders. Travis looks harder, rougher, has acquired an Antarctic edge. He hovers over the table. 'Anything for me?'

She checks the bundle in her self-appointed role as post-mistress. 'Nothing, I'm afraid. Sorry.'

He slumps into a plastic chair beside her and extracts a crumpled wad of paper from his pocket. 'Do me a favour when you get back? Type this and email it to my wife.' He unfolds the pages. 'The address is at the top. If she writes back you can send it over on the next plane.' His hands tremble.

Freya hesitates. '*If* she writes back?'

Travis nods. 'If you ever decide you want to fuck things up at home, try phoning your wife from a floating ice shelf in the middle of nowhere on a ten-dollar-a-minute satellite phone that keeps cutting out.'

'Those nosy little satellites have a lot to answer for.'

Travis barely reacts, devoid of the eager optimism she remembers from the ship. 'That'd be the same night,' he says, 'you've come *this close* to being wiped out in a crevasse on a skidoo, because you have this stupid idea that wouldn't it be good to hear Leila's voice after being marooned out here for three months.' He shakes his head. 'Who, as it turns out, is off her tree at a nightclub, along with one of your white ant mates who's promised to look out for her while you're away. She's screaming at you from her mobile, bawling you out because you weren't there for her twenty-third birthday, or for Christmas, or New Year, or right now when she really, really needs to feel close to someone.'

Freya closes her eyes against the image, only to picture Marcus at home, oblivious to her deceit. Whether you're the one away, or the one waiting at home, everything hinges on trust.

'Life was good when I left home. I came down here thinking this would be the chance of a lifetime. What a joke.'

Their voyage south feels an age ago. 'I'm so sorry.' She's sorry for them all: Travis and his wife, she and her husband. And Chad, leaving tomorrow because of her. 'Travis, the Casas leave for Mawson Station tomorrow. As I understand it, they won't come out here again before they bring you guys back to Davis Station in February. Shall I ask Charlie to radio you any news we hear?'

'Depends what kind of news.' Then he shrugs. 'Who gives a flying fuck. Give the comms guys something to laugh about.'

'Charlie's not like that,' she says quietly.

DURING THE RETURN FLIGHT FREYA'S camera rests on her knees, the vibration of the plane's engines burring through her limbs. Adam dozes in the seat in front, his feet resting on the buckled red skidoo. It feels ludicrous to admit that she was once attracted to a man as vain and boorish as Adam, his charm surface deep. She thinks of Travis—damaged and altered—and begins to see how Antarctica affects people in odd, unpredictable ways. She looks out the window but her focus turns inward, replaying conversations. She feels, within the waves of sadness, a double-edged admiration for Chad, for his strength and self-reliance: he has the courage and conviction to turn and walk away. She thinks of her marriage and questions whether she would have the fortitude to do the same.

They fly over endless rifts of ice. Directly below, three frozen rivers converge into the headwaters of a glacier. From here the mass of ice begins its slide towards open water, set in motion by its own colossal weight. Only when it reaches the ocean will the river of ice complete its course, unfolding like a Herculean hand and releasing immense frozen fingers into the sea.

The birthplace of bergs. Ice bobbing and turning. Weightless. Free.

GINGER EASES DOWN AMONG THE hills of the Vestfolds and lines up the plateau pegged out with black blocks. Freya can see the bank of fuel drums and beyond them the figure of Elisia Hood hurtling snowballs at the two engineers. The plane pulls down on skis and bounces once, twice, before sliding over snow and easing to a stop.

The door of the Casa opens to a beaming, breathless Elisia, clumps of snow tangled in her hair. Freya wishes she could bottle some of Elisia's cheer, take it home and keep it by her side.

Elisia takes one look at the broken skidoo and whistles. 'What happened to the poor driver?'

Adam shrugs and gives the bumper a kick. 'It's cactus. If it had been up to me I would have left it in the crevasse. Let the plateau swallow it up.'

Elisia has a deft way of flaring her nostrils to show disdain. 'And how exactly would that solve the problems of the world, Dr Adam?' She bellows into the plane. 'You don't just chuck something out the minute it's busted. You'd never get anywhere in life.'

'Well, excuse me for living,' his voice booms back.

Freya climbs down the ramp and jumps into ankle-deep snow. 'Can it be fixed?'

Elisia shrugs. 'Won't know until we try.'

21 miles south
January 1913

A LEADEN GLARE, SAGGING CLOUDS, a sharp rise in temperature—the first swirl of snow corralled him to a halt, a stern reminder that he was scarcely strong enough to pitch the tent in calm conditions, let alone in gusts of wind and flurries of snow that would soon wind up to blizzard.

The euphoria of crossing the glacier had propelled him onward to the beginning of the western slope, two miles, three, each terrace a harder, steeper goal than the one before. Seized with hope at glimpses of coastline and a berg-studded bay, he had turned a deaf ear to caution running through his weary, weary mind and discarded his worn crampons and alpine rope. He had flicked his crevasse stick at the glacier and watched it skittle downhill.

It was unfair that he should be held back now by changing weather when he was eager to go on—caged within a wilting tent with a saturated bag and freezing feet.

Hair, human and reindeer, formed a russet halo on the snow around his head. The lining of the tent held a skin of rime from exhaled air. Outside, torrents of snow pressed down until the whole enclosure stood no higher than a coffin. The base of his skull hammered out a strange new pain that brought an image of blood vessels swelling in his brain. The perpetual craving for food racked his body and addled his mind when he tried to calculate how long it was humanly possible to spin out the remaining two and a half pounds of food—a normal day's rations.

Providence had let him come this far, had dragged, cajoled him, drummed him on, step after step, with endless rhyming lines of Robert Service: *Have you suffered, starved, and triumphed, grovelled down, yet grasped at glory, grown bigger in the bigness of the whole?*

Providence had chafed his body raw until it bled, punished him with the science gone to waste—three hundred miles of surveyed coastline, notes on glaciers and ice formations locked inside his head.

Done things just for the doing, letting babblers tell the story, seeing through the nice veneer the naked soul?

It had shamed him with an imagined sea of admiring supporters and an image of forty thousand pounds scattered to the wind by the festering hands of a man with grandiose ideas. Up every slope and over every ridge the voice dragooned like a drill sergeant, *Duty! Duty! Duty!*—kicked him when he crawled.

Only when he held out the sun compass and angled his thoughts to Paquita did the world ease to a hush. In warm, glinting light he remembered her capacity for kindness and love. In the refraction of sun on a circle of glass he knew that nothing meant more than honouring a pledge sealed with a diamond ring and upholding his promise to return.

The simple things, the true things, the silent men who do things; then listen to the Wild—it's calling you.

He had paid his dues to the Wild. Let him reach the plateau and find his bearings; let him make it home.

HE TRUDGED INTO WIND WITH petticoats of drift flouncing at his waist. He moved like a hobbled mule over last year's worn sastrugi that finally marked his direction beneath his feet.

He had marched five miles over undulating ice on a bearing north 45 degrees west when a flash of black ticked the corner of his eye.

He turned and paced closer; he held his breath, uncertain that his mind was not betraying him, believing in miracles only when he touched the cairn with its bunting of black cloth wound through hewn blocks of ice.

Douglas seized a red bag weighted beneath the snow, the frisson of recognition as sweet as the promise of its contents. He ran his thumb across a seam, seeing, for the first time, the painstaking labour and devotion in Paquita's careful stitches.

The note inside the tobacco tin made him catch his breath. The date: 29 January 1913—today. He scanned the plateau for figures, tempted to abandon the sledge and run to catch the party but seeing only ghosts swirling in the drift. When had they left?

29-1-13

Situation   21 Miles S 60 E
of Aladdin's Cave.

Two ice mounds one
14 M S 60 E of Aladdin's Cave
the other
5 miles SE of Aladdin's . . .

—the first has biscuits
chocolate etc.

Please find biscuits,
pemmican, ground biscuit
tea etc.

Aurora arrived Jan 13th.
Wireless messages received
All parties safe.

Amundsen reached Pole
December 1911

—remained there 3 days
Supporting party left
Scott 150 M from Pole in
the same month

Bage reached 300 M SE
17' from Magnetic Pole

Bickerton—160 M West
Aeroplane broke down 10 M

out

Madigan went 270 M East

Good luck from
Hodgman
Hurley
McLean

A. McLean

Possibilities swirled through his head. Twenty-one miles to
Aladdin's Cave, another five to the hut—it would take him
three, four days if the weather held. Would the ship wait?
All parties safe! Wireless messages received! Those
Hannam tapped out before the masts came down, night
after night, with nothing in return? Amundsen's triumph
at the pole—but what of Scott's return? For now he

couldn't think. He didn't care. He was bursting with joy, intoxicated with gratitude and the exquisite sensation of ginger biscuit warming his gut, explosions of flavour as sweet and giddying as each glorious line of news on which he gorged.

A
MEMENTO

CHAD PAUSES AT THE BASE of the studio steps to gauge the cast of early morning light. The helicopter engineer ambles around the Squirrel, yawning as he kneels to release the clamp that tethers a blade. Chad contemplates the thudding in his chest, unsure if it comes from the knowledge he is leaving, or this other act, the offering in his hands positioning him, surely, for pity or silent ridicule.

The station still sleeps and he is glad to have left this deed for last, certain there will be no chance of an encounter now.

It seems odd and sad that he has not set foot inside her studio before. The dimness of the room makes him feel more of a trespasser, hushed into furtive steps. He places the gift on her chair then shifts it to the desk. He studies how it looks then returns it to the chair. The urge to linger, to savour, to look around, staves off his compulsion to bolt.

Stacked along the shelves are countless numbered and dated film canisters, beside them spindles of DVDs. Atop an old steel cabinet lies a hand-embroidered cloth, upon it mementoes from their field trips: snow petrel and skua feathers, an adélie tail quill, a strip of weathered elephant seal hide from the wallow, a collection of pebbles and stones—among them the garnet rock he so self-righteously declined. He wills himself to believe she will leave it at the station, on neutral ground, like her books from the library: articles on loan.

Bolder now, he takes up a hinged photo frame from her desk. On one side is a woman remarkably like Freya except for hair coloured golden and spiked with darker tips. The face looks unfinished without its spread of wine. Draped across the woman's lap, a teenage girl reclines in a theatrical pose. Chad turns the perspex frame to a portrait of an older woman with porcelain skin, her silver hair swept into a roll. Beside it, in the saturated colours of old Kodak prints from his parents' family album, is a younger version of the same woman; the man beside her, fair-haired, slight in build, stands pointing at the nameplate of a ship—*Fram*—Amundsen's ship.

The last photograph smarts. He holds the frame to the light, driven to measure this other man's face. Older than he'd imagined, her husband looks studious with rimless glasses and a mild face, a city man in his collared shirt and jacket. Chad's eyes are drawn to the remarkable fineness of his hand placed on Freya's shoulder, comparing the man's unblemished skin with the coarseness of his own—nails ragged, thumbnail black, knuckles wide and knocked about. He returns the frame to the desk, despondent at the ocean of difference between them, his gloom deepened by Freya facing him in the photo: the admiration in her gaze.

Chad uncovers a photograph lying on the bench and feels a jolt to see a black and white portrait of himself. Not a shred of sophistication in sight, more your good-for-nothing loafer leaning back on his bike in a govvie-issue wool shirt, arms propped behind his head, grinning like a galah. Beneath this image lies a second, smaller print of Freya, photographed by him despite her protests. He feels poignant pleasure in the portrait, at the joy in her face, alive and intense.

Chad hears the rotors whine, the silence of the station broken by a whirring that quickly heightens to a squeal. The studio floor hums. Only now does it dawn on him that Freya works hours on end with this ear-piercing scream penetrating body and mind. Little wonder that at nights, once the whirligigs are laid to rest, he sees her studio lit up; if he stares long enough he will catch her shape moving past the glass.

Five-fifteen. He peels a post-it from the pad and scratches a note. BIRD'S EYE HUON PINE. A MEMENTO OF YOUR SUMMER IN THE VESTFOLDS. He moves the gift back to the desk and places the note alongside.

Chad opens the studio door, one foot on the threshold, his helicopter shuttle to the skiway shrieking its readiness to leave. His feet refuse to work, held fast with indecision, lured by desire for something not rightfully his. He returns inside, closes the door, his pulse quickening with this final act of stealth. He takes the portrait of Freya, working quickly to roll it up tightly, scrabbling through the top drawer of her desk to find an elastic band.

He turns at a sound: Freya stands framed in the open doorway. The sorrow in her eyes—*Look at you*, they might be saying, *no better than a thief.*

'I've been searching the station for you.'

'You found me. Red-handed.' He holds out the portrait.

She shrugs. 'It's yours if you want it. You took the photo.'

She closes the door, the pitch of the rotors still ringing in his ears.

'Adam told me you were leaving. Not even goodbye?'

He shakes his head, afraid to speak, his focus on the wall, on a line of loose and missing studs.

'I didn't want this, Chad. I didn't want you to go.'

'It's no big deal,' he says. 'I'm looking forward to a change of scenery.'

'No big deal? It meant nothing?'

That wasn't what he said. The walls shudder as the second helicopter fires up. 'You're the one that changed your mind, Freya. Overnight. I'd just like you to have told me why.'

'This.' She holds out her ring finger. 'Because of this.'

'You said you didn't want to go home.' He raises his voice above the second engine. 'One night with me and you change your mind?'

'It wasn't like that. Everything happened so quickly. It scared me, Chad. When I get home I have a lot to talk over with Marcus. Whatever the outcome, I want it to be for the right reasons. Nothing between Marcus and me has anything to do with you.'

'I was more of a diversion, eh. A fling to tide you over. Did you ever stop to consider how I might feel?'

'Nothing like this has happened to me before. You have to believe that. I need some time and space to get things worked out in my own head. When a person is married, it's not so simple.'

'Call me naive, but I think it is simple, Freya. I know nothing about your marriage or your husband, but I've got to know something about you and you don't strike me as anybody's prisoner. It might not be easy, but you're as free to make your own choices as the rest of us. The way I see it, the only person holding you back is you.'

'What about you?' she shouts above the duelling rotors. 'You're so sure of yourself. What would you have happen?'

He wants it all. The whole unattainable, happy-ever-after bundle. 'There's a chopper downstairs screaming for me to get in it. It's too late to be asking now.'

He moves past her, pulls on his gloves, has his hand upon the door.

'So that's it, Chad? You're running away?'

'That's it,' he says. 'I'm bailing.'

He steps onto the landing, the blades of the chopper a blur. He takes a last look back, 'Call it self-preservation,' and shuts the door.

FREYA STANDS AT HER STUDIO window, the drone of the helicopter reduced to an echo, the speck on the horizon disappearing into sky. She returns to the desk, noticing the parcel wrapped in cloth, and her photo frame that no longer sits as she left it. For a moment she considers ignoring the parcel, leaving it unopened, refusing to take part in this final act of severance.

She unties the lashing and the cloth falls away. Freya turns the snow petrel in her hands, studying the curve of wings tucked close, absorbing every feathered line, running her hand over the glassy finish of the pine. His hands inhabit every ridge and line. She holds the bird to her cheek, remembering the first snow petrel she saw nestled beneath rocks at Bandits Hut, how she'd imagined then cupping the fragile creature in her hands.

She sets the carving down, presses her fingers across the ridges of her breastbone and listens to her heart. *Thud. Thud. Thud.* Only the feel of his presence lingers in the room. She drags her fingers across her blemished cheek and throat. Her mark of birth never was a blessing; it never was a charm. She has spent her life trapped beneath a glacier, searching for a way out, led and misled by refractions in the ice. The darkroom and camera, the college where she first met Marcus—an admiration she once mistook for love: all paths in search of light.

After that single, sorry night of marital separation, she dutifully returned home from the refuge of her parents' to a man wretched with despair; his manic talk, his threats of doing harm to himself, have haunted her since. *Everything can be exactly as it was*, he begged, when all the while it was she who had turned unannounced and changed direction, she who craved for more. Flowers, cards of eloquent devotion: *she* had reduced her husband—through her guilt and pity—to a man with a suffocating need to please. An untenable storm of turmoil and uncertainty that abated with a *please don't leave me*, the simplest and saddest of words that finally wound her in. *Alright, Marcus.* She didn't give her promise lightly.

She passes the snow petrel between her hands, raises it to breathe in the perfume of wood, to feel its loveliness sensuous against her cheek. She winds the cotton wrap around sorrow and regret and all that she can never have and places the carving deep inside the drawer.

>> Freya, I've been thinking things through these last weeks. I am so very sorry for the way I spoke to you on the phone on Christmas Day. You have every right to still be upset, but please, don't cut me out. You reply to my emails, but it seems a long time since I felt something from *you*. I don't know what else to say to make things right again.

   If nothing else, work on the exhibition moves forward at a good pace. Hurley's *Fury-lashed waters of Commonwealth Bay* gives a glimpse of the conditions that *Aurora* encountered on her return in January 1913. Captain Davis spent weeks battling the weather, searching up and down the coastline. He not only had Mawson's missing party to worry about, but the safety of Frank

Wild and his men, who were 1500 miles west along the coast, their hut built upon a floating ice shelf. Joe Laseron, the biological collector, conveys the mood at winter quarters in his journal.

This is 2.30 a.m., and perhaps the last night I shall spend in Adélie Land. For the last week every night was to have been the last, but we are still here. The same old stove in front, the same old corner where the nightwatchman sits and reads—or thinks maybe—be it for the last time. I feel unutterably homesick—home and the green trees and sunshine and the little water. The same old bunks are occupied by the same old chaps, that is nearly all—but there are three vacant. The poor old chief—we loved him with all his faults, Ninnis, cherub as we called him, and X whose Swiss heart was one of gold, are up on the plateau somewhere. Oh that awful plateau, blizzard ridden, treacherous, the most desolate, cruellest region in the world. January has entirely gone, and winter is practically on the land again . . .

*Fury-lashed waters of
Commonwealth Bay*

Aladdin's Cave II
8 February 1913

WOULD THE SHIP WAIT? DOUGLAS had taken to sitting outside Aladdin's Cave huddled like a child with his back to the wind, waiting for a lull. He weighed up the likelihood he was strong enough to stop the sledge from hurtling downhill and toppling over in a sixty-mile-an-hour wind against the unthinkable gamble of severing his lifeline to shelter and going down alone, leaving the sledge behind. With good crampons he might make the five miles to the hut in a single march, but he had only a miserable pair fashioned from a packing box with nails that cut into his feet; they, and he, would give out in the first five hundred yards.

He'd spent a week eating and sleeping in a cave whose walls no longer sparkled with magic but had blackened with smoke and soot from boil-ups of ground plasmon biscuit and glaxo milk powder. He had eaten chunks of pemmican straight from the tin. Two oranges and a pineapple whose verdant scent had filled the cave on his arrival, and spoke of

Aurora's return, did more to upset than bolster his constitution. Diarrhoea, blood spouting from his nostril and a watery concoction bursting from his fingertips set him questioning whether he had scurvy, or if stale supplies were doing him lasting harm.

Could Captain Davis afford to wait?

To sit on the sledge and be blown downhill, whatever the result, would be infinitely better than another wasted day.

True to the unpredictable nature of Commonwealth Bay, no sooner had he made the decision to take the risk and go, strapped gear to the sledge and begun the downhill march, than the drift subsided and the wind dropped.

After he'd walked a mile the weather cleared and he could see enough of the ocean to know that no ship lay in the offing.

For another hour he held onto the thought that *Aurora* had headed east along the coast to search. Better still, she had swung inshore to anchor and now was obscured from his sight in the lee of the ice cliffs. But a harsher voice that grew more convincing with each laboured step, told him Captain Davis would do right to abandon the Far Eastern Sledging Party. Douglas's instructions, left in the box in his cabin, would have confirmed he was now four weeks overdue. In the same box were personal letters, one for Paquita and the other for his brother Will, *to be delivered in the event of my non-return.*

Davis had already done as any good leader would and sent out a search party to scour the plateau. McLean,

Hodgeman and Hurley would have returned to the hut a week ago with nothing to report.

It would be beyond cruel if Providence had let him come this far only to be given up for dead.

BOAT HARBOUR EASED INTO VIEW below, a cloudburst of light shimmering across the water and onto the ice. He could see the apex of the hut and beside it two newly erected wireless masts. Along the ice edge clusters of adélies conferred at the foreshore. When three of them straightened into human figures he felt himself swim to the surface of a dream and heave a cry of air.

It felt like an eternity before the figures finally turned and answered his wave. He watched the commotion as they bolted from sight in the direction of the hut as if running away to hide.

He continued slowly downward, even now not daring to relinquish his sledge. On the horizon, he caught sight of a dark smudge far out to sea. A head rose above the brow of the hill and as the man closed in he recognised Frank Bickerton, red in the face beneath his dark beard and puffing like a locomotive from the climb. Bickerton slowed and tilted his head in puzzlement, waiting, no doubt, for Ninnis and Mertz to appear.

He sprang once more into motion and bounded through the snow like a man across hot coals. 'My God! My God! Cherub!'

Douglas felt his knees buckle in the warmth of human embrace. 'It's Douglas,' he cried but Bick didn't let him go, a circle of arms threatening to crush Douglas's bones that felt loose inside his skin.

He felt himself unravel with the shuddering of sobs. 'The ship?' he asked.

'Waited as long as she could,' Bick blurted. 'They went to go then waited some more. She left just a few hours ago. Captain Davis had six of us stay on, on the off-chance . . .' He drew back. 'Ninnis and Mertz? They're at Aladdin's Cave?'

Douglas shook his head, letting Bickerton absorb through his silence the confirmation of their death. He would have wept with Bick if his train wreck of a body had any more to give.

He looked beyond Bick, hearing the welcoming cries of Bob Bage and Cecil Madigan, Archie McLean and Alfie Hodgeman, and a sixth man, a newcomer, who joined the soft sea of faces as they crowded in.

Feb 1, 1913

Dr. Douglas Mawson, Commander
Australasian Antarctic Expedition
Winter Quarters
Commonwealth Bay
Adelie Land

My dear Mawson

I sincerely hope that you will read these lines which are to tell you that we are leaving for Wild's base today. What these last days have been I cannot tell you. I have followed out what I consider to be the best plan of operation under the circumstances and hope same will meet with your approval. On our return to Australia if we get back all right I will get things going as well as I can . . .

We spent the last few days searching the coast for you and seeing flags on every point which always turned out to be mirage. Everything has been remarkably successful since we left this base last year that your detention is a heavy blow as it is totally unexpected. I only hope however that you will get in safely or that the search party may tumble across you in time. It has been blowing a gale ⅔ of the 19 days we have been here, what it has been on the plateau God knows. I am keeping your box of private papers here as I think I had better have it than to leave it at the hut. When we get back it will be placed in safety and nothing disturbed . . .

Trusting you will get this all right. We shall not be able to return here in March as I had hoped, our coal will not allow it so you will have to try and get through until I shall be down D.V. by Dec 1.

Yours JK Davis

ANOTHER
WOMAN'S PAST

MID-FEBRUARY AND SUMMER IN ANTARCTICA is winding down. Adélie penguins are leaving for the winter and all but those chicks hatched too late to survive have moulted and followed out to sea to take their chances. Nothing, Freya thinks, when she takes her camera from its bag, not even the icecap continually in motion, is here to stay. From the front seat of the helicopter the Vestfold Hills stretch before her, splayed with pattern and light. The cobbled pathways of mafic dykes—intrusions of darker rock—trundle along as if to guide their course northward, rolling over hilltops, spilling down slopes, dipping beneath the water to cross submarine floors. Even the fjords—arms of glistering white when she first arrived—have thawed and appear from this height as shallow as shoals. By March, she is told, a new season's ice will form.

They fly along the edge of the plateau, over the site of the Casa skiway. Freya might have missed seeing it altogether had Elisia, seated behind her with Adam Singer, not touched her shoulder and pointed down at the single line of fuel drums—all that remains to mark the skiway's presence—waiting to be slung beneath a helicopter and ferried back to station.

Freya has been witness to one cycle of change—an Antarctic spring unfolding to summer, summer closing down. She came here to understand the nature of ice, to record the texture of a place. She now has to remind herself she can have no lasting presence here; she will leave no trace behind. She feels weighed down by the prospect of going home, sickened by the thought of never coming back. The *Aurora Australis* is somewhere out there now.

The sea ice at the northern tip of the Vestfolds remains intact. Ahead of them a blackened nub of mainland protrudes from the plateau. Walkabout Rocks, Freya's final Antarctic destination and the site that has eluded her all season, lies within reach, rising from a pillow of white.

ELISIA CARRIES FREYA'S TRIPOD WHILE Adam, the last in the entourage, brings her waterproof case. Freya lays down her pack and races Elisia to be first to Walkabout Rocks' stone cairn, the pair clambering over boulders.

They stand together on the rocks, Freya's eyes fixed upon the plateau, Elisia looking out to sea as she hums.

'What things have you missed the most?' Freya asks her.

'My husband. Followed by, let's see . . .'

'Your husband?'

'Insects, actually.'

'Insects?' Freya laughs.

'The music of a Queensland night. Dragonflies, cicadas, even the drone of a good old blowfly. Up at the skiway there's wind hammering off the plateau or there's silence. Take your pick. They both get to you after a while.'

'Heard anything from Chad?' Freya asks nonchalantly.

'Had an email a few weeks back. He's all settled, says it's a nice group at Mawson, sounds like there's plenty to do. He's already put his hand up for next year's winter. Not me, babe. One more week and I'm on that ship and outta here, homeward bound.'

Adam beckons Freya and Elisia down from the cairn to the rocks below. Freya watches him drag an aluminium case out of a crevice.

'What's the story on all this?' Elisia asks him. 'Charlie says you've been swotting up.'

'Do you genuinely want to know?'

Freya settles on a rock and wraps her arms around her knees. 'Of course we do, Adam. Go ahead.'

He postures before them, his knee on the case. Adam clears his throat. 'Hubert Wilkins was an Australian polar aviator and explorer—and a photographer—who joined a private US expedition back in the late thirties. When the ship left Cape Town, the Americans informed Wilkins that they were going to claim any land they visited in Antarctica for the US, even though they'd signed a pre-departure statement saying they wouldn't make any claims. Douglas Mawson had already claimed this whole coastline in 1930, 31, during his British and New Zealand expedition. Even back then,' Adam says, 'the Yanks thought they could commandeer the world.'

'Unlike our own imperialist forebears,' Elisia says.

'Douglas Mawson came *here*?' Freya exclaims before the two of them can begin to bicker.

'He sailed right along the coast, took a number of flights in a biplane they brought along. It was a different place by 1930, the Antarctic water teeming with whaling ships. This was almost twenty years after Mawson's expedition to Commonwealth Bay, when he and six men were forced to spend a second winter there.' Adam winks at her. 'You'd know the story of Mawson's fiancée waiting for him all that time? *This Everlasting Silence*.'

So Adam was her Secret Santa. Did he steal the book of letters from the station library? She can't help the shameful thought.

'Mawson and JK Davis,' he continues, 'were middle-aged men by then. They sailed to Proclamation Island, west of where Mawson Station is built, then motored all the way back east to Commonwealth Bay. They claimed that whole section, except for the bit the Frogs got to first.' Adam nods at Freya. 'Now you know why Australia lays claim to forty per cent of the Antarctic pie.'

'Good old Douglas.'

'Don't forget JK,' Elisia says. 'They say Davis was the unsung—'

Adam talks over her: 'Hubert Wilkins, the Australian pilot, wasn't having a bar of the Yanks' bullshit. Once they got down here he took off in his plane and landed at several places along the Vestfolds, including Walkabout Rocks.'

'He couldn't have been on his own in the plane,' Elisia says. 'Where did he land?'

Adam sighs at the interruption. 'He would have landed up there on the plateau or down on the sea ice. Either way,' he says, 'Wilkins climbed to where we're sitting right now and raised the Aussie flag.'

'You know something else, Freya?' Adam stands and puts his arm around her shoulder. He points to a black dot rising from the sea ice. 'See Tryne Island way out there? That's the site of the first landing by a woman in Antarctica. Karoline Mikkelsen, the wife of the Norwegian captain who named the Vestfolds. She hailed from your corner of the world.'

'Adam,' Elisia thumps him on the back with a force that shunts Freya off balance, 'you're full of surprises, boy.'

ELISIA AND ADAM CLIMB DOWN to the sea ice and head off in separate directions. Freya savours her time alone at the cairn. She breathes in the chill air, slowly looks around. She cannot remember a sky so flushed with colour, its reflection bringing the plateau so alive.

Freya is jolted by the scene before her into remembering that Hurley's Antarctica was as flooded with colour as her own is now. In 1912, colour photography had been available in Australia for less than five years. The muted, pastel hues of Lumière autochromes—the first commercial colour plates—would have touched the core of an artist like Hurley. One precious box was all he had to trial at Commonwealth Bay; less than a handful of plates have survived to this day, not one of them published.

Hurley's vast collection of black and white photographs define their time and place in photographic history. It dawns on Freya how influential his images have become in *shaping* a collective understanding of the past: they do not simply preserve the memory of Antarctica and the first Australian expedition, they compel the mind into imagining the past in black and white.

Freya did not envisage, when she conceived of this project, that her photographic collection would be a celebration of colour. When Hurley photographed the blizzard, he offered people at home a vision they had never seen before; similarly, of the thousands of Antarctic images she has captured in these last months, she singles out her summer auroras as her own, unique expression. For Freya, they embody Antarctica's kaleidoscope of colour.

The sky presses down on her, saturating her in jewelled light as if she were part of the garnet-studded rock she holds in her hand. It was never hers to keep, though for weeks she has carried the stone as an amulet, waiting for the right moment to restore it to the ground.

She returns to her tripod and searches through her viewfinder, photographing scurries of snow, drift rising from the crest and spiralling into sky. She widens her lens, craving more, but no eye can take in the expanse. She abandons her camera and faces the sea. She turns in circles, muddled with colour, drunken with light; she tilts her head to swallow the sky. She lets the light wash through her, absorbs the giddying, weightless heliotrope hue until she feels herself afloat. She rises above her grounding of rock, relinquishing land in search of more. She hovers, feathered with luminescence, wings agleam. She glides, diving and wheeling, expansive as she dips and curls, the ice around her spangled with lustrous light until she is spread so far she belongs to the plateau's nacreous glow.

The sun tracks below the horizon, the deepening light resisting its pull. Elisia points to their ride home beating through the sky—always too soon. Elisia makes her way down the rocks but Freya lingers, loading her last roll of large format film, only now registering Adam sitting quietly beside her. She photographs the fading shimmer of the plateau, her motor drive burning a ribbon of exposures until she has no more frames to shoot.

'DETOUR.' THE VOICE OF THE helicopter pilot crackles through the headphones as he veers away from their path home. 'One of the science teams has left their GPS and a pair of boots at Bandits Hut.'

'How does anyone leave their boots behind?' Elisia squawks from the back seat. 'Or a GPS.'

Adam laughs. 'That's the boffins for you.'

Bandits Hut glints in the last of the sun. The rotors form shadows across its roof as the helicopter descends upon the wooden landing pad. The first time Freya laid eyes upon this hut was during field training; she was so struck with disappointment that she had to force herself to photograph it. People at the station had spoken in glowing terms about weekend jollies to Bandits—a favourite escape from the station. She had romantically imagined it to be the kind of cabin published in calendars her auntie sends from Norway, a fairytale vision that fell as flat as a poorly told joke when she set her eyes upon this metal box—a shanty, she had deemed it then— driven into a hillside of rock.

From the front seat of the helicopter she has easy access to the door and offers to retrieve the truant articles. She cowers as she passes beneath the spinning rotors; even after a season in her studio beside the heliport she'll never grow accustomed to the way the blades cut the air to pieces.

The inside of the hut looks dim, timeless, achingly familiar. She picks up the GPS from a shelf but can't see the boots. She checks the porch, peers into the darkness below the deck. She returns inside and finally notices the boots staring at her from beneath the table.

Field training could be a time from another woman's past, as if then she were a painter's wash of who she has become. Her second visit to the hut was at New Year, when she rolled her bike crossing the rift in the fjord. That night the hut offered refuge, a sanctuary she had never wanted to leave. Her body aches with the memory of touch, the pain of her injured leg eclipsed by bodily pleasure so sensual and sweet that now, alone in the room, she is reduced to tears. Afterwards, they had lain entwined, midnight light golden on the walls. She spoke of her girlhood, of images and light, he of timber and boats and his life beside the bay—his trust in her, giving up the sadness of his past, each exchange, every offering, tender and true. They talked until morning, as leisurely as lovers with all their lives ahead.

Dusk deepens to twilight as they fly back towards the station; Venus, the first night light, sits low in the sky.

The rotors wind down, this time to close her season on the ice.

'That's everything.' She thanks the pilot, taking her tripod from the hold and wishing, as she does so, that she could wind back time.

'I'm off to wash my hair before the rush hour,' Elisia shouts, slinging her pack onto her shoulder. Freya watches her stride towards the road.

'With you bevy of beauties on station,' Adam says, 'it's no wonder we're on water rations.'

The echo of the rotors still rings in her ears. Her back and shoulders ache from the weight of her pack.

'Thanks for coming out today, Adam. For all your help.' She feels ashamed of her prejudice against him. Before turning to Adam she had asked two other trip leaders to join her today. Everyone was frantic finishing projects, packing gear inside containers ready for the ship. Adam had put aside all he had to do to accompany her.

'Hey, we're not finished yet. Let's haul this gear upstairs.'

At the landing she pulls open her studio door. 'I'll miss this old rust bucket.'

'You know you've been here too long when you're growing sentimental over a sea container.'

She turns to him. 'Adam, I'm sorry about the start of the season. That you didn't get to come out earlier.'

He holds open the door. 'Ancient history.'

He lays his bags on the floor and slides the pack from Freya's back. 'That's way too heavy, even for an independent woman.'

She stretches and releases the tightness in her shoulders.

'Am I allowed a sneak preview of your exhibition?' he asks.

'I can show you some digitals from our day at Beaver Lake.'

He stands behind her chair, humming as she fires up her laptop.

'Glacier.' She tilts the screen so he can see. 'Here we go. Landing on Beaver Lake. Apple field huts . . . more Apples.' She swivels on her chair. 'You still awake?'

'No chance of losing me.' He squeezes her shoulders.

Freya tenses at his touch. 'Grab a chair, if you like.'

'I'm happy here.'

She opens a new folder of images. 'People photos. Here you are on our walk.'

He leans down, his chin brushing her hair. 'The Devil's Teeth.'

She hears her voice flutter. 'They were remarkable.'

Click.

'Snow petrels.'

Click.

'More snow petrels. My favourite.'

'My favourite, too.' He rests the palms of his hands on her shoulders and presses down. She feels his thumbs knead the flesh around her scapulae.

'Adam.' She murmurs the warning.

'Hush.' He rolls his knuckles along her spine. 'Other women say I should be paid to do this. Two minutes of Adam Singer therapy and you'll feel brand new.'

He massages her shoulders again with both hands. His thumbs work harder through her shirt, the pressure increasing until it edges into pain, the coarse woollen fibre chafing her skin. She winces.

'Too hard?' He eases off.

She shakes her shoulders free and clicks to the next photo. 'Pagodroma Gorge. My husband says that *Pagodroma nivea* is the Latin name for snow petrel.' She's babbling now.

'Those small white birds were a long way from home.' She feels his hand glide under her collar, his fingers slipping beneath her bra strap.

She catches his reflection in the screen. 'Please don't.'

He gives her a wounded, puppy dog look. She shakes her head. But Adam won't stop. He takes the nape of her neck in one hand and crawls the fingers of the other over her scalp. When she tries to squirm free his fingers fasten like a clamp.

She forces her chair back against him and yanks free of his hold. She stands to face him. 'I don't want this,' she says. 'Don't you understand?'

'I understand, alright,' he says. 'Did you put up a struggle when McGonigal fucked you? Is that what you like?'

Freya edges past her desk. The strength of her voice belies her fear. 'I want you to go.' She pushes on the door handle. A wall of cold air rushes in.

She stands in the doorway with one foot on the landing so she is in view of the helicopter team. 'I don't want to make any trouble. I just want you to go.'

'Trouble.' He smirks, reaching for his pack. He raises his knee hard between her legs, pushes into her, his breath warm on her face. 'Your troubles, cunt, have only just begun.'

FANG
PEAK

IS THERE ANYTHING AS DRIVEN as a katabatic wind hell-bent on scouring snow from the icecap, hammering Fang Peak as it rolls downhill from the plateau, and blowing the stuffing out of a work crew who are struggling to patch the field hut's leaky roof? Though Chad positions his weight against the flashing of the roof hatch, squalls from all directions threaten to knock him from his knees and hurtle him on his belly across the blue roof like a tobogganing penguin. *Welcome back to Mawson Station*, the wind might be yelling. *May we take your coat?* Make that peel his coat—whose dodgy zipper Chad has neglected to fasten—up over his head like a spinnaker set to sail him across to Casey Range. Chad drags off a glove and clenches it between his teeth. As he battles with the zipper of his coat he catches Barney's smirk. Barney Foot, fellow chippie and Chad's best mate, rolls his eyes and grins.

It's not even close to dinner time and Chad's worn out, not just from lack of sleep, but from the physical effort of the day:

the weight and restriction of layers he's compelled to wear against a minus-forty windchill, from aching fingers no gloves can keep warm. Most of all he's fed up with this mad dash against time—winter closing in, the *Polar Bird*, his ride to Hobart, due in Horseshoe Harbour any day—to finish repairs to this last field hut in the midst of a gale that refuses to let up. The squeal of the wind pierces his dreams and stalks him through the night until even the otherworld of sleep offers small reprieve. Too late he grabs for a screwdriver that skittles across the roof out of reach. *Welcome back to Mawson, McGonigal. Anyone mention the wind?*

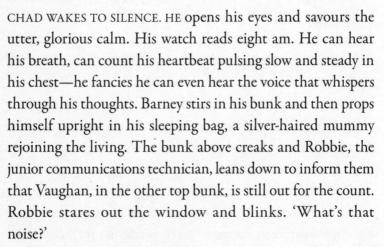

CHAD WAKES TO SILENCE. HE opens his eyes and savours the utter, glorious calm. His watch reads eight am. He can hear his breath, can count his heartbeat pulsing slow and steady in his chest—he fancies he can even hear the voice that whispers through his thoughts. Barney stirs in his bunk and then props himself upright in his sleeping bag, a silver-haired mummy rejoining the living. The bunk above creaks and Robbie, the junior communications technician, leans down to inform them that Vaughan, in the other top bunk, is still out for the count. Robbie stares out the window and blinks. 'What's that noise?'

'That's the sound of silence ringing in your ears.' Barney scratches his balls.

CHAD'S BODY FEELS WEIGHTLESS AFTER days encumbered by windproof layers. He wears overalls and a woollen shirt; thin gloves are all he needs to protect his hands. Chad, Barney and Vaughan, the wintering plumber with a perpetual yawn, finish the roof in the space of the morning. They forgo lunch to help Robbie remount the radio mast and stays that snapped off during winter.

Fang Peak is the last of Mawson's field huts up for repair; by mid-afternoon Barney, coordinator of the summer maintenance program, declares their work complete.

'Barney, think it's worth driving all the way back to station today?' Other than field training, it's Robbie's first time off the station. Who can blame him for wanting the chance to stay out? 'We're not officially due back until tomorrow,' Robbie angles.

'Ask Chad,' Barney says. 'He's the one with a ship to catch.'

'Okay by me,' Chad tells him.

Barney elbows Vaughan whose jaw, agape, snaps shut like a flytrap. 'What d'you say, young fella: first up the mountain?'

All four of them climb up to the saddle of Fang Peak. *A million-dollar view*, Barney says, across to the Masson Ranges, before them Mount Parsons running down towards the coast. For the first time in weeks Chad feels the warmth of the sun radiating through him.

Though Robbie could be easily persuaded, he shows allegiance to Vaughan who won't be talked into climbing to the top, no matter how Barney ribs him about being twice his age and fitter by half again. Finally Vaughan speaks the magic words. 'Carn, Robbie. Let's take the bikes and drive down to the wind scour.' Offer Robbie a quad and he'll follow you to the end of the earth.

'Stay well away from the edge!' Barney barks after them. He turns to Chad. 'Do you suppose that pair have a fully functional brain between them?'

'Nowhere near as cluey as you and I were.'

Chad and Barney rope up at the final section to scramble up the couloir. Fang Peak's tip looks sharp enough to pierce the sky and rises one thousand metres above sea level. Up here the Antarctic air feels noticeably colder. Chad exhales vapour as he levers his body upward through the final cut of rocks.

At the crest he turns in a full circle, absorbing each degree of scenery. He pulls his camera out of his pack to snap mountains that burst through the icecap; rivers of rippled blue ice give way to snow banks, the flow lines of the plateau run steadily downhill to the coast. A real photographer would think herself in paradise up here.

The Mawson hinterland has the most raw and rugged feel of the three continental bases. Beyond the cane line the plateau becomes a crevasse-riven field of ice. Through his binoculars he pans over the blue ice to the east until it gives way to waves of sastrugi that roll on forever. This region has an ominous quality—fiercely beautiful, hostile, unforgiving—you feel it the first time you step off the station, as if it could be warning you, *watch out*.

He and Barney cradle mugs of sugared tea, backs to the sun like a pair of old dogs. The air in Antarctica is so clear that someone might guess it a ten-minute drive from Fang Peak to the coast, yet here they are twenty-six k's inland, alone on top of the world. There's no whisper of yesterday's wind, no calls of birds, no drone of planes winding through the sky. The Casas left Mawson Station weeks ago and by now will have gone from Davis, their summer of field work complete. Davis Station must seem like a ghost town this week, with Freya and the other summerers aboard *Aurora Australis* and on their way home.

Each evening the sun dips down below the horizon minutes earlier than the evening before, a presage of winter closing in. On a clear evening Venus shines through the twilight—give it a few more weeks and the night sky will cascade with stars, auroral lights will sway.

Barney produces a hip flask from his pack and pours a slug of amber liquid into his tea. He passes the flask to Chad. 'Mother's milk.'

Chad runs his finger over the initials inscribed in the stainless steel, a little cartoon foot etched below. 'Maggie give you this?'

'A long time ago now.' He gestures to the ice: 'Thought I'd give it all away after Mags. Yet here we are, my friend, still fools for the place.'

The shimmer of icebergs dipped in golden afternoon light, brings Freya to the surface of Chad's thoughts. The two men sit in silence long past the time it takes to finish their thermos of tea.

'What's on your mind, lad?'

If a person hadn't known Barney Foot for as many years as Chad, they might think him an odd choice of confidant, his manner gruff, questions harsh, a man seemingly as rugged as rock. But on this cold, clear afternoon above the plateau, Chad speaks for the first time of Freya, knowing anything he says will go no further. He speaks to ease the heartache that won't go away on its own, to shift the weight that builds up from keeping things held down too long.

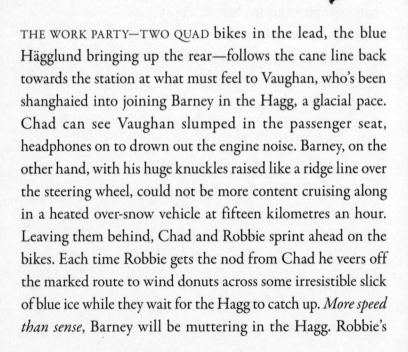

THE WORK PARTY—TWO QUAD bikes in the lead, the blue Hägglund bringing up the rear—follows the cane line back towards the station at what must feel to Vaughan, who's been shanghaied into joining Barney in the Hagg, a glacial pace. Chad can see Vaughan slumped in the passenger seat, headphones on to drown out the engine noise. Barney, on the other hand, with his huge knuckles raised like a ridge line over the steering wheel, could not be more content cruising along in a heated over-snow vehicle at fifteen kilometres an hour. Leaving them behind, Chad and Robbie sprint ahead on the bikes. Each time Robbie gets the nod from Chad he veers off the marked route to wind donuts across some irresistible slick of blue ice while they wait for the Hagg to catch up. *More speed than sense*, Barney will be muttering in the Hagg. Robbie's alright, he's a good guy; his first season down here, been cooped up at the station too long.

Chad sees it first, a kilometre away down the hill: the bronzen sheen of the Russian aircraft wreck glinting in the sun. In the late sixties the DC3 landed on the plateau to refuel. The old colour photos in the yearbook show it readying for takeoff on its way back to the Russian station. One second the plane was taxiing down the skiway, the next a katabatic gust shunted it off course, its starboard ski smashing through the lid of a crevasse and damaging a wing and a propeller. A forlorn crew of Russians escaped unscathed but their plane lay in the ice for the remainder of summer. Finally, the katabatic took charge of the plane one last time and flipped it belly up.

Yet in a slow, quiet way the plane's journey continues. The great dome of ice, two and a half thousand kilometres from pole to coast, three thousand metres thick at its deepest, gradually ferries the wreckage seaward as it inches downhill.

Even with the snow blown away, it's a fluke Chad even spotted the wreckage—apart from a wing, a ski and half an engine—the wreck is buried in ice. He pips his horn to catch Robbie's attention and points out the plane. He doesn't for a moment expect Robbie to interpret his gesture as a signal to bolt down towards the wreckage, which he does at breakneck speed. Chad shouts after him, then blasts his horn. He can see the Hagg approaching, Barney through the windscreen shouting and throwing up his hands.

Chad signals that he'll bring him back.

As he follows warily over the same bumps and ridges that Robbie bounded across, he wants to wring the young guy's neck. Robbie finally slows, sensing something ahead. He brings the bike to a halt and stands tall on the foot braces. Chad swings his bike and brakes to avoid a ridge of névé obscured momentarily by the glare. His quad slides onto a patch of blue ice and he feels the front wheels spin. A sound like shattering glass cuts the air. Robbie turns to look back. But Chad already knows what it means. Too late he knows.

As the snow bridge gives way Chad loses his grip on the handlebars, slides backwards, his limbs flailing as if he were backstroking through sheets of tinted glass. He has time only to register the glow of ice, the surreal hue of the crevasse, before the wind is punched from his lungs by the bulk of a two-hundred-and-fifty-kilogram bike rammed up against him. Time ceases to be linear but curls around itself as the shine of red metal dims. *So this is the end*, Ma says matter of factly—hers is the voice that winds through his head.

He feels the bike's petrol cap grinding into his belly like a biscuit cutter, pictures its scalloped edge imprinting his gut. He shifts his eyes to the left and then to the right; he can't turn his head, the adze of his ice axe digging into his throat. He thinks, though he has no way to be sure, he is wedged vertically, entombed upright (an odd predicament) between the bike and the wall of the crevasse. The seat crushes his chest, the petrol tank presses on his abdomen. He wets himself, hot against his groin; he cannot tell if his legs remain attached. He hears himself pant, thin and shallow like a tired dog. He ought to panic with the effort it takes to move air through his lungs yet he feels little concern. He begins to feel dreamy, neither afraid nor alone.

He remembers Ma trouncing him at Monopoly, and he, retaliating, launching himself across her as she counted out her properties, tickling her relentlessly until she collapsed into her belly laugh. She wasn't fast enough to escape, so she resorted to lying upon him—plastic hotels, paper money, dice and Chance cards falling about—her arms pinning his on either side. He remembers wanting to laugh and not being able to—he could barely breathe beneath her weight. He remembers the smell of lotion on her skin, the trace of coffee on her breath, her hazel eyes so close to his he couldn't focus on them properly. She is here with him now, in the crevasse, trying to pin him down again—him, a grown man. And though her face is as close as it could be, he has no trouble seeing. He can make out the laughter lines radiating from the corners of her eyes, webs of mulberry veins crowning her shiny cheeks. He has not before realised how young Ma is, or how her skin glows. But he wants her to stop, needs her to get up off him and call a truce so he can tell her something he didn't get the chance to say before. He wants her to know how sorry he is that she is gone, that for the longest time he thought the weight of it would crush him. He wants to hold her, cradle her. If he could change things, he tells her, if he could return to Go and collect two hundred, he would take more care pulling the net, would avoid the whip of a stingray's tail as easily as that; she'd have no need to drive to Hobart for a prescription—his legs don't hurt at all.

Ma smiles as he speaks, her gaze full of grace. *Love, it's no one's fault*, is all she says. He can tell, just by her eyes, how much she loves him. She holds out her hand and strokes his hair, over and over until he feels light enough to float away.

Something is winding itself around his neck and he feels Ma must be there, within his reach. It surprises him that she is so much stronger than he, her hands enormous on his back. She pulls him upward, as if he were a child, lifting him in jerks, saying, *I've got you, lad. I have you*, over and over. Ma's voice sounds gruff but not unkind. The layers of tinted glass begin to peel away until all that surrounds him is the palest veil of baby blue. Ma whispers she will have to leave him when they reach the light.

I know, he says, though it hurts to speak and he wishes she could stay.

ERECTED
TO COMMEMORATE
THE SUPREME SACRIFICE
MADE BY
LIEUT. B.E.S. NINNIS, R.F.
AND
DR. X. MERTZ
IN THE
CAUSE OF SCIENCE

A.A.E. 1913

Dearest Dougelly,

The Aurora leaves on Tuesday & I must add a last letter to my little pile. And I do hope it will be the last letter I'll need to write you for a very long while. This separation has been quite long enough. We shall feel almost estranged . . .

We sent you a joint wireless—perhaps you didn't get it? I met Eitel, Hurley and Hunter. I like Hurley. They were very good & I had a private view of the film the Aurora brought back in 1912 when we were away . . .

Dearie I hope you & I are going to be happy. There is so much to discuss before we are married that I can't write in a letter. You understand, don't you, quite, when I repeat that it isn't Paquita of 1911 you're coming back to? I may have changed in ways you won't like but on the whole I don't think so. We are very different in some ways—but that shouldn't prevent our happiness. Its to be 'give and take' on both sides.

I'm longing for your return to put me at rest. It is very difficult not to think of the future. 2½ years is a very long time out of our lives. Oh well 3 months only now. Heaven give that we aren't disappointed in each other. Our wants are different now we are both older. Oh my dear man, come back and reassure me that all will go well with us. I have lost confidence, not in you, but in the future. I want your love again. It has been hard to do without it so long.

I wonder will you return to Hobart or Adelaide. In February the former would be the pleasantest but Adelaide seems the likeliest. Capt. Davis has promised to let me know. It is no good depending on you to. If you had wanted to wire you could have. To answer mine & your brothers wire would not have upset the men down there. However everyone has their own way of thinking.

Mother & I will be waiting for you wherever you return. If we know in time, of course . . .

My dear, dear man. Until February—I love you & the next time I say that it will be in your arms. And will be responded to, I hope. One sided correspondence is the limit.

Your own

Paquita

NORTHWARD
BOUND

THE VOYAGE SOUTH HAD OPENED her eyes to the ice. Now, the passage home—the last of the bergs wound in fog, stretches of pack ice giving way to achromatic sea—reduces Freya's field of vision as if she were looking through a soft-focus lens. On the ship's helicopter deck, she stands with her eyes set astern, looking through a veil of mist, drawing images from her memory. With each increment of latitude they cross, her recollections of Antarctica feather at the edges. Even the sharpness of her final days at Davis Station has receded. It seems foolish, now, to have worked herself into a panic after her trip to Walkabout Rocks and woken Kittie in the middle of the night. As secretive as thieves they had removed from Freya's studio every DVD and canister of film, locking irreplaceable images in Kittie's office for fear they might be tampered with. The echo of Adam Singer's threats still murmurs in her dreams.

Aurora Australis crosses the Convergence, that innocuous blue line winding over the ship's chart to define the boundary of Antarctic waters. Only now does it undulate with meaning, for never has she felt so cast adrift. In the space of a day crisp air dissipates, the atmosphere warms, air turns sultry on her skin. She folds polar layers away, and though it's only nine or ten degrees Celsius outdoors, the dress code around the ship turns summery.

A wandering albatross appears to track their route, weaving over the wake, swooping to pluck some glinting morsel churned to the surface, rising briefly to wheel around the ship. With each monotonous hour of ocean, Freya's thoughts are tugged at and pulled askew. Most of those aboard turn their gaze northward, their anticipation of home palpable, but her eyes stay fixed on the bird. She contemplates the number of days and degrees it will take before the albatross peels away, a sign that the ocean is running out. Other than to breed the wanderer has no cause to turn to land; this body of steely water is its domain.

Freya sleeps during the day and walks the decks at night. So quickly now, evening light fades. As she climbs the outside steps of the ship she sees a faint smattering of stars across the southern sky. Only when she reaches the ship's bridge does she set her sights forward, gaining some comfort from the substantial span of ocean that still buffers her from the prospect of home, from a decision too life-changing to begin explaining to her husband in an email.

Some of the ship's crew are new this voyage but the captain, with the same boyish sweep of hair, remembers her from the trip down and nods as if they've been sailing this ocean together half their lives.

'Down next season?'

'A one-off,' she says, failing to sound bright.

'That's what they all say. Eh, Parksie?' The sailor at the wheel, his face ruddy with acne, blushes in reply.

The captain flicks fair hair from his eyes. 'I signed on for one summer. Same as Parksie. That was eighteen years ago.' He nods at the ocean. 'Once a place gets into you . . .'

❦

AURORA AUSTRALIS DOWNLOADS EMAILS TWICE each day. The communications room swarms with bodies; screens flicker, computers hum, keys click-clack. Three messages wait in her inbox, not one of them, Freya registers, from Marcus.

Dr Ev writes from Davis Station:

>> Now that things have quietened down around here, I've finally found some time to clear the backlog. A while ago you asked about the effects of starvation, why Douglas Mawson survived while Xavier Mertz did not. I can't offer anything conclusive but here are some thoughts to consider. The photos in various publications show Mawson as a tall, wiry fellow. Alongside him, Mertz looks considerably shorter with a stocky build. All things being equal, Mertz should have fared better on starvation rations than Mawson, given their different body types. Mertz, though, found eating the dogs—who he had come to love as pets— repulsive, the meat indigestible. It would have been as tough as old boots given the emaciated state the poor creatures were in. Perhaps when they divvied up the food Mertz ate a larger portion

of softer, more 'palatable' pieces, i.e. the liver. Neither men had any way of knowing then that Greenland dog liver contains toxic quantities of vitamin A. Mawson had a harrowing trek home, hair falling out in clumps, festering boils, skin peeling away. Although he was savvy about nutrition in terms of calories and sledging rations, the effects of vitamins were not understood for another fifty years. He died in 1958 so would never have heard of the debilitating effects of hypervitaminosis A.

I should add a proviso that the vitamin A theory as the cause of Mertz's death has been challenged, with reasonable cause, in recent years. One peer-reviewed article in the MJA calls for a re-evaluation and proposes severe food deprivation as the outstanding contributor. It also suggests that Mertz was affected emotionally after Ninnis's death, and suffered from cold after losing his burberry trousers and helmet to the crevasse. In my view, this last factor plays a big part in the equation. You can appreciate what a dramatic difference the wind in Antarctica makes. Mertz's ability to maintain his core temperature would have been seriously compromised, particularly with an insufficient diet. Mertz was an elite athlete in terms of cross-country skiing and he was an experienced mountain climber, but that didn't necessarily equip him for a 500-km march through snow. Mawson, on the other hand, had proven his abilities on a record 2000-km man-hauling trek during Shackleton's 1907–09 expedition.

Some say Mertz died from exhaustion, that Mawson survived because he simply refused to die. Incidentally, Mawson set out on his trek weighing 95 kilograms and returned to Commonwealth Bay, thirteen weeks later, weighing 51.

Robert Scott's men (1910–13 South Pole Expedition) were likely vitamin C deficient before they even began their race to the pole. During the winter leading up to the trek, in addition to poor food choices, they all smoked like geysers. I remember a radio interview that said Scott's provisions included 35,000 cigars!! (Makes the Davis Station chocolate rations look paltry.)

There's a suggestion that this lack of vitamin C, and also of B-group vitamins and total kilojoules, exacerbated by smoking, contributed to the failure of Scott's group on their return trek from the pole—they died in their tent on the plateau just 11 miles from One Ton Depot.

How does this relate to your question? Mawson also took tobacco and cigarettes to Commonwealth Bay and rationed them out weekly to the men, but he himself was a non-smoker (albeit a passive one with a hutful puffing away). If Mertz smoked—and I believe he did—then a deficiency in vitamin C, on top of a long winter of inactivity, may well have contributed to his demise out on the ice.

In any case, there's more to survival than physical ability. Some people derive extraordinary strength from their belief in a higher power. Then there are the stories you read of Holocaust survivors and prisoners of war, how those who had someone to come home to—a reason to keep living—withstood astounding privation while others around them perished. Mawson was a determined leader, an ardent scientist. I'd hazard a guess that on both counts he was a force to be reckoned with. Perhaps his will, sheer bloody-mindedness, call it what you will, helped get him through.

Best wishes for your exhibition—Ev

Freya prints out the email to file with her list of things to follow up. Already her imagination is off on a tangent—she will travel to Commonwealth Bay, photograph winter quarters, all the polar explorers even start on a larger study of Scott, Shackleton, all the polar explorers from the Heroic Age, and their huts, from Commonwealth Bay south to Cape Royds. She couldn't possibly do the field work on her own.

In the second email, Astrid, ever the big sister, writes to confirm Freya's arrival time in Perth.

>> Prepare yourself. Mama's organising an Antarctic slide presentation and you're the guest speaker. It started out as a book club gathering, now she's talking about hiring the Kalamunda Hall.

Sigh.

Freya's niece, Sophie, has her own news to add.

>> We have a dog! Maximillius (Max to his friends) is an adorable beagle with velvet-soft ears. Some low-life abandoned him at Dad's work. Bestemor says he's as good as her ducted vacuum system because he hoovers up every crumb in sight. Max is waiting to meet and greet you. xxxxooxxxx

>> Astrid again. It's been 40-plus for three days straight (one guess who's been left to walk the hound). I thought we might all have an early barbecue at our place the first evening, if you're not

too tired. I've left several messages with Marcus but he hasn't phoned back.

Freya feels a flutter of homesickness and pictures herself with Astrid and Sophie, the three of them floating in the pool. Sophie would be doing her utmost to entice her grandmother in but Mama would be shaking her head, waving her hands, shooing her granddaughter away—*the weather's too hot*; *the water's too cold*.

Freya scrolls to her last email, from Kittie.

>> Greetings Freya,

How's life on the AA? Here at Davis, we've had our first official blizz—winter's on the way.

The following may be second-hand news by now. If not, I'm truly sorry to be the bearer of crap tidings but you need to know what's been happening around here.

The night before last, Adam Singer called your home in Perth and spoke to your husband. Adam gave some bogus name, claiming he was a friend of yours down here. He apparently talked to your Marcus for ages, chitchatting about the season and Antarctica, buttering him up as only Adam knows how. He eventually went for the jugular, asking was there anything he could do to help because your affair—Adam's words, not mine—with Chad McGonigal had become public knowledge around the station and you'd left on the ship in a very distressed state.

I know, unbelievable.

BTW, the above came from Dr Ev who heard it from our esteemed station leader. Adam didn't count on the fact that your husband would phone Family Support at AntDiv. They were brilliant. The Division sprang into action and traced the call back to Chad's phone PIN, which was a crock because Chad's over at Mawson Station and apparently working out at the field huts. It was like a courtroom here last night, seventeen of us assembled in the dining room presenting our alibis to Malcolm. After the conversation you and I had had about Adam it was obvious who the culprit was and I was all set to have a quiet word in Malcolm's ear. As it turned out Ev beat me to it. She'd gone over to the Green Shed the night in question to organise the chocolate rations and saw Adam going into your studio, which at the time she thought was odd. Then during last night's 'interrogation' Adam dug his own grave by claiming he was out on a walk to Lake Dingle at the time, saying, when Malcolm quizzed him, that he must have forgotten to turn over his tag. The next thing we knew, Adam was hauled into Malcolm's office and read the riot act. Methinks Adam's working days for AntDiv are numbered. Charlie always said he was the one bad egg in the basket.

I'm sorry, Freya. I figured you'd rather hear this now than face things cold when you get home.

Calm seas—xx Kittie

PS Keep in touch. I'm an email away.

Freya sits benumbed, oblivious to the bustle around her, staring past the monitor, through the porthole that reveals a surge of ocean each time the ship rolls. She pictures Marcus answering the phone, responding to the friendly tone in the stranger's voice. She shudders at the stealth of Adam's attack—words honed razor sharp to cut a husband's faith in two. She gauges, by her own anaesthetised shock, the hurt Marcus would have felt as he'd sat alone through the night, reflecting, filling in the blanks from her dwindling emails, replaying her evasive answers to his questions, systematically putting things in place until he pieced together a core of truth from Adam's words.

She rereads Kittie's email and feels a sorrowful kind of pride in her husband for summoning the courage to phone the Division. She pictures them talking over the ugly allegations.

The ship rides up at an angle and runs along the swell. Freya grips the table edge and waits until it levels out. Perhaps strangest, at odds with this wave of protectiveness she feels towards her husband, is the easing of the burden of a lie now that Marcus knows. This is not as she has planned to tell him, yet she feels she has been dragged out from under a tonnage of deceit.

Charlie appears at her side. 'Got a minute?' He directs her along the hallway to the empty dining room. 'Quieter in here.' He sits down beside her and slips his reading glasses into the case clipped to his pocket. 'I've had an email from the radio officer at Mawson Station. Scally's an old mate. He told me something on the quiet—it concerns a friend of yours and I think you ought to know.'

She raises an eyebrow at how quickly gossip spreads in Antarctica. 'You're ten minutes too late, Charlie. I already heard from Kittie.'

'Kittie?'

She reminds herself Charlie is only being kind. 'Kittie told me what's been happening. Adam Singer; the phone call.'

Light from the porthole filters through his faded eyes. When he shakes his head Charlie seems older than his years. 'Love, this has nothing to do with Adam. There was a prang over at Mawson Station. Up on the plateau.' His eyes comb her face. 'Chad McGonigal and his bike went into a crevasse.'

❧

THE TALK ON THE SHIP is of *Aurora* turning around, a dash to Mawson Station to bring Chad home. No, the captain shakes his head. The scheduled vessel, *Polar Bird*, is only eighty nautical miles away from the station. Already her ship's doctor has flown in by helicopter to assist the doctor at the base.

An official release from the Division is pinned to the dining room's notice board. *Fell fifteen metres into the crevasse . . . evacuated to the station . . . acute injuries . . . emergency surgery.* Freya closes her eyes to see an image of two doctors heading a surgical team comprising plumbers, chippies, sparkies, diesos.

Over the next days news trickles in from Kittie. But the most detailed accounts originate from Scally, Charlie's radio mate at Mawson Station. The list of injuries alone is more than she can stand to hear. *Compression fracture of the lumbar spine vertebrae, fractured pelvis, broken ribs, abdominal tearing, internal bleeding*, and on it goes.

She paces the decks, climbs to the bridge, is unable to settle and returns outside to start all over again. The wandering albatross still follows in their wake.

THE INMARSAT SYSTEM IS DOWN and no emails reach the ship. Freya's mind races with panicked speculations. She overhears the two women who work in the galley. The fair-haired woman stacks plates onto the racks. *Spinal injury is what he told me.*

The Portsmouth woman sighs. *Words to chill a mother's heart, dear.*

Aurora's doctor registers the tremor in Freya's voice and sits down beside her.

'Of course any spinal injury is serious,' he says gently, 'but it doesn't automatically mean damage to the spinal cord. From what we know, your friend has a stable fracture that can likely be treated with a brace and physiotherapy. The concern, as I see it, is the extent of the mesenteric tearing, any other abdominal injuries, and whether they can stabilise him and stop the bleeding.' He pats Freya's arm. 'We have to hope, send him our prayers.'

'A BLIZZARD,' CHARLIE TELLS HER. '*Polar Bird* has boarded the summerers going home and headed out from the coast to ride it out.'

'How long will the ship wait for him?' Freya asks the captain.

'Depends on weather and ice. Her captain will have the final say. *Polar Bird*'s been out half the season doing oceanographic surveys. She must be low on juice.'

Freya returns each evening to the bridge, guided through the darkness by the scarlet glow of instruments. She stands at the corner window where she can see both forward and aft. The captain joins her and points astern. 'See there, low in the sky, this side of the Southern Cross? Barely a whisper, but it's there.' Freya has to concentrate, search until her eyes accommodate the night, until she too can see the faint auroral glow.

She climbs the outside steps to the flying bridge. She leans against the railing, the midnight sky a swathe of stars. Within the hour, others join her to watch the sky stretch into life.

The aurora begins as nebulous bands of mist and brightens to vertical folds coloured emerald green through to aquamarine. For a time the lights hang motionless, as a drape, the intensity greatest along the lower edge where it glows lucent and iridescent, more vivid than the stars. Filaments of quartz pink rise from the upper folds into streamers that fray at the ends before fading to darkness above. The sky begins to pulse. All who watch are stilled to reverent silence, following the celestial array as it waxes and wanes in its dance across the heavens.

To be certain of her bearings Freya locates the Southern Cross and its pointers. She conjures all she has to give, collecting everything inside her that can mend and heal and soothe and sends it as a prayer, deep into the aurora and across the southern sky.

'THAT'S NOT THE BIGGEST ISSUE anymore.' Charlie holds court before the early risers. 'They're saying Chad's stable enough to be moved if they can only get the ship back in.' Gesturing to Freya to pull up a chair, he bites off a corner of Vegemite toast and continues. 'The *Polar Bird* went out to sea to escape the worst of the weather. The current problem is she's been trying to get back into Mawson for three days—she's stuck in heavy pack-ice sixty k's out. Scally says they've had both engines chewing through juice like there's no tomorrow—she doesn't have the grunt of the *Aurora*. They've had one hell of a battle getting in that far. The ice is causing them no end of grief and now with this new blow, there's the risk the ice will hem them in.'

'Causing *them* grief,' says one of the field assistants loading his spoon with rice bubbles. 'What about our guy half dead waiting for an ambulance ride home? Why can't they send the choppers in to pick him up?'

Charlie scoffs. 'Mate, it's blowing eighty knots off the plateau. The katabatics haven't let up for days.'

'It's simple triage,' puts in Ian. Even Charlie leans in to hear the physicist's softly spoken words. 'The ship is in a vulnerable position and low on fuel, thirty other expeditioners need to get home, and some level of confidence—or resignation—has been reached that the chappie with the injuries should be left to take his chances.'

Freya closes her eyes. 'What does it mean, Charlie?'

'It means a second winter, love. It means he's there to stay.'

THE MORNING OCEAN IS ALL sapphire curves and silver tips. Freya sits on the deck in the shelter of the hangar, the sun warming her legs. *Aurora* rides the waves of a running sea— each surge lifts and propels the ship forward.

She holds a pen, a pad of paper propped upon her knee. Give her a camera and Freya can show you what she feels, but she has always laboured with the imagery of words. She chooses this way knowing it is arduous, understanding as she writes that, once posted, the letter will not begin its journey south until the spring, eight months from now. A circuitous mode, when a message can be emailed with a click. But for all her letter's poorly turned phrases and flawed expressions, she likes to think a residue of Freya will remain through the slant of the cursive, the loose-knit whorls. She rereads her sentences, pausing over words that comfort, that affirm her deepest feelings. The ship's hull rises with a rush, hinging, momentarily, on the shoulders of the sea. She braces as *Aurora* begins its downward slide, gathering speed to skitter down a wave. She returns to the page, deliberating how to finish, looking for words that state her intentions, but cast neither obligation nor regret, nor place promise, upon the expression of a wish. She scans the ocean, looks towards the sky, searches the blue; her wanderer has gone.

Antarctic Ocean
26 December 1913

True One—

What a lovely time I have had reading your letters over and over.

It has not been unalloyed pleasure, for though the joy bells have been ringing through my head in admiration of you, there has been an undercurrent of anguish—that dull pain in the heart, a constraint upon its free beating—for the anxiety I have caused you.

Believe me, Paquita, I would not willingly have caused you any of it—but my Antarctic plans were laid before you and I were blended, and then under those circumstances it appeared to me right to go straight ahead . . .

My very dear Girl, my winter letters will explain the absence of more wireless news. Nobody seems to have understood our difficulties.

Darling I thought that you had at least one letter from me by the Aurora of March 1913, else would I have endeavoured to send you a few more words by wireless. Before sledging I wrote several letters including one to yourself and one to my Brother. These were written with the idea of delivery in case of my non-return . . . Well, Capt. Davis took the box off with the letters and they were all delivered but mine. I now find them still in the box undelivered . . .

Now Dearest all else can remain till we meet except perhaps a few references to your letters. Here goes.

'Did my love help you then' My love for you and duty to you was the real insentive which finally availed my reaching the hut—so far it helped—I shall never regret the struggle through which it dragged me.

'So young and silly. How could you love me?' Perhaps there were a few things that I wondered at, but if they were part of a large and true heart such as I knew yours to be, I was amply satisfied . . . Rather should I beg your forgiveness for my thoughtlessness and shortcomings.

'Wireless messages . . . unsatisfactory, want a letter.' I could never have given you my heart's feelings by wireless. Had I really been incapacitated to be your Husband, I should not have reached the Hut. My love you had to trust—that you need never fear for unless miracles happen to yourself. Always trust me. Will you? I believe I begin to see how you have changed—I felt that any change would be so . . .

'You won't go again, will you?' No dearest, nothing like this will happen again—rest assured.

No! I am not frozen in heart you may be sure, this is where the warm hearts are bred . . .

Believe me Paquita. I have never at any time loved anybody as I love you. Never had it entered my head before I met you to wed anybody. This is perhaps one reason why I love you so much.

Your 3rd letter tells of a visit to the ship. You are quite right, Davis is inclined to be pessimistic . . .

'Everlasting silence' indeed it has been unbearable. I do miss you dreadfully but would not have you here for all that life holds. It is my love that wishes you not here . . .

'Only 3 or 4 wires.' You should have had that letter and, besides the wires referred to, many assurances of our being 'all well' from various quarters intimated at the end of business telegrams. I would not have been 'all well' had my love for my Darling wavered even the least bit. Perhaps they did not tell you—Eitel and David are both very remiss. Oh; I cannot talk further about the horrid wireless—wait till we meet . . .

'Dearie I hope you and I are going to be happy'. My Darling, it lies with You—Can you be happy with me. I have aged in appearance with this strain and may not appeal to you now. My body tissues have been strained and cannot be so good. But at heart I am just the same though perhaps more impressed with your qualities. Size me up critically, and don't let us get married unless after reflection you feel nothing but attraction and an abandonment to my desire just as I feel to yours. This is so important for after marriage the merest indications of splits are apt to widen to become fissures and crevasses in which all hopes of married bliss are dashed to pieces . . .

The joint wire from yourself and Will never came. There has been scarce a message through since early October on account of daylight interference on top of all other troubles . . .

The first time I read these letters, I rushed through proud for news. The second time I don't know why but I shivered & all the blood seemed to go to my heart in one great whirling eddy. Your love made me shiver.

I must turn in now and just wait and long for our meeting. Perhaps better not on the ship—really better not until I have a wash. My domestic life has been very miserable now for 2 years and I long for a clean up—ordinary clothes and a good bed— above all a carefree sleep—not dozing with one eye open as it has been for so long. Nay much better still a sleep in your arms my Love.

Douglas

*A radiant turret, lit by the
midsummer midnight sun*

THE
BAY

AFTER TWO YEARS OF NEGLECT, the bush has taken hold of Chad's shack at the bay. Bracken lines the gravel driveway. Overgrown branches grate against weathered boards. The water tanks are camouflaged beneath a crust of tinder-dry needles of she-oak. Even the gutters of the boatshed and workshop are jammed with leaf debris untouched so long it has composted to mulch.

Chad pours soapy water into a nest that has taken over the honeycombed cement of the back steps. Wasps bubble and seethe, filling the air and sending him running for cover.

Lines of sugar ants march along the worn railing of the front verandah and down the wooden joists to a damp bed of moss beneath the tank stands. A film of salt coats the windows. Inside and out, cobwebs droop like hanks of yarn. Chad drags at the threads with a broom, conscious of a residual weakness in his back and arms. The remains of huntsman spiders, desiccated things as weightless as tissue, litter the floorboards beneath the sills. He thinks of the morning's grim discovery, the remains of a pygmy possum unwittingly trapped in the boat shed when he locked up the place so long ago to leave for the ice.

It takes all day to air the shack and sweep and rake and clean, and though he's hungering for a meal and could knock back an ale without persuasion, he treads the road through the dimness of dusk to take a look around. Light in the western sky hangs by a thread of magenta; wind whistles through the tops of gums. Soon summer will be here, but seasons in Tasmania are capricious and bring a shiver to the air any time they please. The bush edging the road forms a canopy of kunzea and tea-tree whose branches hang heavy and pungent with petals of white. He snaps off leafy sprigs and returns to the shack, filling vases and jars with the heady scent.

The knock at the door startles him. The November long-weekenders have headed back to town and won't return until December holidays begin. Only a handful of residents— retirees, arty types—stay on through the quieter months. Roma Buckle, his neighbour from the other side of the bay, stands stooped at the door cradling a plate of flathead fillets.

'Saw the lights on,' Roma says in her offhand way, as if arriving home twelve months late is neither here nor there. She hands him the fish and gives him a once-over. 'Looks like you could do with a jolly good feed.'

When Chad asks her in she brushes him off. 'Can't stay, Chadwick. Jim'll be twiddling his thumbs if I'm not back in time for *Millionaire*.'

Chad studies Roma's gait as she totters up the driveway, her bad hip and the sou'westerly causing her to list and meander like a rudderless vessel. Perhaps with his injuries he walks the same. 'It's good to see you,' he calls after her. Roma and her husband Jim are the only ones who call him by his christened name—possibly the only ones left, barring the old man, who've known him long enough to remember the wretched thing. After Ma died, the Buckles kept an eye on the shack for several years, stopped it falling into disrepair, until Chad was old enough to drive a car and come back on his own. Roma reaches the road and turns, huddling inside her duffle coat. She seems smaller, frailer than he remembers. Yet: 'It's blowing straight off the ice,' she yells at a pitch that could waken the dead.

These first days back remind him it takes more than physical travel to coax mind and body home. He stands beneath the kitchen light looking over Davis Station photos taken last summer, the prints developed only this week after he returned to Hobart on the ship. He lingers on the image of Freya kneeling on the ice, jubilant, eye to eye with an emperor penguin. He studies a handful of prints from Mawson Station, a photo of himself that Barney Foot took at the summit of Fang Peak the day before Chad's world collapsed. Chad sees how, in the space of nine months, his face has changed, aged in ways not governed by time. He runs a finger across his throat, feels the knotted scar left by the blade of his ice axe. He has reduced sensation in one leg and walks with a ponderous step. Cheloid scars from the surgery are hidden by his clothes.

Deeper scars from the crevasse are there beneath his skin— marks fretted and raw that still pick at his dreams. He packs away the photos, resolving not to dwell on them again.

Chad sets a match to bone dry kindling laid in the fireplace two years ago. The sticks flare with a whoosh, an explosion of crackers spitting sparks against the screen. He kneels on the hearth, logs crackling, flames licking the chimney, warmth radiating through the room.

TEESHIRT AND SUNNIES FOR THE drive down to Hobart in December, his list as long as his empty trailer. For years he has mulled over changes he wants to make to the shack. During his winter of recovery at Mawson Station he sketched diagrams, talking through the renovations with Barney Foot, as if it really were a plan.

He questions why it's taken him this long.

'Change,' he utters as he motors down the highway; the fear of change has stopped him all these years. Fear that has resided within him so long now it's turned into a great stagnant dam holding him to the past in want of something that can never be regained. Now, after hanging onto life by a thread, he refuses to let the rest of it slip by.

Shooting through on the sly had been the old man's fucked-up way of relinquishing the past and moving on. Thinking back, it had begun when the two of them left the shack without locking up, the news of Ma still unconfirmed. *Get in the bloody ute, Chad. The place can go to blazes for all I care.* Returning shell-shocked from the memorial service to their family home in Hobart, to a year of going through the motions without Ma, sandwiches to fill, school shoes to clean, a bath before bed and don't forget the soap. Dad would grip him by the shoulders so hard it hurt but still he couldn't speak Ma's name and would not meet his father's eyes, when each morning as he left the house for school, and each afternoon as he walked home, and through the sunroom windows and from the kitchen porch stood the bridge, the guts of it gone, the great gulping chasm at its centre mirroring the collapse of the McGonigal home.

Dropped off at Nan and Pop's to watch Greg Chappell bat against the Windies on their new colour TV. *Australia by 165 runs, you bewdy!* Then Nan at the sink, all flushed and teary, pulling him into her apron. Her tears, this time, were not just for a lost daughter. It was all prearranged. She'd been crying for him.

Pop's voice from the doorway, *You'll be staying on with Nan and me for a spell*; Chad's confusion subsiding to relief then anger at his father.

BARNEY FOOT AND LACHLAN, HIS youngest, drive down after New Year, Barney's FJ ute brandishing P-plates, his tray and trailer laden with sheets of roofing iron. Despite Chad's protests that he's strong enough to help, Lachlan and Barney move the fridge and stove and all the heavy furniture to the boat shed where the three set up camp. *Our own little field hut*, Barney coos before turning in.

Chad sands thick and weary layers of history from oak floorboards while Barney and Lachlan extend the line of the roof, doubling the size of the two front rooms. They replace old sash windows and the patio door with new custom-built jobs. The Glass Ballroom, Barney names the living room, whistling at the fancy bi-fold doors.

By the end of January, after two more runs to town, they have laid the foundations for a grand new Oregon pine deck. Even with nothing but the frame in place, Chad can stand on a ladder at the corner post and see beyond the point.

Barney's ute, with Lachlan at the wheel, chugs up the drive loaded with shack furniture tired when even he was a boy, destined for the Campbell Town tip—*better known*, Lachlan says, *as Dad's Shed*. Chad waits on the road until the ute drives out of sight; until he hears the toot of the horn at the turnoff and knows they're on their way.

He returns to his house of oak and glass, a man with a beginning who can see far across the bay.

ON HIS FINAL RUN TO town in March, he parks down near Constitution Dock. Thirty minutes is all the time it takes to swagger out of the optics store the owner of a flash new pair of binoculars. Not your everyday lenses: these are top of the range.

He sits on a bench beside the river with his cheese and salad sandwich. He slides the binoculars from their felt-lined case and sets them on his knees, then picks them up and pans along the opposite shore, marvelling at the clarity of vision. His thoughts return to an image of the winter left behind.

After the surgery at Mawson Station a drip hung beside his bed pumping fluid through his veins. A nasogastric tube drew sludge from his stomach, a catheter line curled over the edge of the bed, the drain from his wound ran as relentlessly as his pain. Hell was not a chasm of icy blue but the weeks that followed his accident, trapped in a world that began and finished at the edge of his bed. It took all his will and the extraordinary care of those around him—it chokes him still to think of it—to continue breathing in and out. When it seemed a miraculous feat to shuffle to the bathroom, half-carried by two bearded nurses in Carhartts, Chad was beyond caring that his reflection showed a man with sallow skin whose gaunt face he barely recognised. Winter's darkness passed before he gained the psychological stamina to revisit the site of the crevasse—first in his mind, and then, when he was strong enough to leave the station, with Barney. Even still, so much remains a dream.

He turns his new binoculars this way and that, holds them up one more time to feel their weight in his hands. He wipes the lenses with the silky cloth before replacing the caps and packing his treasure away. He declares such extravagance a blessing of life.

THE EASTER THRONG HITS THE bay and with it comes a run of sun-kissed days. He listens to splashes and squeals from kids on the beach, takes in the aromatic smoke from a neighbouring barbecue, gives silent thanks at the close of the day when the whining of a chainsaw splutters into silence.

He mulls over his father's once-cherished transistor radio, doubtful it will be fixable; it has no material value—the ivory bakelite discoloured and cracked, the aerial hanging by a steel thread. When he arrived at the tip this morning, he set the wireless aside from the pile of junk, thinking a collector might see it there and take it home. He drove out through the exit and then did a U-turn and drove back through the entry again, peevishly hauling the wireless into the car. *Someday your father might call and want it back*, Ma's voice still visits him. Someday pigs will fly.

It's six-thirty and almost dark when he watches the last shivering kid, wrapped in a beach towel, scamper up the track that leads from the beach. Chad stands on his new pine deck with a mug of tea warming his hands. The big room remains unfurnished except for a pair of easy chairs and a blackwood dining set crafted long ago by Pop. He's grown used to the lack of clutter in the room. Lamplight spreads a honeyed glow across the boards and freshly painted walls. Beyond the point, Jim Buckle's old Seagull outboard whirrs like an eggbeater wending him home. The time is nearing for Chad to return his attention to building boats. He looks to the northern sky and counts the seconds before the cape lighthouse winds its beam out across the ocean, its faraway glow a ghostly echo behind the hills.

He unpacks milk, bread and the paper from the co-op and sorts through his mail. He lays aside bills and magazines and then pauses at the sight of the package wrapped in plain brown paper, postmarked Melbourne GPO.

Chad guesses the contents before he has the wrapping peeled away. He moves to an easy chair and sits beneath the lamp to study the catalogue from Freya's exhibition.

THE NATURE OF ICE
—IMAGES OF ANTARCTICA—
BY FRANK HURLEY AND FREYA JORGENSEN
EDITED BY MARCUS FITCH

Chad rubs at the knotted scar on his throat.

The front cover features a turreted iceberg tinted in blues, soft around the edges like a dream. He turns the book over to an image of the plateau on the back cover, a glorious thing with scurries of drift curling into sky, the ice alive with crystals of garnet light. Inside it is a full-page photograph of Hurley's. He's seen it before, but never as now—a man entombed in an ice cavern, wound in light, in the foreground a canopy of ice waiting to collapse. A glimpse, a memory, a flash of blue from the crevasse shudders down his spine. A post-it note falls from the pages and flutters to the floor. For a moment Chad ceases to breathe; his heart loose in his chest, he pins the note with his finger.

Break a leg—Charlie.

A wry smile to Charlie boy; the last glimmer of hope snuffed out.

Freya's colour images sit opposite Frank Hurley's black and whites: a weddell seal basking in sun, the hurly-burly of the adélie rookery, Antarctic light streaming over sea ice; each of them delivering a wave of nostalgia.

Chad pores over the section of her portraits that unfolds like a family album: Elisia welding, Malcolm in the laundry, a towel draped around his shoulders, directing proceedings while being given a crew cut. Charlie sits in the radio room frowning over the top of his specs as he does when deciphering the garble of an HF radio call from hundreds of kilometres away. A team of limnologists stand in a circle on Crooked Lake, the jiffy drill as tall as the woman who cores the ice. There're two scientists down on the sea ice working at the tide gauge, Kittie at the met building sending up the weather balloon. Chad turns the page to see himself in the demisted cab of the bulldozer, crooning some song the day he met Freya and nearly wiped her out. The D8's blade is so close he can practically count the crystals in the ice it holds.

The series titled 'Summer Auroras' catches his eye. He distinguishes the blues of the bergs and the white of sea ice, but travelling across the frozen mass—even through it, it seems—are streamers of colour so vibrant they dazzle him. He is about to turn the page when he recognises a shade of green as that of the groundsheet that billowed behind his bike the day they drove to Zolatov Island. The impression the photo creates is truly that of a brilliant green aurora, alive as it dances through the sunlit ice. The groundsheet has turned into a luminescent cloak swirled across the ice, and through it runs the wheel of his bike—only here it appears as a corona, its steel hub a body of silver surrounded by an aureole of black. The green folds onto itself just as an aurora might drape across a darkened winter sky. Within the folds he deciphers other tinges of colour as the duco red of his bike, the yellow of the quad's kitbag.

He turns the page to reveal ridges of cerulean that dissolve into light, dips and rises of turquoise. He sees an orange sleeping roll unfurled in an arc.

Freya had become gripped with the notion that the southern and northern lights occur concurrently. When the aurora borealis dances vivid in the dark of an Arctic winter sky, the aurora australis, at the identical moment, sways in rhythm unseen across Antarctica's sunlit sky. *A summer aurora*; she held her arms to the sky, her polarised glasses mirroring the glare of the sun. *Just imagine if we could see the colour of its light.* Here she has created it, a summer aurora cavorting and swaying, waxing and waning.

Though he has always considered photographs still and quiet things, before Chad are images alive, pictures in motion, swirling shapes, liquid light. He will always picture Freya behind her camera, physically distanced from her subject yet an integral part of it, the same connection he feels to the ice no matter where he is. Through these images the essence of the artist shines, Chad feels it like the presence of a ghost, her aura luminescing through the glow.

IT'S LONG PAST HIS BEDTIME when he puts up the fire screen and flicks off the lamp. From his closet shelf he takes down a storage box labelled ANTARCTICA IX–X. Inside it are two journals and an envelope crammed with medical reports, as well as the rolled-up portrait of Freya he pilfered from her studio. For all his gall in claiming it, the photo was never his to display; now he unrolls it one more time to study her face.

Afterwards, he takes from the box a letter delivered to him at Mawson Station by the ship that finally brought him home. He traces a finger across impressions in the paper. Words a winter old before they reached him, relinquished, surely, even before he read them. The letter has aged, the folded pages limp and fragile from touch. He knows the words by heart but still they overwhelm him, the closing lines reopening a wound of want. He slides the letter between two pages of the catalogue and packs it in the box.

A mopoke owl hoots across the creek gully. Another *mopokes* back. From his bed he can look through the silhouette of branches and see Orion. Tonight the southern sky is a starry vault stretched to the edges of the hemisphere. So many things intervene. Truly, he thinks, for all our desire and ambition, lives mapped out, pledges made, in the end we live from day to day, as fragile as twigs, needing to be loved, urged on by hope and acts of kindness.

Returning from the edge of the world
February 1914

AFTERNOON HEAT SHIMMERED OFF THE pavement. Douglas
moved along Adelaide's North Terrace, his senses full of the
city air, an orchestra of passing conversations. His attention
was seized by the spotless white of men's shirt sleeves, by the
wonder of lightweight skirts and dainty linen blouses. He
was mesmerised by trills of laughter beneath coloured
parasols and wide-brimmed hats. He was a man returning
from the edge of the world, taking new steps upon a
civilised land. All that kept him grounded in the surreal
lightness of being here was his herringbone jacket,
outmoded and too heavy for a summer's day; inside his
pockets were fifteen letters written to Paquita during his
second year at winter quarters, and his sketches for a home.

A store window decorated with millinery. The clatter of
a tram.

He turned into the South Australian Hotel where
he found his luck had been too good to hold. Cries of

Dr Mawson! escalated, footsteps sharp as tacks across the tiled foyer.

He agreed with the first newspaper man that a second enforced year had been a trying time indeed, not for him alone but for all six of his fine comrades who had stayed at the hut and tended him—and not forgetting too the pain of the unexpected delay for the dear ones at home.

Captain Davis's actions had his full support, he told the second reporter. On top of which, Davis's decision to relieve Frank Wild's western party instead of his own had possibly saved Douglas's life. In hindsight, he doubted he would have survived the voyage home a year ago.

An undeniable success! The sledging parties had opened up large areas along the coast and obtained magnetic data inland to the vicinity of the south magnetic pole. During the second year a new wireless operator had added to Mr Hannam's pioneering work of 1912 by conducting regular telegraphic communications between Antarctica and Australia.

Yes, with great sadness he had relayed wireless messages from Commonwealth Bay to the people of Lieutenant Ninnis and Dr Mertz. He would be visiting the families in London and Basel later in the year. He feared the meaning of Scott's non-return from the pole—he had come so close to death himself.

It had been a blow to return to the hut and learn the news that his father had passed away. (He would tell no one but Paquita of the night, in a tent on the plateau, that his father had appeared before him in a dream.)

Indeed it was grand to be home. Why, he planned to see Miss Delprat as soon as was humanly possible. He hoped, nodding at the wall clock, she might forgive him for arriving for their appointment twelve months late.

He threw a pleading eye to the man in hotel uniform who obliged by crossing the tiles to shepherd the newsmen away.

Douglas scaled the guest stairs two at a time, pausing at the landing to reply to a last opportunistic question pitched up to him. *No fear!* he cried back to the reporter. Dr Mawson would not be returning to the ice.

THE PULSING IN HIS CHEST engulfed his body in the seconds between knocking and waiting for the door to open. It was not Paquita but her mother, Henrietta, who welcomed him with a hug, crying, *Dear, dear boy* and gesturing with a sniff and her handkerchief towards the sitting room doors.

The image of the girl he'd left so long ago now blended with the woman edged in light at the window, taller than he remembered in her frock of ribbon and lace. He chose to ignore the flicker of shock that Paquita blinked away as she traced his haggard body with her eyes.

Words momentarily failed him. He felt at risk of breaking down.

'You have had a long time to wait,' he whispered, not trusting his voice to deliver more words. Paquita slowly nodded.

He reached inside his jacket; his fingers turned to butter, letters and his house plans slipping to the floor.

Then Paquita stepped towards him with open arms, drawing him to her with the strength of her smile. He closed his eyes to the press of her body and the gentle folds of home.

Frank Hurley

A NEW WAY
OF SEEING

FREYA RISES WITH THE LIGHT. The trail, once a railway line linking the Darling Scarp to Perth, leads her through bushland chill with shadow; it's too early in the day for June's winter sun to warm the face of the escarpment. These morning walks through the bush, beyond earshot of the drone of commuters pouring westward to the city, away from the hisses and groans of road trains lumbering up Great Eastern Highway, clear Freya's head and resurrect a world beyond the acrid turmoil at home.

Freya leaves the trail and scrambles uphill through bush. She reaches her favourite outcrop of granite that looks across the tops of jarrah and marri, down through a sweeping valley to the Swan Coastal Plain. She turns an ear to the rush of a distant waterfall revived by winter rain. The first gleam of sunlight touches her back and silvers the brook snaking through grass trees and scrub. She sits for a time, drinking in the view. She will miss these things, will crave them, even.

Freya doubles back to the opening of the abandoned railway tunnel, where a kookaburra peers down at her between the branches of a tree.

The date carved into a limestone block reads 1895. She has entered this masoned archway only once before, Marcus gripping her hand in his, rallying her through the eight-hundred-metre-long enclosure. Now Freya walks once more through the blackness, the frigid tunnel closing around her in a press of lifeless air. Water drips and echoes. Her boot catches an aluminium can and sends it rattling over stone. For a moment she thinks to turn and run but when she looks back towards the entry, the daylight beyond is no longer defined by an arch of stone. She has come so far that the blackened lens of tunnel has reduced the light in the distance to a pinhole, to an aperture closed down.

MUSIC FROM THE FAR END of the house belies the dissonance.

Freya spends the morning reclaiming her shambles of a studio, filing remnants from the photographic exhibition, archiving the last of negatives and proof sheets. She is thankful, now, for her husband's insistence (ultimatum, her sister called it): *We will finish what we began, Freya.* She owed him that and more. She, in turn, has behaved above reproach, has, for longer than the agreed-upon trial—*if you still want to go after the exhibition I won't stand in your way*—dutifully played out the futile charade.

She spreads an armful of proof sheets and prints across the work bench—ocean and icebergs, shots around the station, a man's black and white portrait she refused to destroy.

When she studies her photographs of Davis Station, she can see that the spirit of community is as vibrant now as it was in Douglas Mawson's day. The portrait she has of Frank Hurley, dressed in full sledging gear, reminds her that though aircraft and vehicles have replaced sledges and dogs, the terrain they cross is a layer of the same. She has learned from her summer on the ice, that for every hero of the past, another waited at home for their return. And for her own small part, through some gradual, curious process that has you absorb a place until it forms a part of you, Freya has been vested with a new way of seeing. Her concept of Antarctica began with Hurley's black and white images from a century ago. Her vision now flourishes with colour, and will forever hold an image of two people upon a limitless expanse of ice. Truth and understanding, she sees, perhaps a glimpse of love, can be found in frozen places.

Freya sorts through proofs of a broken red skidoo retrieved from a crevasse on the Amery Ice Shelf and flown back to Davis Station for repair. She hears the garage door, sees Marcus make his way towards her studio with a satchel of papers, his head down. She won't let his heartache undo her. *No, Marcus*; without hesitation she turned down his offer that they start a family—*begin again*—a forlorn and desperate plea. Freya knows now that some things can't be fixed, no matter how you try.

WINTER
SOLSTICE

DAWN. THE JUNE SUN PALE and low. The water is a shimmer of glass, broken only by a pair of wooden blades that form coronas of bubbles as they dip and rise. The oars are evenly weighted in his hands. On this, the winter solstice, the sounds are of the bay, nothing more. Chad listens to the cry of gulls, glides over baubles of kelp, hears the gurgle of water beneath the newly varnished planks. He nods to the silver-haired lady in tartan pants who stands at the end of the new timber pontoon that has replaced the crumbling granite breakwater, for years the bay's single eyesore. Each morning at this hour she does a sprightly walk to the rocks, on to the pontoon, then returns along the beach to her easel and paints to catch the light. What began a few days ago as an insipid wash and a few wavy lines, this morning, when he wandered over to say hello and take a look, captures refractions of winter light thrown across the bay.

Jim Buckle's boat is hauled high up on the beach, tethered to the hub of an old tractor wheel. Come winter the Buckles, and others of their ilk, leave the bay to escape the cold. Revived by Queensland sun, the pair will stay north until Roma can be convinced that spring has thawed the last skerrick of frost from this small southerly isle.

When Chad pulls on an oar to veer the boat down the bay he feels the morning sun touch his face. Through the trees he can see the oiled wood of his deck, now completed. He's been home eight months. He passes the old dead gum where this time each year a pair of white-bellied sea eagles adds new scaffolding to their nest of sticks. Time feels as steady and smooth as the stroke of an oar.

The water at the stern flashes between aquamarine and cobalt blue when a mollymawk crisscrosses the sun. The big bird trails his wake as Chad makes his way past the quarry; it quickly learns the pattern of a man's day, discovering the treasures a net can hold.

Chad rests his feet against the wooden foothold repositioned to suit his height. He's as happy as Larry with the new lease of life he's given his grandfather's old dinghy. He spent the last month—time he should have put into a shamefully long-overdue delivery—restoring the wood: sanding back timber and planking the floor with new King Billy pine. He honed smaller handles from the original Huon pine oars he'd watched his grandfather turn before Chad was old enough to use the lathe on his own. If Pop were here now he'd run the flat of his hand along the planks to judge the kind of varnishing job the kid has given her. He'd not find too much to tut-tut about; the waterproof skin of the dinghy gleams.

Chad rolls up his sleeves and reaches down beside the dinghy to retrieve the wooden buoy. The mollymawk skims the water, tucks its wings in close, bobbing a respectful distance away. Man and bird peer down through the water at the glint of silver held fast in the mesh. Chad frees the remnants of a parrotfish and throws it well away. The mollymawk, in a flutter of wings and gangling legs, squawks across the surface and stakes its claim before any marauder dares approach. Chad pulls in fistfuls of netting, and with it a trevally and two good-sized trumpeter, the last struggling to shake free of his hold in a shower of glassy scales.

HE RACES AGAINST HIS BEST time home, working his arms and upper body, stretching and flexing his back. When he rounds the point to the bay he lets the dinghy drift, regaining his breath, absorbing the sun, water burbling beneath the keel. He can see the artist on the beach in conversation with a second woman.

Chad rows leisurely across the deeper water towards the pontoon. At the shoreline the figure of the new arrival treads across the sand, keeping step with the pace of his oars. Her movement seems distinctive and for a moment his breath stops, but when she takes off her hat he can see her hair is darker, that she wears it cropped, that this woman in jeans is slighter than the one who lives in his thoughts.

He hooks the dinghy's painter around a cleat and sits on the edge of the pontoon, his feet dangling inside the boat. He holds the fish bucket in his lap, admiring his bounty that continues to flip and flop. He turns to see that the woman has reached the rocks and stops to stare in his direction. She tilts her head quizzically, her face divided by shadow. With a start he realises the puzzle she ponders is *him*. Chad is in peril of being winded; he stands, clutching the handle of his bucket, stepping forward, lingering, hesitating, unsure still if his mind is playing tricks. She scrambles over the rocks, jumps barefooted from one stone to the next as lightly as a bird. He just has time to think, *Of course it's Freya*, before he becomes dizzy and has to firmly tell himself to concentrate lest he careers off the edge of the pontoon.

She steps onto the planks and raises her hand. He feels her steps vibrating through the wood, the distance between them dwindling. She strides towards him, fearless, and though he tries to move he cannot, apprehension ringing in his ears like shattering glass.

Freya stands before him, smiling, crying, flyaway strands of her hair floating in the sun. He pushes the bucket to the crook of his arm and takes her outstretched hands—he grips them hard, incapable of less. He feels fifteen years old, his limbs ungainly. He shakes his head, tongue-tied, looks downwards for words, certain his voice will quaver when he speaks and finally blurting, *You waited a long time*.

His utterance echoes as a couplet; she speaks the same words in return.

Chad meets her iceberg-blue eyes and it's Freya who laughs first. He stands fixed to the pontoon, fish slapping the bucket, his hands covered in scales, but he's not letting go.

ACKNOWLEDGMENTS

THE NATURE OF ICE WAS written as part of a PhD in Writing at Edith Cowan University, with the support of a Postgraduate Research Scholarship and a stellar supervisor. For wisdom, guidance and goodwill, my heartfelt gratitude goes to Richard Rossiter and to fellow writers Amanda Curtin and Annabel Smith.

While *The Nature of Ice* is a work of fiction, it rests on a foundation of research reinforced by the expertise and experiences of colleagues and friends who shared information, material, anecdotes and views.

Nancy Robinson Flannery, along with Ian Flannery, contributed in myriad ways to my understanding of Paquita Delprat and Douglas Mawson. Nancy also permitted me to use and research her ideas on smoking as a factor in Xavier Mertz's demise.

I am indebted to Gabrielle Eisner of Switzerland who translated Xavier Mertz's German diary transcript in its entirety and to The Friends of Mawson for financial assistance.

Particular thanks go to Maya Allen Gallegos, the ANARE club (especially John Gillies, Bruce McDonald and Selwyn Peacock), Philip Ayres, Sasha Boston, Henk Brolsma, Ingolv Bruaset, Dave Burkitt, John Bryan, Mike Craven, Amy Cort, Chris Forbes-Ewan, ECU library staff and the Document Delivery Service, Malcom Foster, Pete Gill, Stephen Haddelsey, Deborah Kerr, Syd Kirkby, Estelle Lazer, Elle Leane, Lynne Leonhardt, Ben Manser, Gary Mason, Dave McCormack, the late Jessica McEwin, Alasdair McGregor, Doug McVeigh, the late Mollie Mundy, Thomas Pickard, Estelle de San Miguel, Bob Silberberg, Max and Muriel Sluce, Mike Staples, Clive Strauss, Tashi Tenzing, Amanda Till and Rosy Whelan.

The South Australian Museum/University of Adelaide allowed me to publish Hurley's and Mertz's photographs, and with Gareth Mawson Thomas, kindly consented to me reprinting archival material from the Mawson and Delprat Papers. The generosity and enthusiasm of Mark Pharaoh, curator of Mawson's Papers, added to the enjoyment of the research process. I am grateful to the Mitchell Library for assistance with archival material, and permission to publish Hurley's and Mertz's images from their collection. Bill Hunter granted permission to reprint extracts from his father's diaries held at the National Library of Australia; Allan Mornement allowed me to use several excerpts from Belgrave Ninnis's diaries housed at the Scott Polar Research Institute. While these and other quotes have since metamorphosed into scenes and dialogue, they have been an invaluable part of 'getting it right' within the creative process.

Much of my polar experience I owe to Greg and Margaret Mortimer of Aurora Expeditions, with whom I first travelled in 1996. They have since included me as part of their expedition team on ship-based tours to the Antarctic and Arctic. In the summer of 2003–04 I worked for the Australian Antarctic Division as a field assistant at Davis Station, and while this was a scientific role researching south polar skuas, the experience of living at a station and working in the field provided the scaffolding for the novel.

I am indebted to Allen & Unwin for accepting the novel and for their efforts in its development. Thanks to Annette Barlow, Peter Eichhorn and Catherine Milne for guidance and encouragement, and editors Siobhán Cantrill, Clara Finlay and Ali Lavau, whose expertise and patience have steered the manuscript through its final evolvement. Sandy Cull produced the striking cover and interior designs, while Bookhouse typeset the pages.

Finally, I thank my lucky stars for my loving partner Gary Miller, who has enabled me to participate in Antarctic science, and whose knowledge of and passion for Antarctica has helped foster my own understanding.

ARCHIVAL
SOURCES

Depositories: LaT: La Trobe Library of the State Library of Victoria, Melbourne; MAC: Mawson Antarctic Collection, University of Adelaide, Adelaide; ML: Mitchell Library of the State Library of New South Wales, Sydney; NLA: National Library of Australia, Canberra; SAM: South Australian Museum; SLSA: State Library of South Australia, Adelaide; SPRI: Scott Polar Research Institute, Cambridge

Correspondence: AAE Staff Agreements, 1911. MSS 171/19. ML; Close, J. Application to Douglas Mawson, 1911. MSS 171/14. ML; Collier, M. Application to Douglas Mawson, 1911. Scrap book 257.1.7 (8). MAC; Davis, J.K. Correspondence with Douglas Mawson, 1913. 43AAE. MAC; Davis, J.K. Correspondence with Roald Amundsen, 1912; Percy Gray, 1911–1913; John Hunter, 1913. MSS 171/23X. ML; Delprat, P. Correspondence with Douglas Mawson, 1912–1913. 52DM. MAC; Gaumont Co. Correspondence with Douglas Mawson, November 20, 1911–December 31, 1913. MSS 171/21X. ML; Hurley, F. Correspondence with Douglas Mawson, 1911. MSS 171/14. ML; Hurley, M.A. Correspondence with Douglas Mawson, 1911. MSS 171/14. ML; Madigan, C. Correspondence with Douglas Mawson, 1914. 175AAE. MAC; Mawson, D. Correspondence with AAE suppliers and sponsors, 1911: Farrahs, Dr, Jaegar's Sanitary Woollen System Co. Ltd., Sunlight Soap, London Aluminium Company Ltd., Marmite Food Extract Co. Ltd.; Correspondence with Professor Orme Masson, 1911; Correspondence with Xavier Mertz, 1911. MSS 171/4. ML; Correspondence with Frau Mertz, 1914. Lennard Bickel Papers. MAC; Correspondence with Inspector General Ninnis, 1914. 175AAE. MAC; Correspondence with John King Davis, 1913;

Correspondence with T. W. Edgeworth David, 1914. 43AAE. MAC; Correspondence with Kathleen Scott, 1916. PRG 523, Series 4–6. SLSA; Correspondence with Paquita Delprat, 1911–1914; Belgrave Ninnis, 1913; Ada Ninnis, 1914; Alec Tweedie, 1911; Kathleen Scott, c. 1914, 1920. 52DM. MAC; Correspondence with Paquita Mawson (nee Delprat), 1911–1920. PRG 523, Series 3. SLSA; Correspondence with Walter Hannam, 1911; Gaumont Co., 1911; Frank Hurley, 1911; Charles Laseron, 1911; Herbert Dyce Murphy, 1911. MSS 171/14–15. ML; Telegram to Mertz family, 1913; Telegram to Inspector General Ninnis, 1913. 29AAE. MAC; Telegram to Paquita Delprat, 1913. 28AAE. MAC; McLean, A. Field note to Douglas Mawson, 29 January 1913. 48AAE. MAC; Mertz, E. Correspondence with Douglas Mawson, 1914. MSS 171/18. ML; Mertz, X. Correspondence with Douglas Mawson, 1911. 13AAE/2. MAC; Scott, K. Correspondence with Douglas Mawson, 1926. PRG 523, Series 4–6. SLSA; Southcott, R. Correspondence with Fred Jacka, 1983. 70AAE. MAC; Toutcher, N. Correspondence with John King Davis, 1912. MSS171/24. ML.

Diaries: Davis, J.K. AAE diaries, December 3, 1911–February 26, 1914. MS 8311. LaT; Gray, P. 'Letters Home', December 2, 1911–February 26, 1914. Typed transcript with a preface by Francis H. Bickerton. MSS 2893. ML; Hannam, W. AAE diaries, November 21, 1911–March 14, 1913. MSS 384. ML; Harrisson, C.T. AAE diaries, December 2, 1911–April 12, 1913. MSS 386. ML; Hunter, J.G. AAE diaries, November 21, 1911–March 1, 1913. MS 2806. NLA; Hurley, J.F. AAE sledging diary, November 10, 1912–January 10, 1913, with a typed, edited transcript. MSS 389/1–2. ML; Kennedy, A.L. Diary. December 2, 1911–July 26, 1912. 80AAE. MAC; Laseron, C. AAE diary and related papers, November 21, 1911–February 24, 1913; Sledging diary, November 8, 1912–January 6, 1913; MSS 385. ML; Mawson, D. AAE diaries, 1912–1914; AAE sledging notebook November 10–13, 1912; AAE notebook 'Glaciology' (n.d.). 68DM. MAC; McLean, A.L. AAE diaries, December 2, 1911–February 26, 1914. Typed transcript. MSS 382, Vol. 2 (2). ML; Mertz, X. AAE diary, July 28, 1911–January 1, 1913. 70AAE. Typed German transcript. MD752/1. MAC; AAE diary, July 28, 1911–January 1, 1913. English translation, 2005, from typed German transcript MD752/1. (G. Eisner, Trans.). Author's collection (copy held at MAC); Moyes, M.H. AAE diary, December 2, 1911–February 23, 1913. MSS 388/1. ML; Ninnis, B.E.S. Diaries, May 11, 1908–November 8, 1912. SPRI; Webb, E.N. AAE sledging diary, November 19, 1912–January 11, 1913. MSS 2895. ML.

Documents: AAE Photographic Equipment List. (n.d.). 13AAE/2. MAC; Auroral sightings at Adelie Land, 1913. 43AAE. MAC; Bickel, L. Research Report on Xavier Guillame

Mertz. (n.d.). Lennard Bickel Papers. MAC; Hunter, J.G. Biological Report, c. 1913. 63AAE. MAC; Mawson, D. Lecture notes and captions accompanying public lantern slide presentation, 1914. PRG 523, Series 11. SLSA; Meteorological Log: Far Eastern Sledging Journey in Adelie Land and King George V Land, summer 1912–1913. 63AAE. MAC; Newspaper clippings, 1914. Scrap Books 257.1.2 (3). MAC; Note regarding unsuccessful recall of ship on February 8, 1913. 43AAE. MAC; Southcott, R. Three folders relating to vitamin A poisoning. Lennard Bickel Papers. MAC; Webb, E.N. (1965). *Magnetic Polar Journey 1912*. Typed transcript including cover letter. MSS 6812. ML; Winter quarters departure note, 1913. 43AAE. MAC; Winter quarters hut notices, 1912: Routine Duties; Nightwatchman Duties; Messman Duties; Kitchen Department; Clothing; Desiderata in Aurora Observations. 43AAE. MAC; Winter quarters library books, c. 1912. 43AAE. MAC; Wireless Log, Adelie Land Station, 1913. 43AAE. MAC; Wireless messages transmitted from Macquarie Island, February 14, 1912–November 22, 1913. MSS 171/40. ML.

Photographs: Hurley, F. Australasian Antarctic Expedition 1911–1914. ML: pp: 52, 154, 203, 344; SAM: pp: 20, 30, 60, 66, 88, 141, 294, 323, 361. Mertz, X. Australasian Antarctic Expedition 1911–1914. ML: p. 2; SAM: p. 112.

Recordings: Antarctic Pioneers: The Story of Australia's First Conquests of Antarctica, narrated by Frank Hurley [Video]. (1962); Home of the Blizzard [Video copy of Cinematograph]. (1913). ML: VB 2743; *Nutrition Lessons From Antarctic Tracking.* Transcript from *Ockham's Razor.* Radio National; *Portrait of a Scientist: Sir Douglas Mawson.* c. 1962. [Audio recording]. ABC Radio; "Ready Boys Mush" [Video]. (1987). Mawson Station, Antarctica.